CW01483711

NINE O'CLOCK BUS TO BROMPTON

THE COUNTY MOUNTIES BOOK 1

KEVIN FITZPATRICK

To Janice

Special thanks to Helen Susan Swift, without whose help this book would never have been completed.

PRELUDE

BELGRAVIA, CENTRAL LONDON - MID 1960S

From the outside, the house appeared perfectly innocent. A grey stone building, exactly like so many of its neighbours. Located in an exclusive area of the city, it was conveniently situated a short walk from the nearest Tube station and, for all intents and purposes, had the appearance of being the home of a highly paid accountant or maybe an exclusive private doctor.

The street outside had recently been furnished with coin-operated parking meters, and smart wardens, wearing hats with yellow bands, were frequently seen patrolling the area, much to the disgust of drivers hoping to park their cars. However, parking was rarely an issue for these premises. Clients, mostly middle-aged men in smart suits, almost always arrived and departed by taxi.

There was a flight of three marble steps that led up from the pavement to an imposing front door made of oak, painted black and sporting a highly polished brass handle. There was also an old-fashioned bell-pull, however, there was no nameplate on the stone pillar next to the door. The house was discreet and anonymous.

• • •

At a gesture from Steven, the two young women in Waffen SS uniforms, complete with miniskirts and jackboots, put down their whips and the taller of the two picked up a key ready to free the prisoner from his bondage. It took the woman a couple of minutes to undo the four padlocks that held the poor man securely chained to the X frame. However, even after he was free, he was very stiff and needed assistance to walk over to a chair and sit down. The girls giggled as they helped him massage some life back into his aching limbs.

The "prisoner," a fair-haired man in his twenties, was tall, muscular, and completely naked. The oil that coated his body glistened in the bright lights and gave the appearance that he had been sweating profusely. The marks that covered his body that were made to look like cuts and bruises were, in reality, nothing more sinister than clever make-up. But the ball and chain that had been attached to his testicles was a real device – and he was very relieved to have it removed with no harm having been done to his greatest assets.

"Was that okay then, Steve?" the man asked the photographer once he had somewhat recovered from his ordeal.

The man to whom he spoke, Steven Hoskins, was a meticulous little photographer with a compulsive attention to detail. Although only thirty-five years of age, he looked, acted and dressed like someone far older. His outlook on life was similarly old-fashioned, and he considered himself a perfectionist.

Other people, his models in particular, thought of him as a fussy little so-and-so who was very hard to please. Steven didn't care what they thought; he would much prefer it if they didn't think anything at all. As far as he was concerned, the less the world knew about him, the better.

"Yes, pretty good," he replied, actually smiling for once. "In fact, very good. Well done, Andy. Are you all right, though? I'm sorry we had to keep you chained up for so long."

"No problem, I've had a lot worse." Andy grinned. Then, having quickly checked that the women had by now left the room to go and get changed, continued, "I wouldn't want to be on the wrong side of that Irene though. I got the distinct impression she'd rather be doing it for real than just posing."

"Suzanne says she's priceless," Steve replied. "Most of the women who work here do it just for the money. But Sue reckons Irene's the real deal, a genuine sadist. Believe it or not, they're hard to come by, even in this game."

Andy nodded. "You down the club tonight?" he said, changing the subject.

"No, I'm staying in with Suzanne this evening."

Andy laughed. "I can't imagine you married. She definitely knows you're ginger, right?" he said, using the contemporary expression Ginger (ginger beer) to refer to a homosexual.

"She's actually perfectly happy with that as it happens, and so am I. We just get on well. There's more to life than sex, you know."

Andy shook his head and went to the corner to get dressed from a pile of clothes that he'd left there earlier.

Andy had known Steve for several years; they'd even slept together a few times. The photographer was a "face" in the local community of West End sex workers; well-liked but known to be quiet and of a somewhat introverted disposition. The society they both moved in was extremely tolerant, by general standards, but they were still bemused by the fact that he wanted to marry, and spend his life with, a female dominatrix.

For his "day job" Steve made his living as a freelance photographer for the advertising and property industry. That was the employment the tax man knew about. However, what the authorities did not know about him (he hoped) was that he also ran a lucrative side-line in off-beat pornography. The session just finished had been shot in a room known to the "models" as The Dungeon; and The Dungeon was located at the business premises of Steven's fiancée, the senior dominatrix known to her clients as Mistress Stern.

Steve carefully removed the exposed film from the expensive Pentax camera which he then unscrewed from its tripod. He placed it into its felt-lined metal case, closed the lid, and snapped the catches shut. The Pentax had cost him hundreds of pounds, and the lens alone was worth more than his car. He knew he had to be careful around here.

In his own studio, all his photographic equipment was solidly mounted and protected from any harm. However, inside The Dungeon, it was a different matter altogether. Things could get out of hand in here. Especially when the sessions became ever more energetic and the excitement mounted. Violent action could easily lead to unintended consequences – and optical equipment was eye-wateringly expensive to replace.

Not only that, but Steve wouldn't have put it past one or two of the working girls to take a perverse delight in his despair should any of his precious kit get damaged. He knew he needed to be vigilant around this place.

However, the shots that were now safely captured on the two rolls of film tucked away in a leather case had posed no particular risks. Andy was a regular. A professional young porn actor, and the two girls, employees of the establishment, had obviously not really been beating a confession out of him. The fearsome-looking canes and whips had been genuine enough, but the fluid that was liberally spread around the place was nothing more sinister than chocolate sauce – the perfect substitute for blood in black and white photography.

Steve was very happy with the day's work. Once developed, those pictures would be worth a small fortune in the seedy little back street shops in Soho. Andy was extremely well-endowed, so his naked body would have huge appeal to the "ginger" fraternity. And the sadomasochists would love the girls with their evil postures and expressions. The women had gleefully projected into the camera sufficient cruelty and sadism to satisfy even the most ardent followers of that particular fetish.

About twenty minutes after the shoot ended, Steve heard the sound of shouting, banging, and clanging emanating from somewhere along the corridor outside the Dungeon. It appeared to be coming from a room used by the girls as a dressing room.

Andy, now fully dressed, was totally nonplussed. He simply shrugged his shoulders, blew a kiss to Steve, then made his way towards the front door, ready to go home. Steve, on the other hand, was more concerned.

Wondering what on earth was going on, he decided to go along the corridor to investigate.

He put his head round the door of the changing room just in time to see Irene, the woman he had been talking about with Andy, brandishing a vicious-looking riding crop that she slammed down with terrifying force onto the top of the wooden table in the middle of the room.

"What the hell's going on?" shouted Steve. "Irene, what's got into you?"

"Oh, it's you is it? Tell me, are you really going to marry that fucking bitch? I feel sorry for you if you are, the fucking cow!"

Irene was still dressed in her fetish outfit and looked a fearsome sight as she marched towards the hapless photographer – with her whip still in her hand. For a moment, Steve feared for his safety, but he stood his ground and held up his hands in a gesture of appeasement.

"Calm down, Irene, what's Suzanne done to upset you? I'm sure it's nothing we can't sort out."

Irene was still furious but, with a visible effort of will, she stopped, threw the crop across the room, then clenched her fists by her side and stamped her foot. She grunted in frustration.

"I went up to tell her we'd finished the session, like she told me to, and she's only gone and bloody fired me!" she said through gritted teeth. "Paid me off and told me to get out. After all I've done for her! Fuck off, Irene, you're not wanted. Just like that."

"I don't believe it." Steve was genuinely shocked. "She told me just yesterday you were the best girl she had. A natural, she called you, worth your weight in gold. Why on earth would she want to fire you?"

Irene's fists were still clenched, but now angry tears sprang from her eyes. Her naturally red hair seemed to stand on end.

"I need a fucking drink," she said finally. "Take me down the road and buy me a drink – unless you're scared the precious Suzanne might object. I need to talk to you anyway."

"Give me a minute to speak to her, then I'll go with you. I need to find out what this is all about. Hang on here, and I'll be right back."

While Irene changed out of her outfit, Steve climbed the stairs to the top floor of the innocent-looking three-storey Victorian townhouse. This was the part of the house where he and Suzanne Blenkinsop (aka Madame Stern) shared a flat. There was a small box room just off the landing that Suzanne used as her office, and the lady herself was currently sitting on a swivel chair, with her back to the door, looking out of the window.

Like Steve, Suzanne was aging before her time. After years of work in the sex industry, she was no longer the stunningly attractive woman of her youth. But she was certainly still beautiful and, with her trim figure, well capable of turning men's heads whenever she ventured out of her lair.

She spun her chair around to face Steve as he entered.

"From all the noise, I gather Irene's told you what happened?" she said.

"She says you've given her the push. She wants me to take her out for a drink."

Suzanne opened the top drawer in her desk and withdrew a wad of notes.

"Here," she said. "Have the drink on me. I owe her that much; she's made me enough money over the past couple of years."

"So why are you getting rid of her?"

"I've no choice. You know who some of our clients are. They've all been scared shitless since that Profumo business, and now one of them's been tipped the wink that Irene is a security risk."

"Bollocks! That Profumo thing was a Secretary of State sharing a prostitute with a Russian spy. Not quite our scene. Oh, but wait a minute…" He paused, then said, "Could it be because she's Irish?"

Suzanne sighed. "As if they'd tell me! All I know is they don't trust her all of a sudden. You know what these pervy politicians are like, none of them have any balls when it really comes to it."

"It does seem a bit unfair, though…"

"Steve," said Suzanne, cutting him short, "do me a favour, take her for that drink then give her the rest of this cash. I've already paid her what she's due, but it won't keep her for long. Tell her if she needs any more she knows where to find me. I think she may struggle to find work from now on – in our line of business anyway."

The pub was beginning to fill with early evening customers, but Irene and Steve were lucky and found an unoccupied table in a quiet corner. There were three chairs at the table, and Steve was about to allow another customer to remove the extra one when Irene stopped him.

"Leave it there!" she snapped. Steve was concerned to note that she hadn't calmed down much since her earlier outburst.

"Why?" Steve asked. "We don't need it."

"There's someone joining us that I want you to meet. I phoned him while you were up with Suzanne. I was planning to introduce you to him sometime later on. Of course, now the bitch has forced my hand, and I need to get things moving."

"Suzanne's told me what happened," said Steve, wondering who the chap might be that Irene wanted him to meet. "I had no idea."

"The reason you didn't know about it is because she only knew herself this morning. The fucking bitch had her chain pulled, and that was it."

"Any idea who pulled her chain?"

"I don't know exactly which one it was, but it was definitely one of those high-up politicians we've been servicing recently. Whoever it was, he complained about my Irish accent. He told Suzanne she'd be blacklisted by his friends if she didn't get rid of me."

"Well, like everyone else, I'm aware of some trouble brewing in the North of Ireland," said Steve, leaning forward so their conversation couldn't be overheard. "But you're from the Republic, aren't you? How does it affect you?"

Irene remained silent for a moment then looked Steve directly in the eye. She took a deep, theatrical breath.

"There's only Ireland, Steven, no north, no south, no republic, just Ireland. Don't you ever forget it – or you and me will be falling out. Got that?"

"Okay, steady on, no offence intended. You know how I feel about the old country. My mother's family suffered dreadfully during the Troubles, you know."

Irene took a long swig from her drink and motioned over to the barman to pour her another. She gave Steve an icy stare.

"Yes, you've told me. Well, you never know, you may just get a chance to do something about that injustice. You'd like that now, wouldn't you?"

"What do you mean?"

"I think you know exactly what I mean. There's a war coming, and you and every other man of Irish descent is going to have to decide which side he's on. If your mother ever taught you anything, then you'd know that. And if you've got a pair of balls, you'll stand and fight."

A cold knot of fear gripped Steve's stomach as the realisation struck him that Suzanne was probably right to get rid of Irene. Prominent politicians sometimes had strange desires, needs that only women like Irene could satisfy. It made these men very vulnerable. People in Irene's profession had access to knowledge that would be invaluable to a blackmailer – and solid gold to a terrorist.

"I–I don't know what I could possibly do to help," Steve stammered. "I never even get to see the customers. The photos I take are posed by models and actors – nobody of importance would ever let himself be photographed."

"But you're an advertising executive, aren't you? In your day job, I mean. There are other pictures you could take without arousing suspicion. Pictures that could be useful to us in our plans. Locations in the City, for example. You'd just have to carry on as normal. All you'd have to do is do your job, carry on as normal. You stay out of trouble; you stay invisible to the authorities. You're lily-white until we call you. We may never call you – but one day, we just might. That isn't too much to ask is it, you know, for the Cause?"

"But, Irene, the authorities probably know about me already," Steve protested. "I must be on their radar with my little side-line."

"Exactly, and it's that that gives you the perfect cover. They expect you to be secretive, but they'll assume it's your perverted snapshots you'll be protecting. They'll take no notice at all of your legitimate photography. We'll even give you genuine commissions. So stop worrying and get yourself another drink."

The enormity of what this woman so calmly suggested was overwhelming. Steve felt physically sick. He stared at the door of the bar as though looking for a means of escape.

"Do I have a choice?" he asked quietly.

"No, Steven, not any more you don't. Not now I've spoken to you." Irene spoke evenly but her voice was loaded with menace.

She looked over into the gathering crowd where a smartly dressed young city gent was weaving his way towards them with a glass of beer in his hand.

"Ah, here's your man now," said Irene.

"Brendan, come over here!" she shouted. The young man nodded to her. "This is Steven," she said to the newcomer as he reached the table. "He's the chap I was telling you about."

"Hello, Steven." Steve was surprised to note that Brendan spoke with the middle English public-school accent of a stockbroker. He even probably played "rugger" instead of rugby, Steve thought sourly.

Brendan held out his hand. "I'm very pleased to meet you at long last, Steven. Irene here's told me so much about you. We're delighted to have you aboard."

CHAPTER ONE
WEST BERKSHIRE – MID-1960S

Despite it being a bright, sunny day, the wind had a keen edge. Gusts of cold air, like whispering thieves, rhythmically drifted over the countryside and stole away any warmth that the rays may have produced. In response to one particularly icy blast, Emily Pritchard shivered and pulled her cardigan closer around her shoulders. She was still the right side of sixty years of age, but her painfully thin body constantly struggled to retain anything like a comfortable body temperature.

That is not to say that Emily was at all frail. She was an energetic lady and her level of fitness, from years of cycling, would put many younger women to shame. However, she did feel the cold.

She was frequently cold – and often lonely.

Emily was a widow; her husband had been killed in war, and she had never remarried. For many years she had lived alone but, as the secretary of a local high school, she was kept reasonably busy and looking after the garden of her secluded cottage kept her fully occupied in her spare time.

She sighed. She had to admit the flowers were lovely; however, like so many pretty things, they were becoming rather unruly and needed a firm hand to bring them under control. Emily very much believed in the use of a firm hand when it was called for, as many disrespectful children at her school had learned to their cost. The boys and girls knew that it was best behaviour only when Mrs Pritchard was on the prowl!

Her quick, deft hands worked the secateurs with surgical precision as she clipped and pruned. After half an hour or so, she paused and straightened up for a minute to ease her back. It was then that she heard the sound of a motorbike approaching in the distance. As her cottage was the only dwelling for some miles, she surmised she was about to receive a visitor.

Hands on hips, Emily watched as the Triumph motorcycle of the Berkshire Constabulary pulled up outside the wicker gate that led into her garden. She'd had a good guess as to which policeman likely to be visiting her, but, even so, her heart missed a beat as she recognised the rider to be PC Fred Weston. Fred was a special friend.

The officer killed his engine and dismounted, swinging his leg across the seat of the machine in a movement so entirely masculine that Emily could only approve.

Having effortlessly hoisted the heavy machine onto its centre stand, the powerfully built policeman slowly took off his white-backed leather gauntlets and placed them, fingers outward, on the tank of his bike just in front of the radio handset. He then removed his black "Corker" crash helmet with the word POLICE emblazoned across its front. He gently placed the helmet into the crook of the handlebars, on top of the gloves.

Emily was no stranger to police procedure and knew what to expect next. She was aware Fred wouldn't even acknowledge her until he'd checked in with his control room a few miles away at constabulary headquarters.

The radio on the 650cc Speed Twin was located behind the

wide leather rider's seat. The set's telephone-like handset, and other controls, however, were mounted on the top of the petrol tank. There was a small switch that, in one position, permitted the operator to use the handset discreetly like a telephone, whilst in the other position it switched on a loudspeaker that, in theory at least, permitted the rider to hear whilst travelling along the road.

Fred flicked the switch to the private setting and spoke briefly into the handset, telling his controller, in his slow, broad Berkshire accent, that he was engaged on crime enquiries and would be off the air for some time.

He concluded by saying, "You can get me on Brompton three one seven if required."

"Thanks, Fred," came the reply from the operator. "Give us a shout when you're back on the air – just so we know you're okay."

Although he possessed incredibly quick reflexes, Fred routinely did nothing in a hurry. For him, everything had to be done right – and rushing things meant mistakes could be made. He switched off the radio, secured the motorcycle, then, finally satisfied, he made his way through the gate and over towards Emily – who by now had grown tired of watching him and had gone back to tending her flowers.

"Hello, stranger," she said over her shoulder. Then, sarcastically, "To what do I owe this honour?"

"Now, don't be like that, Milly," said Fred with a large smile. "I've just called by for a cup of tea and a bit of a chat."

"Yeah, I bet!" she said harshly, but nevertheless stood up, latched the secateurs in the closed position, and put them away into the pocket at the front of her tweed gardening skirt.

Emily opened the front door but, before entering, she turned and faced her visitor.

"You can take those boots off," she said, slipping out of her green Hunters wellies.

Fred did as he was told. He unzipped then stepped out of

his shiny, black leather, calf-length boots and placed them next to Emily's wellies on the metal grill under the porch. He followed Emily into the cottage. Then, without waiting for permission, he unbuttoned the heavy uniform "thorn-proof" jacket, took it off, and hung it on a hook behind the door.

Emily took a long, hard look at him. He was just a few years younger than her, and he was a fine figure of a man. Lean, but broad-shouldered and strong. However, despite his youthfulness and energy, age was catching up with him. In a couple of years, once he reached fifty-five, he would have to retire whether he wanted to or not. The same grim prospect faced her when she hit sixty. She was not looking forward to it.

But now, seeing him standing in his shirtsleeves, riding breeches, and stockinged feet, she started laughing.

"You look like a tortoise that's been winkled out of its shell," she said. "Will the police force ever join the twentieth century, do you suppose? They actually make shirts with collars these days, you know. I'm surprised you can still get collar studs for those things."

"These are top-quality Van Heusen shirts, I'll have you know," he said pompously. "They're all the rage in Chelsea, or so I'm told. And Langston's in Reading still do a very nice range of studs, thank you very much. Anyway, it makes sense, doesn't it? It's only the collar that ever wears out; the rest of the shirt doesn't. It's stupid throwing away a whole shirt when you can just replace the collar."

Emily turned around and began making the tea whilst Fred sat himself down comfortably at the large, well-used wooden table that dominated the room.

"Now then, Fred," Emily said, "why are you really here? And don't tell me it's just for tea."

"No, not just the tea," he replied slowly. "To be honest, I was hoping you'd have a little word with Mr Headley for me. A couple of your boys have been up to mischief again."

Mr Headley was the headmaster at Brompton High School where Emily was the school secretary. A few times over the past couple of years, Fred had arranged, through Emily, to have misbehaving youths punished by the school for misdemeanours committed whilst wearing school uniform. Everyone agreed it was preferable to them being sent to juvenile court and acquiring a police record – besides which, it saved PC Weston a great deal of paperwork.

"So, what is it this time?" said Emily. "More rowdiness on the bus?"

Fred stood up and walked over to his jacket. From the extended inside pocket, known as a summons pocket, he withdrew a folded piece of paper that he placed face-up on the table.

Emily brought two steaming mugs over from the kettle, handed one to Fred, then sat down herself before picking up the paper.

"It looks like a photo-copy of a five-pound note," she said.

"Exactly, and it was used to defraud old Jenny in the village Tuck Shop out of a load of sweets. The poor old dear is as blind as a bat and had no idea it was a dud until the bank rejected it."

"Little sods! But what's this got to do with the school?"

"Well, the culprits were in school uniform, and it seems the original five-pound note was 'borrowed' from the music teacher's bag during break. Oh yes, and it was the school Xerox machine that was used to make the copy."

"Yes, but even so, shouldn't this be put before a juvenile court? It seems quite serious."

"I agree, but Jenny won't hear of it. She totally refuses to make a complaint – and without her statement, we're buggered. The fact is, I really don't want the little shits getting away with it."

"Okay, I'll do what I can. I'll speak to Mr Headley for you. Who are the culprits, or do I need to ask?"

"No, I'm sure you've guessed. It's the Churcher brothers again."

"Oh dear. Poor Mrs Churcher, she's tried so hard to bring them two up since she lost her husband, but they seem determined to let her down."

"Does she still work at the school canteen?"

"Yes. She's actually a very good cook. This will break her heart – again."

"What will Mr Headley do, do you think?"

"Well, with something this serious he could expel them, but my guess is they'll both get six of the best... for all the good that will do."

"What do you mean? I thought Headley was a bit of a demon with a cane."

"Oh, he is. Most of the boys are terrified of him – he refuses to cane girls, you know. However, the last time those two got into trouble, I had the older boy waiting his turn in my office while his brother was getting thrashed in the next room."

"And?"

"Well, you could clearly hear the cuts being delivered, but when I looked over at the little monster, he was grinning like an idiot and openly playing with himself."

"No!"

"It cost him an extra two strokes when I reported him – but he didn't seem to mind a bit. There's something very odd about those two boys. More tea?"

"Maybe later." He paused and looked directly into her eyes. He smiled. Then he gave her a wink before he allowed his gaze to travel down her body.

"You've got a bloody cheek!" she said. "Where have you been these last few weeks?"

"I haven't had an excuse to get over here until today – and I'm too close to my pension to take too many chances."

"I know, Fred, but I do like to see you."

"Come on, Milly, we both agreed there'd be no commitment, didn't we?"

"I know, Fred. Don't worry, I'm not some silly schoolgirl who's going to get all emotional and clingy. It's just that I get so lonely, sometimes, here on my own."

She stood up and walked over to an interior door. "Come on, then," she said.

"You needn't think I'm going in there with you while you've got those things," said Fred with a huge grin.

Emily blushed. She'd forgotten all about the secateurs that were still poking out of her skirt pocket.

"You're right," she said. "Too much temptation." She unfastened her belt, and her skirt fell to the floor.

Within a minute they were inside the bedroom and naked. Emily could see that Fred was visibly aroused.

"You must be desperate if the sight of a skinny old lady can have that effect," she said with a grin, but it was obvious that she was pleased with herself.

Fred grew serious. "Milly," he said, "you don't need to say things like that. You're all the woman any man could ask for. If things were different…"

"I know," she said, wistfully, "I know."

She walked over to him and allowed her hand to run down his chest and beyond.

She closed her fingers around his rock-hard erection and led him gently over to the ancient feather bed that they had shared so many times in the past.

CHAPTER TWO
WEST BERKSHIRE – 7 YEARS LATER

I t was 9 pm on a warm evening in mid-June, and the brightness of the day was finally beginning to fade to twilight. PC Don Barton, working the late shift, decided it was time to stop to take a short break and bring his pocket notebook up to date. He pulled the Morris Marina patrol car over into a field entrance at the side of the road and then reversed a few yards, turning the wheel, so that he ended up facing out towards the currently deserted country road.

Don did not like this car. The Marina was British Leyland's replacement for the much loved and reliable, but sadly out-of-date, Morris Minor. The car itself was nicely designed, but for one reason or another it had gained a bad reputation for finish and reliability.

To make matters worse, police drivers were notoriously critical of any vehicle they used. Any faults (and the Marina had several) stood no chance of being overlooked or forgiven.

It had been a quiet evening on the Hampstead Norreys rural section and Don was bored. He was in his mid-twenties and he felt that the world was passing him by. Was it really almost a full year since he'd been kicked off the Traffic Department and dumped into this dead and alive country beat? The days and weeks were flying by, and Don could feel himself growing old before his time.

He knew it wouldn't take long to bring his notebook up the date, but if he didn't do it now there was a danger that he would forget to record something. He removed the little journal from its pigskin cover and took out his pen. He placed both items on the seat beside him and reached into the pocket of his tunic for his cigarettes. A smoke would help him reflect and recall the events, such as they were, of the afternoon.

He wound down the window of the car and lit up. However, before he began writing, he decided to radio into his control room and advise them of his location, just in case he should be required for anything.

Although his area was part of the Newbury Division, Don's rural beat was well out of range of the local control room's UHF radio system. This meant that for radio communication he had call in to the main Headquarters Control at Kidlington via the much more powerful VHF set fitted to his car.

He lifted the handset from its cradle and depressed the toggle. "HT Control from Foxtrot Golf Five Zero, over," he said into the mouthpiece.

There were three main channels constantly supervised by Control Room staff, and HT was the frequency that covered the southern part of the Thames Valley force area.

"Go ahead, Five Zero," a female voice answered him.

"Booking ten-five on the Brompton to Bucklebury road, available for commitment if required—Bloody Hell!"

"Is everything all right, Five Zero?"

"Er, yes, all okay. Sorry about that, I was startled for a moment. A white horse has just trotted past me. It's running along the middle of the road heading towards Brompton. There's no saddle or bridle, so I don't think it's thrown a rider. It's probably escaped from a field. However, it is obviously a danger to traffic, so I'll have to try to stop it. Any chance of some assistance, over?"

The Control Room operator put out a general call: "HT Control to any unit available to assist Foxtrot Golf Five Zero with a horse on the highway, please acknowledge with call sign, over."

"X-Ray Delta Two One, resuming from the break-in in Didcot, I'll start making, over," came a male voice through the ether.

A dog handler! Just what the doctor ordered, thought Don. But he's a long way off.

Control: "Thank you, Two One. Did you copy that, Five Zero?"

"Yes, all copied, many thanks. I'm following the horse now. I'll advise Two One with more precise details as he approaches this location, over."

"Obliged, Five Zero. I'll leave this channel on talk-through and see if we can get other units to put some traffic control in place. Meanwhile, please keep me updated with progress, over."

Because they transmitted and received on different frequencies, patrolling units could usually only hear the Control Room side of a conversation, but with "talk-through" engaged, they could clearly hear both sides. However, the protocol was that they would stay off the air themselves except for an emergency, or to contribute something to the unfolding drama.

Don had thrown his cigarette out of the window and was stealthily following the horse along the road by the time the radio conversation was completed – but he was already having difficulty. The horse was trotting at around 15 mph and kept speeding up every time he drew closer to it. The animal was also sticking to the centre of the road and showed no sign of slowing down or stopping.

Don was getting anxious. Two years previously he'd been

patrolling the M4 when a horse had escaped from a field and somehow found its way onto the motorway. It was in the early hours of the morning, and a lorry coming out of London had struck the animal before crashing into the metal barrier on the central reservation.

The driver had been uninjured, but the horse had suffered a catastrophic laceration that had cut its stomach wide open and left it lying, pouring with blood, on the carriageway.

Don had never seen so much blood. He ruined his uniform when he tried in vain to attend to the poor creature as it lay whinnying piteously on the road. It had taken the vet over half an hour to arrive and put the animal out of its misery, then another forty minutes for a trailer with a winch to turn up and take the body away.

Meanwhile, the motorway had been at a standstill, and huge jams built up as the early morning rush hour approached.

Don vividly recalled seeing the Fire Brigade hosing the blood from the motorway as he now tried, cautiously, to get past this animal. His plan was to attempt to control it from the front. Pressing the accelerator, gently so as not to create too much noise, he crept closer and closer.

He gently eased the car over to the offside. Just a little more and he would be level with the horse's rear quarters. Gently, gently, closer and closer; just another few more seconds and he'd be in front of it.

The horse suddenly became aware of what it perceived to be a strange creature creeping up alongside him, and it panicked. It tossed its head in the air and let out a loud whinny.

"Easy, boy," said Don, knowing the animal could not hear him. "Stand still, you stupid thing!"

The horse suddenly bucked, then it kicked out behind itself and began to trot even faster.

By now, the light was fading rapidly and, with the sun

setting low in the sky behind him, Don knew the horse would be almost invisible to anyone driving towards them.

The animal trotted even faster.

"Come on!" shouted Don, becoming frustrated, "I'm trying to help you."

Don was getting worried that another vehicle was bound to appear on the road ahead of them before long. He would need to find a way to warn any oncoming traffic of the danger, but he realised he couldn't dare use his rotating blue light for fear of spooking his quarry even more.

However, Don knew he had to think of *something* to highlight the danger to other road users – and fast. The horse still showed no sign of slowing, so Don decided it was worth the risk to experiment with operating his hazard warning lights.

He held his breath and flicked the switch. Amber light from the four-way flashers instantly bathed the road in front and behind the moving vehicle.

"Blast!" he shouted. The flashing light had spooked Don more than the horse, and he fumbled the switch off almost as soon as it operated.

Without warning, the horse slowed right down and stopped dead in the road. Don was forced to slam on his brakes. The car slid to a halt only feet away from the tail of the frightened animal. He was close, too close. Don began to gently back his vehicle away, but the horse began to shake his head and look all around.

Displaying amazing agility, the animal spun around and reared onto its hind legs. Don flinched as metal horseshoes thrashed the air a scant few yards in front of him. He stamped on the pedal and slewed the car backwards out of the way.

The horse suddenly leapt forward and ran full tilt past the startled officer. It was now heading back the way they had come. This was getting out of hand. There was no time to radio the control room, so Don performed a hasty three-point turn and, once again, gave chase.

Thankfully, the sun had completely dropped out of the sky, so although he was heading West, he wasn't blinded as he would have been a few minutes earlier. However, without the light of the setting sun, visibility was becoming very poor.

"Oh, shit!" Don shouted aloud. Through the gloom, he could make out the headlamps of an approaching Land Rover – a mere few hundred yards in front of him.

Don knew he had to take a risk. He flashed his headlights. No response. He flashed again, then repeatedly, all the while praying it wouldn't scare the horse into an even more dangerous frenzy. To his immense relief, the driver of the Land Rover flashed an acknowledgement and pulled up onto the grass verge to its nearside. A few seconds later the horse, followed by the police car, raced harmlessly past the now stationary vehicle.

After a further quarter of a mile or so, the horse, finally exhausted, slowed to a trot then to a sedate walk. Amazingly, it calmed right down and now appeared not to have a care in the world. It quietly ambled into an entrance at the side of the road and stopped just in front of a five-bar wooden gate.

Don pulled up across the entrance, hoping to use his vehicle to cut off the animal's access to the road. The horse started looking around but made no attempt to run off. Cautiously, Don got out of his car.

He had never ridden a horse in his life and, still fairly new to the rural area, he had no idea what to do next.

Then he had a brainwave. He opened the boot of his car and began to look for a towrope among the untidily packed road signs and other sundry equipment that had been thrown carelessly inside. Don sighed. As someone who had so recently worked as a Traffic motorcyclist, he hated seeing kit not being cared for properly. My own fault, he thought to himself. I should have checked the car when I picked it up.

After a minute or so, he found what he was looking for. However, the thick rope was a bit short as well as being somewhat greasy with oil. Nevertheless, it would have to do.

Don worked feverishly. Thankfully the rope had a metal eye at one end, and he was able to thread the other end through the hole to fashion himself a crude noose. Armed with his makeshift lasso he walked nervously towards the horse. The animal whinnied and tossed its head but didn't kick out. Don held the rope in both hands ready to throw it over the horse's neck. If he succeeded he intended to tie the horse to the gate and await the arrival of the dog handler.

As Don walked forward, the horse once more began to fret and shake his head more vigorously. Don paused when it started to paw the ground with its foreleg. Did he dare risk moving further forward, or would the horse try to kick him?

Suddenly, "What the Hell do you think you're doing? Get out of my way!" came a sharp voice from behind.

Don spun around to see that the Land Rover from earlier had turned around and followed him along the road. It was now parked a few yards from the police vehicle.

A very irate young lady wearing a green Barbour jacket, having alighted the vehicle, marched purposefully past the bemused police officer. Calmly and confidently, she walked over to the horse and put her hand under its chin. She then stroked his nose. The horse was instantly comforted and nuzzled the woman. Don was impressed.

"You've been watching too many cowboy films," the woman said scornfully to Don, pointing at his length of rope. "Open the gate, will you."

Without waiting for a reply, she turned around while Don operated the metal lever and opened the gate. The young woman led the horse into the field where it dropped its head and began to chew grass, perfectly contented, as though nothing had happened.

"Thank you for that, Miss," said Don. "I'm not much good with horses."

The woman dropped her stern countenance and smiled.

"I can see that," she said. "You could have scared the poor thing to death, you know."

Don estimated her to be in her late twenties and, from her accent, a member of the local gentry.

"Any idea who he belongs to?" he asked.

"Monty? Oh yes, I know who owns him. She's a local girl – and she'll be getting the sharp edge of my tongue tomorrow. It's not the first time this naughty boy has made it out into the traffic. There'll be an accident one day, then she'll be sorry."

"Do you know who owns the field, perhaps I should tell him he has a visitor."

The smile vanished. "Why do you assume it's a 'him'? I own this field. Or don't you think women should own land?"

"I didn't mean…"

"Don't worry, you're no different to anyone else around here," she said brusquely. She then brushed past Don, walked back to her Land Rover and, without further ado, climbed in, slammed the door, and drove away.

Too late, having finally regained his composure, Don realised he should have taken more details from the woman – including her name and address.

CHAPTER THREE
A SIMPLE DOMESTIC

"Are you completely mad?" Suzanne shouted, standing in front of her husband. "This was all supposed to be behind us. It's the reason we came to this shithole! Are we never going to be free of it? Well, are we!"

"Calm down, you stupid bitch!" Steve shouted back at her. He stood up from the sofa where he had been sitting and confronted the angry woman." Do you want the whole village to hear us?" he hissed, waving his arms about.

Steven Hoskins wasn't a big man, probably an inch or two shorter than his wife, and he was usually the personification of calm. Infuriatingly so, according to Suzanne. However, that evening, while his wife was out, he'd been drinking a lot more than usual. As with so many other usually calm and equitable people, alcohol released his inner demons.

"I'm a bitch, now am I?" she shouted back at him. Unfortunately, Suzanne had also been drinking. "Well this bitch has had enough, do you hear me? More than enough! They were fucking children for crissake! We could all get sent to prison for pictures like that, you idiot!"

"I didn't know, did I? I was told they were older."

"What! So, you're blind now as well! Perhaps if you stopped playing with yourself for five minutes, your eyesight might improve. How could you possibly think they were older?"

"They could have been jockeys."

"You bloody stupid man! Well, I'm telling you this and you'd better listen. You're completely on your own this time. If you get arrested, I'm washing my hands of you."

"Oh no, you won't. I know a thing or two about you as well, remember? If anything happens to me you're coming down with me."

"You spineless faggot!" Suzanne screamed. "Do you think you can get away with threatening me? I'll bloody show you!"

She picked up a glass vase from the occasional table in front of her and hurled it in Steve's general direction. It smashed to pieces on the wall behind his head, causing a picture to come loose and fall noisily to the floor.

Still furious, Suzanne screamed in frustration and ran at Steve with her fingers extended. He grabbed her wrists as she tried to scratch his face. As he pulled his head back out of reach of her nails, she brought her knee up as hard as she could between his legs. Fortunately for him, she missed her target and made solid, but relatively harmless, contact with the top of his inner thigh.

At this, Steve lost his temper and pushed her away from him. The push was hard enough to make her fall back against an armchair. He picked up a heavy marble ashtray and made as if to throw it at her. At the last moment, he appeared to think better of it and instead threw it at the expensive colour television set in the corner of the room. The ashtray missed the screen, but it hit the controls and knocked the channel selector knob out of its housing.

Still angry, Steve picked up one of the Waterford crystal whisky glasses he'd been drinking from. He smashed it into the fireplace. Now he turned his attention to the furniture and began throwing everything around the room.

"You're lucky I don't fucking kill you!" he shouted.

"You're mad!" his wife screeched at him. "Fucking mad! I'm not safe here with you, you lunatic! I'm off out of it!" She ran to the front door.

"Go on then, fuck off!" he yelled back at her. "See if I care! I should never have married you in the first place."

"You bastard!" she shouted. "You really are a fucking bastard! I'm going to set the law on you, and don't think I don't bloody mean it!"

She ran from the house and slammed the door behind her. There were tears streaming down her face as she stumbled down the gravel drive and out through the wooden gate into the road.

Steve stared at the, now closed, front door for a full minute. Then he took a fresh glass from the cabinet and poured a drink from the half-empty whisky bottle. He knocked it back in one.

The drink calmed him a bit, and he surveyed the damage in the room. He began to tidy up, cursing his bad temper. What was I thinking of? What a bloody shambles!

She won't call the police, he thought to himself. She's not that stupid, she'll be back in a minute.

The church clock softly chimed for midnight.

Don Barton eased his patrol car into the bus lay-by and killed the engine. God, what an evening, he thought. One rubbish job after another.

As well as the runaway horse, there had been a report of vandalism in one of the local cemeteries.

("Bloody Satanists," the verger had said in all sincerity. "There's loads of them around here, you can hear them chanting sometimes. I stay out of the way. It don't pay to mess with that lot.")

Then there had been an abandoned car in a ditch that would need a follow-up in the morning. A search had revealed no trace of the driver, and there was no reply at the home of the registered keep of the vehicle.

Hopefully, it was just a drunken driver keeping out of the way until he sobered up – but one could never discount the possibility of there being an injured person somewhere in the vicinity who needed help.

It was all very time-consuming. Routine, but important in its way.

Reaching for yet another cigarette, Don swore as his fingers found an empty packet. Had he really smoked the whole lot since booking on at six? The car's overflowing ashtray gave him a silent and disapproving reply.

His shift still had two hours to run, so Don mentally explored the hundred or so square miles of countryside that represented his patch for tonight. He scratched his brains wondering as to where he was going to get some more smokes.

Well, there was an all-night garage on the A4 at Thatcham. Slightly off his ground – but not by much. Problem was, if he went there, the Newbury lads might call him in to help with some job or other. They were desperately under-strength, so he could easily find himself tied up all night.

Don wasn't lazy, and usually he'd be only too happy to help his colleagues, but he was on duty at Royal Ascot Races the day after tomorrow. He really wanted a full day off before diving into the tedious, if very well paid, fourteen-hour shifts, including travel time, which went with policing the event.

Then he had a thought. How about the Green Lion pub up on the Wantage Road? When he'd booked-on and phoned in for briefing, the duty sergeant had told him the pub was having a private party after hours. As it was being held on licensed premises, he had every right to call in to check it was legitimate – and ensure they were obeying the rules.

They'd have fags. Kill two birds with one stone, then.

He crunched the Marina into gear and ambled forward. Don would much rather have been driving his Ford Escort van for routine patrol than this horrible motor. However, the saloon car, unlike the van, was equipped with a "repeater set" radio, and as Don was designated the "area car" for the evening, so he had no choice other than to use the hated motor.

The reason for this was that the van was primarily used for routine enquires on Don's own "patch." However, whilst driving the area car, he had responsibility for the whole rural section, and he was required to be available to be deployed to matters that couldn't be left until the local officer was on duty. These jobs usually required a more immediate response.

The repeater sets were important because they allowed the officer to converse with his thirty-mile distant Headquarters Control Room whilst away from his vehicle. The set managed this by relaying short-range UHF transmissions from a hand-held Pye Pocketfone via the more powerful VHF set installed in the car.

This facility could be of vital importance to an officer attending the scene of a serious incident.

The car was supposed to be "double crewed," but manning levels in the force at that time were critically low, and this frequently wasn't possible. This didn't bother Don. As an ex-Traffic motorcyclist, he was well used to working alone – and often preferred it that way.

Don was a conscientious police officer – and he was only too well aware the remoteness of the area was a magnet for town-based burglars as well as so-called joyriders and the all-too-frequent vanloads of professional poachers. Consequently, he drove slowly on his journey to the pub, carefully scrutinising the widely scatted farms and dwellings as he went.

The Green Lion had once been an old coaching inn and had an impressive façade, making it an important landmark in the area. The building itself was set back from the road, and there was some limited parking for cars at the front.

The white painted brickwork of the pub was run through with oaken beams and an archway, large enough to accommodate a carriage and four horses, led into a space in the rear. The old stable block behind the main building had long since been converted into storage units, but the land adjacent to the units had been cleared and tarmacked to provide additional parking for customers.

Unlike most of the licensed premises in the area, the Green Lion was what was called a "managed house," so the landlord was a manager and an employee of the brewery rather than a self-employed tenant or owner.

Managers in the pub world were at the bottom of the landlord hierarchy; they had to be a married couple, and between them were paid a pittance for the hours they worked. Their employers, usually a main brewery, rigidly curtailed the small part of the business they could run for themselves. Inevitably, fiddling was rife, and a hard-pressed manager was disinclined to turn away cash trade, even if it was after hours.

The "private party" was a much-abused loophole of which many landlords took advantage. Legally, it was permissible to carry on serving after hours as long as the persons present were bone-fide friends of the licensee – being treated at his expense. In law, a customer who had been buying drinks could not suddenly become a "friend" once time had been called. Strictly, no money at all could change hands during the "party."

In reality, like so much legislation, the private party rules were impossible to enforce. So, most police areas operated a more common-sense compromise. Basically, all the landlord had to do was notify the local station in advance of the start of the party. Then as long as he locked the doors, kept the curtains closed and the noise to a minimum, all would be well.

Obviously, the landlord of the Green Lion was aware of the rules. From the road, the establishment appeared all locked up with everyone inside gone to bed. However, as Don slid the highly visible police car into the car park at the rear, keeping it well out of sight of the main road, he could just make out clinks of light emanating from the edges of the curtains in the small back bar. He alighted from his vehicle and rapped on the hard, wooden rear door.

From inside a male voice called, "Hello?"

"Police," said Don. "Routine check."

The bolt rasped back, and the door opened a fraction. A youngish looking man in a sharp-looking flared grey suit peered out cautiously into the night. Seeing the officer, he said, "Private party, I've notified the Newbury lads."

"Yeah, I know," grinned Don. "To be honest, mate, all I want is a packet of cigs, Embassy if you've got them."

The man visibly relaxed and smiled thinly back at the policeman. "You had me going there," he said. "Fags are in a machine in the Public Bar. If you've got the right change, I'll get them for you."

Don handed over the coins and, while the man was absent, instinctively took a good look around the car park.

Not much of a party, he thought. Just two cars, a green Austin 1300 and an old, but well looked-after red Triumph Herald. Other than that, the car park was utterly deserted.

The grey-suited man came back with the cigarettes and said, "D'you fancy a quick pint while you're here? You'll have to drink it outside, though."

There was nothing in the world Don fancied more than a

pint at that moment but felt he'd pushed his luck enough already.

"I'd love one," he said, "but not tonight. Maybe another time?"

"Any time you like. Goodnight, mate, stay safe out there."

"Cheers."

"HT Control to Foxtrot Golf Five Zero, over." The Pocketfone in the top pocket of his tunic piped up. Don took the transmitter from his side pocket and pressed the transmit button.

"Foxtrot Golf Five Zero receiving. Go ahead, over."

"Talk through with Foxtrot Yankee, over."

Foxtrot Yankee was the call sign of the fixed VHF radio located at the Newbury Police Station control room.

"Five Zero from Foxtrot Yankee, can you make your way please to the TK at Brompton village. A distressed female has just called in on the nines requesting assistance. Possible domestic. Over."

"Roger that, ETA eight minutes from my present location, over."

"Thanks, Don. Many thanks, HT. Finished with talk-through. Foxtrot Yankee, standing by."

Don knew exactly where the telephone kiosk in Brompton village was located; it was less than half a mile from where his own police house (and little one-man office) was located. For a driver with Don's skill, eight minutes was a generous timescale. Had he been driving a high-performance Traffic car; he could easily have made the trip in under four – but he was in the Marina. So, it was a full five minutes before he actually pulled over outside the phone box and walked over to meet the lady who emerged from it.

"Good evening, Madam, was it you that called us?" Don smiled to take the edge off his rather formal approach. He estimated the woman to be aged in her forties, and he noticed she was very attractive. From her appearance and demeanour, she was obviously from the middle classes. Her dark trouser suit was discrete, elegant, and looked to be expensive. Her hair was neatly coiffed and her, now tear-stained, makeup had been expertly applied.

She made a visible effort to compose herself before speaking. "Officer, I'm so, so, sorry to have bothered you. I've never phoned the police in my life before, but it's my husband. He's just gone berserk. I'm absolutely terrified and didn't know who else to call."

Don said, "Okay, I'll need a few details. Come and have a sit down."

He opened the passenger door of the patrol car and let her in. With the lady beside him, Don became uncomfortably conscious of all the fag ends that littered the inside of the vehicle. As it turned out, he needn't have worried. The lady was a smoker and asked him for a cigarette. Together they christened his brand-new pack.

"So, tell me all about it, "Don asked. "Are you injured at all?"

"No, I don't think so." Don could tell she had been drinking.

"What about your husband, has he been hurt?"

"No, of course not. Look, officer, I think I'm wasting your time. I was just upset, that was all. I'm okay now, I'm sure I don't need any help after all, thank you." She made to get out of the car.

"Hold on, just a minute," said Don sharply, raising his finger. "It's not as simple as that, I'm afraid, Mrs …?"

"Hoskins, Suzanne Hoskins. I live about half a mile away. Our house is the one set back from the road on that bit of a hill."

"I think I know the one, but I don't recall seeing you before. Have you lived in the village long?"

"We've been here a few months, maybe a year," she said. "We've travelled around a bit these past few years. We moved here to take advantage of the house prices. It's also handy for my husband. He uses the motorway to commute to London three times a week."

"Three times?"

"Yes, he stays in town Monday and Thursday nights."

"Okay, so have you anywhere to stay tonight other than your home?"

"No, I don't have friends here. I've no family and all my associates are in London."

"So, what can I do to be sure you'll be safe? Do you want me to arrange for you to go to a women's refuge? The nearest one is in Reading."

"Oh, God, no!" she looked aghast. "I'm sure Steve's calmed down by now. I'll just go back and sort it out myself…"

"Right, well, I'm sure you understand my position. I have to check for myself that everything's okay, I can't just leave you here."

Before driving to the couple's house, Don copied Suzanne's personal details into his official notebook. Don was still smarting from forgetting to ask the horse woman her name.

Suzanne told him that she and her husband, Steve, had been married six years. She went on to say that, two years previously, she had foolishly become involved with another man. Her lover had been less than discrete in writing her a series of hot letters and, instead of destroying them, she had kept them hidden. Her husband had found them, and it had almost wrecked her marriage. One of their reasons for moving to the country was to give them a fresh start.

Don nodded, taking notes, "Carry on." He encouraged her.

Tonight, they had both been drinking. For some reason the whole issue became the focus of a fierce row. Things got out of hand, and Steve had started throwing furniture about.

Thankfully, he'd made no attempt to physically harm his wife, but she was badly frightened.

"Are you sure you're safe now?"

Don knew only too well the difficulties of trying to repair a broken marriage when one party had been unfaithful, but he decided to keep that particular piece of knowledge to himself. He resolved to stay strictly within professional boundaries: protection of life and property and the maintenance of order. Nothing more.

"You're very young to be working out here in the sticks, aren't you?" Suzanne said suddenly. "I thought village bobbies were all fat old men." Her smile lit up the car, and Don could see how easily this woman could attract men if she so desired.

"Sorry to disappoint you," he grinned back at her. "I'll try and put some weight on."

"Oh, don't do that," she said, with a smile that warned Don she could be a very alluring woman. "Ah, here we are. If you pull up next to the Jag, you'll find it easier to get out of the drive when you leave."

The house was a large, three-bed, modern build bungalow set in half an acre of land. There was a dry-stone wall around the perimeter and the five-bar gate, that Suzanne had left open in her flight and through which Don had just driven, led into a loose gravel drive wide enough for three cars.

Obviously, Steve was no motorcyclist, thought Don as he walked across the loose stones. You'd never get a bike parked on this stuff.

The man who answered the front door was bald, below average height and appeared to be a couple of years younger than his wife. He was wearing suit trousers with a blue and white striped shirt tucked loosely into his waistband. Like his wife, he wasn't drunk, but he had obviously been drinking.

"Mr Hoskins? We've had a call from your wife."

Mr Hoskins momentarily glared at the policeman then

visibly withered. He stood back to let the officer into the house.

Don stepped inside and looked around. There were various items that were showing superficial signs of damage, but no serious destruction had taken place. It was obvious that Steve had been tidying up after his outburst.

"I don't know what my wife has told you, constable, but I can assure you your presence here is really not necessary."

"Well, sir, it's not for me to interfere in your private marital affairs, but I do have a duty to maintain the peace. I need to be certain your wife is not likely to come to any harm if she remains here tonight."

"You'd never hurt me, would you, Steve darling?"

Don sighed as he realised that Suzanne had silently, and contrary to his instructions, left the safety of the car and followed him into the house. He really didn't want to be in the middle if a fight broke out between the husband and wife. He'd been in that situation more than once in his career and knew how nasty things could become.

However, in this instance, it appeared violence was off the agenda.

"Of course not, darling. How could you think such a thing? I love you far too much to ever think of harming you," Steve said and burst into tears. His whole body shook with the sobs.

"Oh, darling!" Suzanne rushed forward to console him. Putting her arm around her husband, she glanced over at Don.

"Thank you for your assistance, Mr Barton, I don't think we'll be needing you any further tonight," she said.

"Are you sure you'll be all right?" Don asked.

"Just go!" she hissed at him before turning back to Steve.

Don had been summarily dismissed, but there was nothing further he could do. No offences had been committed, and the woman was entitled to reside wherever she wished. Don grinned to himself and shook his head. Women, he thought, he would never understand them!

Don used the handset on the Marina to call into Control before driving out.

"Foxtrot Golf Five Zero for HT, all in order Brompton Village. Domestic dispute, both parties given advice. No offences, no further action required. I'm now returning to Foxtrot Golf, and I'll pop an entry in the Occurrence Book before booking off."

"Thank you, Five Zero. HT to stand-by."

CHAPTER FOUR
ROYAL ASCOT

I t was 8 am Tuesday morning, and the weather forecast was dry and sunny. Nevertheless, Don decided to take his lightweight Ganex raincoat with him. He had worked at the royal meeting several times in the past and knew full well that sudden and unexpected rain was a frequent occurrence.

His tunic and trousers had been pressed to perfection, and he could see his face in the shine on his boots. This was the first day of Royal Ascot; uniformed officers would have to go on parade and only the very best turn-out would be accepted.

Don drove his police Ford Escort van from his office in Brompton to the section office at Hampstead Norreys, where he picked up his colleague, Ian Jones. PC Jones had also taken great care with his personal presentation and joked as he stowed his helmet, "I'm keeping a sharp eye on that bugger this year. My other one went missing after last Ascot, and I've never seen it since."

"It's probably sitting in pride of place on some mantlepiece in North Carolina by now," said Don.

They both laughed. It was well known that items of British police equipment were eagerly sought-after as souvenirs by the American servicemen at the nearby Greenham Common airbase. Any kit carelessly left lying around could very quickly be traded by unscrupulous colleagues for King Edward cigars and Bourbon whiskey at the PABX. Helmets were in particular demand

Don liked Ian. Ian was recently married, and, being in his early twenties, he was the only other youngish officer on the section. The two men carried on with their chatter until they reached F Divisional Headquarters at Newbury, where they were due to complete the journey to Ascot by coach together with the rest of their contingent.

F Division was affectionately known as F Troop from the American TV comedy about the Seventh Cavalry fort. They were always a welcome addition to the staffing of any major event. With a racecourse of their own in the town, these officers were not only well experienced in dealing with the racing fraternity, but they had a reputation for being self-sufficient and confident – without being overbearing. They could invariably be relied upon to remain good-humoured and to use common sense when dealing with minor offences.

Together with twenty colleagues, Don and Ian boarded the coach to travel east along the M4 to the other end of the county. They were all looking forward to the day's work that lay ahead of them. The event itself was an enjoyable one to police, and the overtime was very welcome.

However, as the coach pulled out of the station car, Don's attention was drawn to a vaguely familiar vehicle parked in the staff area of the police station car park. He leaned forward in his seat and tapped a colleague on the shoulder,

"Here, Tom, any idea who owns the Triumph Herald?" he asked.

"Yeah, it's that new inspector. Mollington, his name is. You want to watch out for him, a right arsehole by the sound of it. On the way up, that one, a real high flyer."

Don sat back in his seat and contemplated. It did look a lot like the car that he'd seen parked at the Green Lion, but he couldn't swear to it. He hadn't taken the registration number, and Triumph Heralds weren't exactly remarkable or unusual, other than the fact that there weren't that many still about.

If a new firebrand inspector was drinking after hours out on the section, it was knowledge worth having. He decided it prudent to keep his suspicions to himself, for now, so he put his thoughts to one side and joined in with the general banter in the coach.

At that time, several officers in the police service in the UK was going through hard times. Young officers especially were finding it hard to make ends meet, and financial pressures meant that resignations were outstripping appointments. For increasingly worried senior management, Special Events like race meetings represented a welcome opportunity to give junior officers some much needed financial relief by means of paid overtime.

Royal Ascot was the most prestigious of these events and supplied the ideal opportunity to loosen the purse strings at bit. The annual bonanza of extra pay meant that a lucky few officers could subsequently afford to fund a short holiday for their families. Others, less well off, used the cash to pay off some of the debts that were giving them sleepless nights.

Don desperately wanted to take his wife away for a break. He needed an opportunity to try and heal the wounds that had recently threatened to destroy his marriage. He resolved to clock up as many hours as he could and earn as much as possible in the week ahead.

The coach got to Ascot around ten-thirty and, although the first race wasn't due to run until 1.30 pm, the town was already alive with visitors. Many of the men were wearing top hats and tails, and the ladies were splendid in their beautiful gowns and crazy hats. Even in those austere times, if anyone doubted there was still money in the country, they only had to look in the reserved car parks that were dotted around the racecourse to see the truth of the matter – for some, at least.

Grey-suited Chauffeurs in peaked caps were busily setting up folding tables that they retrieved, along with the lavish hampers, from the boots of their employers' cars. Rolls Royces, some new, some vintage, were everywhere to be seen.

Elegant family groups were standing around or sitting at the tables. They could be heard to twitter excitedly as they nibbled at their extravagant snacks before they rushed off to the Members Enclosure to rub shoulders with others of their social class, leaving most of the food and drink untouched.

The chauffeur would then take his turn at the table – and it was common practice for any passing constable to join him in the feast, if he could do so without being spotted.

As usual, there was a general parade for the police personnel before the start of the operation, and Don took the time to stroll across the huge parking area to where a long line of gleaming motorcycles stood proudly next to a red brick wall.

The 650cc Triumph Saints that had served the force well for many years were gradually being replaced by the strange-looking BMW R Series machines with their ungainly Boxer flat-twin engines. Whatever the make, every nut and every bolt of every bike had been polished until it shone. The tyres had been blacked, and the writing on the sidewalls painstakingly picked out in gold paint. Don felt a familiar pang as he admired the presentation.

A group of riders from his old Traffic base came over and shook his hand. Strangely, however, nobody seemed to know what to say to him. They all knew what had happened to him and were dying to know what had become of him, but no-one wanted to mention it. An uncomfortable silence followed.

Eventually, Don said, "Has anyone come off on the Tan yet?"

The Tan crossing was a notorious strip of the racecourse

that allowed the royal horse-drawn procession of coaches to cross over the Winkfield Road and enter the final straight of the course proper. It consisted of thick matting laid over the tarmac so that the horses' hooves wouldn't be damaged. Motorists were allowed to use the road until it was closed an hour or so before the first race. Crossing the matting was no problem to cars, but for motorcycles, it was like crossing an icy skid pan in a gusty wind.

The men laughed. "Wilkie's been off twice already. He's round the back now waiting for the mechanic from Taplow to come out with a new clutch lever." Poor old Sergeant Wilkinson, he only rode a motorbike once a year – and always gave the regular riders a good laugh.

Their little reunion was cut short by the local Chief Superintendent marching into the yard and calling for everyone to form up in their units.

An impressive looking ex-Scots-guardsman, Superintendent Jackman, was the Silver (i.e. local operational) Commander that year. The Gold Commander was an Assistant Chief Constable who remained back at HQ, so Jackman was effectively the officer in charge. He had issued all the men and women attending the event with copies of his operational order.

He had also ensured that they had all received meal tickets to hand in to the caterers when they obtained refreshments. Therefore, everyone should already be aware of what his or her role in the proceedings was to be; however, it was a tradition that the officer commanding carried out an inspection of the turnout of the troops before giving them a final briefing.

"Right, you lads," he bellowed in his resonant Scottish accent, "and lasses," he added a bit belatedly, "I'm sure you know what to do, but I'll tell you anyway."

Don, who had heard it all before, tried not to look bored.

"You'd think he was addressing the esplanade at the Edinburgh Festival," he muttered.

But, on it went: Remember the royal family and high-ranking government officials will be all around the place, stay out of the Royal Enclosure, watch out for the telephoto lenses of the BBC, do not congregate in groups of more than two, keep a low profile when not actually performing duty, no visible betting, and so on and so forth. Then finally:

"No doubt some of you will be seeking liquid refreshment. You are to stay out of licensed premises, we have a perfectly good beer tent of our own set up down in the Donkey Field. If you must spend your money, at least do it in support of our own sports and social club."

Don met Ian's eyes and winked.

The briefing was over and, together with more than a hundred other uniformed officers, Don and Ian made their way downhill along High Street towards the Silver Ring where the police caterers had set up a huge marquee tent.

"Looks like the first pull of the day," said Ian, pointing across the road to where two burly police officers frogmarched a fat little man in a loud check suit towards the local police station. One of the officers was carrying a green baize fold-up table, revealing the prisoner to be one of the many card sharps that haunted the streets outside the event.

"His lookouts must have been asleep to let him get nabbed so early," said Don. "He's hardly had time to make enough to pay his fine."

"Don't bet on it!" quipped Ian, and they both laughed.

They arrived at the feeding station and squeezed in at the end of a long line of men and women queueing for the tea and coffee urns.

Don glanced around the throng of people who were milling around inside the marquee and, to his horror, instantly recognised someone he had hoped never to see again. Diane's back was towards him, but there was no mistaking the blonde ponytail that seemed to dance above a pair of shapely shoulders.

"Oh, God, no," he said softly, but not softly enough, for Ian caught the words and saw the look on Don's face…

"I take it you know her?" Ian said.

The remark seemed innocent enough, but Don knew that his marital problems and subsequent posting away from Traffic had been the subject of much gossip across the area – and the quick-witted Ian would have instantly guessed the cause of his friend's discomfort.

"If you'd rather make yourself a bit scarce, mate, I don't mind fetching your tea outside to you."

Don fought the sinking feeling in his stomach. "Thanks, Ian, I appreciate it, but I'm okay. I'm not going to spend all week hiding in a corner."

As if on cue, Diane turned away from the small group of young men she had been chatting with and looked straight at Don. To his amazement, she smiled over to him and gave him a brief wave before returning her attention to her friends.

Don wasn't sure what reaction he'd been expecting from her when she spotted him, but her simple, brief acknowledgement of him, as though he were no more than a casual acquaintance, left him somewhat stunned.

He was, he realised, after all, just another colleague. Their shared past meant nothing to her. Casual sex had apparently not made him special.

After a couple of minutes, Diane walked out of the tent without so much as a glance in his direction. Don watched the swing of her hips as she walked, and he tried not to remember them without the long skirt. He suddenly felt ashamed of his unexpected feelings of rejection. He determined instead to be grateful that she no longer represented a threat to his marriage.

Don and Ian each sat down at one of the places that had been set up on the long trestle tables. They ate their lunch in virtual silence, which they washed down with the traditional half-pint bottle of Courage light ale; then it was time to report for duty.

The operational order had informed the two men that they were assigned to general patrol of Ascot Heath. So, together, they walked to the stands then negotiated the long narrow tunnel that ran under the track and linked the Silver Ring with the large open area known as the Heath.

"Bit of a come-down for you, isn't it, young Don?" Sergeant Williams was the fat, scruffy and unpopular Welshman who commanded the team that Don and Ian had been detailed to join. He smirked at Don. "You're better used to flashing it about with the nobs in their Rollers on a fancy motorbike, aren't you? Not so used to slumming it on the Heath with the local riff-raff like the rest of us, eh, boyo?"

Don just grinned good-naturedly; no way was he rising to this idiot's bait. Not yet anyway, but it looked like being a long week ahead...

The crowds now began to arrive in their thousands, and at 1 pm, Don and the rest of his team marched in a line through a gate in the crowd barriers, then they walked along the grass track itself to eventually take up position, several yards apart, as "route liners."

Emily Davison, the suffragette who had thrown herself under the king's horse at Epsom Derby all those years before, had cast a long shadow and, since her day, the crowds had to be watched whenever royalty was present.

This duty meant that Don and the other officers faced the crowd and were under strict instructions to observe the public and keep their backs turned toward the ornate coaches and horses of the Queen's procession as it made its majestic way along the final straight, before alighting on the grass in front of the Royal Enclosure. Ironically, it wasn't the nobs in the Grandstand but the ordinary folk on the Heath who had the best view of the spectacle – and the Queen usually rewarded them with a brief wave.

With the Queen and her guests safely inside the Royal Box, the route liners marched back off the track to take up general patrol positions among the racegoers. However, Sergeant Williams was waiting like a coiled snake for Don as he walked back through the gate.

"Don, I've just had a message on the radio. You're to make your way immediately to Ascot Police Station."

He paused, waiting for a reaction, enjoying the obvious stress he was creating.

"What, me? Why's that then, Sarge?"

"There's a detective inspector waiting to see you." Williams gave an oily smile.

"Any idea what it's about, Sarge?" Don was perplexed and a bit uneasy,

"I've no idea, mate. You might be in the shit, you might not. You've not been shagging any young woppsies again, have you?"

Don wanted to punch the sergeant in the mouth but, instead, turned on his heel and, with his mind spinning, he began the long walk back up to the local nick.

As Don approached the busy area around the rear door of the small police station, he saw uniformed officers of all ranks to-ing and fro-ing from the building in an endless stream. He slowed down and wondered to whom he should report.

"PC Barton?" came a voice from behind. Don spun around to see who had spoken and saw a middle-aged man of medium height, wearing a smart business suit, who was smiling at him in a friendly manner. The sun glinted from the man's dark hair.

"DS Dave Johnson, Headquarters CID." The hatless man held out his hand. "I thought it must be you when I saw you coming up the road."

Don shook the man's hand and thought: Old-fashioned detective, very professional, what the Hell's going on?

"Let's pop inside, shall we? DI Braden is waiting upstairs in the inspector's office."

Don was aware who DI Braden was, he'd seen him before for various reasons and knew that he oversaw the CID office in Slough. Not a bad governor, known to like a drink.

"Come in Mr Barton, take a seat," the DI said when they reached the office. "I see you've already met Sergeant Johnson. I suppose you know what this is all about?"

Why did they always say that? Don thought. Of course I don't bloody know, you haven't told me anything yet!

"No, sir, nobody's said anything to me," he replied. Then he noticed that the Occurrence Book from his section office was sitting open on the desk in front of the DI.

"Did you make this OB entry?" asked Braden, indicating the couple of paragraphs Don had penned following the domestic at the Hoskins house.

"Yes, sir," said Don, totally puzzled.

"And Mrs Hoskins was alive and well when you last saw her?"

"Absolutely, it was a something and nothing domestic, some damage but no violence – by either party. Why, has she been hurt or made a complaint or something?" Don knew only too well that she wouldn't have been the first marital partner to call the police only to throw them out when they got there – then later complain that they'd done nothing to help her.

"So, it comes as a complete surprise that her body, at least we're assuming it's her body, was found bludgeoned to death in the area known as Bluebell Wood, on the Weston-to-Hampstead Norreys road earlier today?"

"Oh, dear God!" Don was visibly stunned and took a moment to recover his composure. "Yes, sir, a complete surprise."

"The body was found by the owner of the land, a lady out walking her dogs. I believe she's an acquaintance of yours, a Miss Anne Wilson?"

Don shook his head. "Never heard of her," he said.

"Well, she knows you. Apparently, she helped you with a runaway horse the other night."

I knew I should have taken her bloody name! "Oh, her! She stormed off before I could get her name. It was actually the same night as the domestic with the Hoskinses. She was brilliant – but a bit volatile. I had no idea she owned Bluebell Wood. Is she involved at all, do you think?"

"We don't know who's involved at the moment," DS Johnson said.

"And Mr Hoskins, the husband, what does he have to say about it?"

"That's what we need to find out. Problem is, he's done a runner, disappeared completely. Did you see a car when you were at the house?" DI Braden asked.

"Yes, sir, a blue XJ6."

"Well, that's gone as well. You don't know where it is, I suppose?"

"No, sir, not a clue."

"Right, well, Mr Johnson here is going to get you to make a full statement while it's all fresh in your mind – and before you pick up any outside influences. I believe it's already been on the telly once today. After that, you're to go back to Newbury with him and make a formal identification of the body. Continuity, you understand."

"Yes, of course, sir."

Johnson took Don to the small dining room and sat him down at a table that was already equipped with statement form. He gave Don his instructions, then left him to it.

A few minutes later Johnson said goodbye to Braden who returned to his office in Slough. Johnson took the inspector's place at the desk in the office and phoned Newbury to speak to his boss, Detective Superintendent Merryweather, the senior investigating officer for the murder.

"Hello, Guv, how's it going?" he said when the guv'nor answered his phone.

"Hi, Dave. Pretty good, actually, the incident room is just about set up, dog search is ongoing, the forensic pathologist is finished at the scene, and the body is en route to the mortuary. How did you get on with Barton?"

"No problem, he's making his statement as we speak. I'll get it typed up then go through it with him."

"What do you make of him?"

"Pretty reasonable sort of chap, he seemed shocked when we told him about the killing. My first impression is that he's straight."

"Well, of course, I respect your judgement, you know that. On the other hand, Barton is the last person we know for sure to see Mrs Hoskins alive. At best, he may have abandoned her to her fate, and, at this point, I don't want to think what the worst-case scenario is. Apparently, he fancies himself as a lady's man, so who knows?"

"Well, I don't know if it's significant, but he also denied knowing Anne Wilson when DI Braden told him it was her that found the body."

"Did he, indeed? That might be interesting."

"Are we leaving him over here or shall we pull him back to Division?"

"Er, no, leave him to carry on at Ascot. We know where he is if we want him and he'll be out of the way while we're working the villages. Oh, and by the way, there's some very interesting stuff already coming back from SOCCO at the victim's house." He said, referring to the Scenes of Crime officers who were painstakingly searching the property for forensic evidence. "This whole thing looks like being a bit more complicated than we thought. I'll explain when I see you. Meanwhile, total press embargo, got it?"

"No problem, guv, I'll make sure Barton knows to keep his trap shut as well."

"Thanks, Dave, I'll see you later."

Don toiled over his statement for an hour and a half, labouring over every phrase. Johnson had told him to write down absolutely everything from the moment he received the radio call sending him to meet Mrs Hoskins, to the time he booked off duty.

"Forget about the rules of evidence," Johnson had ordered. "I want the ins and outs of a duck's arse. Everything you saw on the way to and from the house, details of other traffic on the road, any pedestrians, and so on. Oh, and include a weather report and, whatever you do, make sure you write a full description of everyone you saw or spoke to – and any comments you want to make about them, just stick them in brackets next to the description. Soon as you're finished, take it down to Brenda, the CID typist. She's waiting downstairs."

When Don finally completed his task, Johnson carefully and slowly went through the statement. Occasionally, he paused to clarify some point or to make a brief comment, but he mostly read in silence.

"Not a bad effort," he said grudgingly. "Have you done these before?"

"No, not for a murder, but I've dealt with a fair few fatal accident on the roads."

Johnson allowed himself a smile. "Fatal road accidents? Of course, you're ex-Traffic, aren't you? We sometimes forget that you lads actually do a bit more than just hound hard-working detectives for driving a couple of miles an hour over the limit."

"Well, speeding may be a minor offence, probably on a par with minor theft; however, shoplifters rarely kill anyone, do they?"

Johnson laughed. "You've got me there, Don. Anyway,

let's get back to Newbury and look at this body. My car's in the field next door; you can drive if you want to."

Don grinned. "No thanks, Sarge. It'll be a treat to be chauffeured for a change."

As it turned out, DS Johnson was an excellent driver with an impressive, and smartly turned out, two-year-old Mark 3 Ford Cortina.

"Is this yours or is it a job car?" asked Don.

"It's mine, but I use it for work and get paid mileage. Have a look in the glove box."

Don did as he was bid and found the car was equipped with a VHF force radio. Johnson explained that the provision of this radio was a condition of being on mileage.

"The main wireless gubbins is in the boot," he said. "They've drilled holes all over the place to fit it all in. Shame really, but they reckon they can fill them all in when they eventually take the set out for me to sell the car."

The conversation continued in this vein for the hour it took them to get back to Newbury town centre where Don had to give directions to the local mortuary.

PC Pete Smith, the local police Coroners Officer, was waiting for them when they arrived. He made a record of the time of their visit in a log on a clipboard then took them into the examination room where a body was lying on a long metal trolley, covered with a sheet.

"Here she is, gents. A bit of a mess after the post mortem I'm afraid."

Smith lifted the sheet back as far as the cadaver's waist. Don could see that the body had been completely opened for the pathologist's examination. The vital organs had been removed, and the chest had then been roughly stitched back together in a jagged line from the throat to the groin. The top of the head had also been removed then replaced, and the face was contorted by a mass of black and blue bruising.

"I see what you mean about the PM." Don said.

However, with all the road deaths he had witnessed, he was well used to seeing mangled bodies. He took his time to look carefully to see if this was, in fact, what remained of the attractive woman who had sat next to him in his police car just two days previously. He felt a tinge of sadness as he recalled the incident and he wondered what could possibly have happened to destroy a life in such brutal fashion.

Once satisfied that there was no possibility of error, he indicated to the others that this was, without doubt, the body of the woman known to him as Suzanne Hoskins.

CHAPTER FIVE
BROMPTON VILLAGE

For the size of the village, Brompton was blessed with a larger-than-average Memorial Hall. Following the murder, the police had requisitioned the hall, and it had been kitted out as a temporary communications centre, or Forward Command Post as it was known.

It was Wednesday morning, and inside the hall, several rows of chairs had been unfolded and placed facing the wooden stage. Along the side of the room, towards the rear, were two typists' desks, fully equipped and ready for use; close to them stood a table on which there was a UHF portable base station, linked by cable to a mast on the roof of one of the vehicles in the car park. Two shirt-sleeved officers were manning the telephones that were sitting by the radio, and, on the desk, were two large wooden trays containing pairs of Pye Pocketfone handsets ready to be handed out to the enquiry teams.

Fortunately, the hall was blessed with generous parking facilities and a grassy area that was sometimes used for picnics. Police vehicles of all shapes and sizes had begun arriving around six am and by nine o'clock the car park, and some of the grass area, was full to capacity.

The forty-plus occupants of these vehicles were milling around inside the building. The officers, both uniform and plainclothes, were chatting with one another and drinking tea. Several were also eating bacon, egg, and sausage baps, distributed from a large baker's tray on a table in the corner. The supply of food was overseen by a sharp-eyed uniform sergeant whose job it was to make sure no-one took more than his or her share.

The general hubbub in the room dropped a fraction when, at nine o'clock precisely, Inspector Mollington, carrying his cap and wearing a smartly pressed uniform, mounted the steps and strode over to a lectern that had been placed on the stage facing the assembly.

The wooden stage he marched across was usually reserved for the presentation of locally produced amateur dramatic performances and, when needed, overseeing polling booths at election time.

That Wednesday, however, a large white screen had been set up at the back of the stage. The lectern had been placed a few feet to the front of this screen, and an OHP (or overhead projector) had been set up on a table next to the lectern.

"May I have your attention!" shouted Mollington as he reached the lectern. "Can we have everyone seated please, we've got a lot to get through and time is limited."

The officers shuffled into the seats and carried on munching their breakfasts.

"Can you hear me at the back?" asked Mollington loudly. "I'm afraid the Tannoy isn't on, so I'm going to ask you all to remain as quiet as you can until we're finished. Please don't call out. There will be ample opportunity to ask questions after the briefing."

The room fell deathly silent.

"Thank you," continued Mollington. "For those of you that don't know me, I'm Inspector Mollington from Newbury, and I've been assigned as the administration officer for the current murder incident room. Now, as you will no doubt be aware, the body of a woman was found at the entrance to some woods not far from here yesterday, and her death is being treated as murder. Your job today will be to assist the murder investigation team with carrying out local enquiries. But, just before I hand you over to Detective Sergeant Johnson to explain your duties to you, may I remind you that this incident has been deemed a Special Occasion. It's important that any claims for overtime or expenses must be clearly marked with the operation code and submitted under separate cover via your own local admin office. Thank you, everybody, have a good day and do a good job. Over to you, Sergeant Johnson."

Johnson, somehow managing to avoid rolling his eyes at this mention of administrative trivia, strolled over to the lectern.

"Good morning, all, thanks for coming, I'm Dave Johnson, Headquarters CID. Our Senior Investigating Officer, Superintendent Merryweather, sends his apologies for not being here. Unfortunately, he's been detained elsewhere."

Johnson placed a transparency on the OHP, and an aerial photograph of a country road appeared on the screen behind him. The image also revealed a wooded area with gravel parking. A white arrow had been superimposed on the picture, pointing to the roadside near the entrance to this parking area.

"This location is known locally as Bluebell Wood," said Johnson. "At ten o'clock yesterday morning the owner of the land was out exercising her dogs when she came across this."

He changed the transparency and the image now on the screen, taken at ground level, was of what could have been taken for a bundle of clothing on a grass verge. The next shot was a close up showing that the clothing was, in fact, the fully dressed body of a woman with her eyes and mouth wide open, reaching forward with her right hand as though beseeching help.

The officers in the audience had seen plenty of dead bodies in their service but, nevertheless, stared grim-faced at the photograph. Violent death was something nobody ever really got used to.

"The grass was quite long where the body was found, so it was quite concealed and could have been in situ for some time," Johnson continued. "That's one of the things we would like to find out today, so anyone you speak to who's been to the woods in the past twenty-four hours is very much of interest to us."

One of the officers put up his hand; Johnson nodded to him.

"Have we any idea who she is, Sarge?"

"Formal identification has yet to take place, but we believe her to be a Mrs Suzanne Hoskins. She moved to this area from London not too long ago, but we don't know much about her yet. Once again, this is where you come in today. We want to speak to anyone who knew her, however slightly. Unfortunately, there are no photographs of her at the property where she lived, so we're struggling a bit until we find out more."

Another hand went up.

"You called her *Missus* Hoskins, is there a Mister Hoskins?"

"Yes, there is, and we would very much like to speak to him. He seems to have disappeared, so any information you uncover about him is to be treated as important and passed back immediately."

"Is there a description of Mr Hoskins?" a sergeant asked.

"There is, but it's brief, and you'll find it in your handout. There's no photograph yet though. He seems to be a very private man. We don't know a lot about him yet."

Johnson changed the image to a black and white map of

Brompton Village. The map showed the village divided into segments, each of which had been designated with a letter of the alphabet.

"Ladies and gents, you'll be working in teams of two and assigned to carrying out house-to-house enquiries in one of these areas. Each team will have a radio and a clipboard with a questionnaire – along with a supply of statement forms. We want a separate questionnaire completed for each member of every household. Anyone answering Yes to questions four and seven is to be asked to make a statement, and you're to radio in if anyone can answer affirmative to question fourteen: Do you know the present whereabouts of Steven Hoskins?"

"How long have we got, Sarge?" a voice from the crowd called out.

"This is not a race; we want you to take your time and do a thorough job. If we don't finish the village today, we'll come back tomorrow. And look, everyone, drink as much tea as you're offered. People open up over a cuppa. You never know what they've got to tell you. But only tea mind!"

A ripple of laughter went around the room.

"So, what I'm saying is don't rush," Johnson went on. "Please, just listen to what people are saying. These questions are not comprehensive, don't be frightened to throw a few in of your own if the conversation is going somewhere we hadn't anticipated."

"How much feedback do you want while we're out there?" A male voice from the audience. "Do you want us to call stuff in or wait until we get back here?"

"I want that radio buzzing all day. Keep us fully informed of your progress – and for God's sake, make sure we know your location at all times. The very last thing we want is to find one of you lot lying in a ditch somewhere just as we're getting ready to knock off and go home." More laughter.

As the group began to disperse Johnson called out, "Oh,

and by the way, Superintendent Merryweather is the best detective this force has ever had. He doesn't like to get beaten and takes murder enquires very seriously indeed. Don't be surprised if he pops up out of the blue at your location. So, stay alert and do a good job."

Don hardly recognised his village as he drove home to Brompton that evening. There were various police vehicles parked up in several of the roads near the Hoskins home, and the two small pubs were overflowing. Despite the lateness of the hour, there were strangers, some of them apparently reporters with cameras, walking around everywhere.

My sleepy little village has developed a carnival atmosphere in the short time since I left it this morning, Don thought to himself. He would normally have welcomed the increase in activity (God knew he'd had enough of being bored lately), but for some reason, he actually felt a sense of foreboding.

Be careful what you wish for, he reminded himself.

He left his van in the driveway ready for an early start the next day, and he entered his police house via the small office attached to the side of the building. He could hear that the TV was on in the living room, so he went straight in there.

Rosemary had been dozing on the sofa but jumped up to greet her husband. She rushed over to him and gave him a hug and a quick kiss.

Rosemary Barton looked a lot younger than her twenty-five years. She was five-feet-four-inches tall and blessed with a firm, slender figure. She rarely wore make-up, hated dressing up, and was habitually seen wearing jeans and a T-shirt. However, despite her lack of sophistication, she was an attractive young woman with a "girl next door" appearance that most people found appealing.

"Don, I'm so glad you're home. It's been bedlam around here all day," she said.

"I know, I've just driven through the village. Has it been like it all day?" he asked her.

"It started shortly after you left this morning and hasn't eased up at all from what I've seen."

Don grinned. "Well, you've been moaning about it being such a dead-and-alive hole, perhaps you should be grateful."

"I didn't want anyone to die, though! Has that poor woman really been murdered?"

Don's smile faded. He became serious. "Yes, I've just had to identify her body."

Rosemary was shocked. "You have? Why, how do you know her?"

"I met the victim last Sunday night when her husband kicked off in that domestic I told you about. But it was a simple married couple's argument, no real violence."

"Is that why he did it, the husband I mean?"

"To the honest, love, if you've been watching the news, you probably know more than I do. CID have been talking to me all day, but they haven't given much away. Has there been anything on telly about it?"

"They've put his picture out as being wanted for questioning. Is he guilty do you think, I mean they haven't said it was him?"

"From what I saw, he didn't have it in him. But, on the other hand, everybody's capable of murder, I suppose, given the right provocation."

"But if it wasn't him then it means there's a killer on the loose. Am I safe here all alone in the day?"

"Well, stay by the phone and keep a whistle handy. There's enough police about so you should be okay. I mean this is the last place a fugitive's going to want to come to, I reckon."

Rosemary wasn't convinced. "If I hadn't started that new

job I'd go and stay with mum. Anyway, I can hardly go off and leave you all alone."

Rosemary suddenly turned cold; her comment had triggered an unwelcome memory. "Was Diane at Ascot today?" she asked abruptly. "Did you see her?"

Don wasn't about to lie to his wife.

"Yes," he said slowly, "she's at the event. Nowhere near me, thank God. I did see her, though. She looked right through me."

Rosemary looked sceptical. "I don't want all that nonsense starting up again," she said. "I couldn't stand it."

Don took both her hands in his and looked her directly in the face "Nor could I," he said, honestly. "I know I was totally out of order, but it was a one-off stupid mistake, believe me. It will never happen again, I promise."

"Oh, Don, I want to believe you, really I do." She took a deep breath. "I know we can't change what's happened, but it's over. It's in the past now."

"Yes, Rosemary, and that's where it stays."

"It better had, Don," she said despairingly, then, adopting a harder tone, repeated, "It better had."

Don said nothing. He knew a threat when he heard one, and this was one threat he intended to take very seriously.

"Morning Ian, you obviously got back all right last night," Don said as his colleague climbed into the van beside him.

"Yeah, no sweat; once I knew you were tied up, I got the area car to call into Newbury and pick me up. I even rescued your Ganex for you, it's in the back with mine. Looks like we may need them today."

"Well, it wouldn't be Ascot without rain, would it?" They both laughed.

"So, what's it like living at the centre of the universe?" said Ian.

"I'll tell you what it's like; it's like being a kid with his nose against the window of the sweet shop. I feel totally out of it. My missus knows more of what's going on than I do – and that's only because she watches telly."

"Really? After the time you spent with CID yesterday, I was sure you'd have the inside track on everything by now, a sharp operator like you."

"You're joking, aren't you? That lot are playing Secret bloody Squirrel as usual. They're more likely to talk to a BBC reporter than they are to a woodentop like me. I do get the impression it's more than a simple domestic murder, though. I had five minutes with Merryweather once I'd ID-ed the body and all he kept asking me about was if I'd seen any strange youngsters in the village recently."

"And had you?"

"No, but I've only been there a few months, so I don't know all the local kids by sight yet."

"Hello, looks like the coach is here already," said Ian as they pulled into the police station car park. "No tea for us until we get there then."

The Wednesday of the race meeting went by without incident, so Don was home by eight o'clock. Rosemary had prepared a cold supper that they washed down with a chilled bottle of white wine.

"It was more frantic than ever around here, today," said Rosemary as they ate. "There were uniforms all over the place. They knocked at every house in the village with a questionnaire on a clipboard. They even came here. I was a bit surprised; it was as though ours was just another house rather than the local police office!"

"Well, they'd look damn silly if they didn't come here, then found out later that you knew something of value," smiled Don.

"Well, there's not much to tell you. Bluebell Wood is

completely closed to the public – and there's been all sorts of odd people in and out of the Hoskins house all day."

"All pretty routine," said Don. "They'll be talking to all the taxi and bus drivers that service the village as well – and don't be surprised if you get held up at a road check over the next couple of days."

"What on earth do they do with all the information?" asked Rosemary. "There must be mountains of paper piling up."

"Well, it all goes into the incident room where trained statement readers go through everything with a fine-tooth comb. Absolutely every item of every statement is indexed, cross-indexed, and double indexed on a card system. It's amazing how clever it all is."

"So, Mr Merryweather is like a spider at the centre of a web?"

"Ha, ha, what a great description! Yes, just like that. He sits in an office and gets constantly briefed by a team of specially trained detectives. One of them, Dave Johnson, a DS, is my point of contact. I deal with him and no-one else."

"Suppose he's off duty?"

"These boys don't go off duty until the murder is cleared up. I've got Dave's home number in my wallet, and the superintendent has moved into single men's quarters in Newbury. He has been known to have a camp bed at the back of his office on other murders he's dealt with."

Rosemary wasn't impressed by that idea. "Don't you ever go on CID, Don, I don't think I'd like it much."

"Don't worry, love," said Don ruefully. "Even if I wanted to join them, I very much doubt they'd have me."

For some reason, Don felt relieved. It was later he realised that, by her comment, Rosemary was seeing them both as having a future together. Hopefully, Diane would soon be totally forgotten.

CHAPTER SIX

A QUIET DAY SHOPPING

T he royal meeting concluded on the Friday of Ascot Week, and Don was grateful for the fact that he hadn't encountered Diane again after that first meeting. The last day of actual racing, known as Ascot Heath, customarily took place on the Saturday, and was a very low-key affair.

The Heath Meeting required only a fraction of the policing presence of the main event, so F Division was not detailed to perform duty on the Saturday. This meant that Don was granted a much-needed couple of rest days that gave him the opportunity to take Rosemary shopping in the nearby town centre in Reading.

Parking in Reading was the usual nightmare, but Don eventually settled on leaving their nine-year-old Vauxhall Viva on the top level of the Minster Street multi-storey car park. From the parking spot they were able to walk a few hundred yards to St Mary's Butts, then along the road past the historic church to Broad Street and the main shopping area.

Despite being with his wife, Don's mind kept drifting back to the village and the missing Steve Hoskins. He couldn't help taking a close look at every middle-aged man they passed. Rosemary gave him a hard look.

"I know what you're doing," she said. "Stop it."

It was a gloriously sunny Saturday mid-morning, and the town was packed with shoppers. The couple took one look along Broad Street and decided instead to cross over to West Street and do their shopping at the enormous co-operative department store.

The shop carried everything from carpets to furniture, food to soft furnishings. It included a well-appointed paint, wallpaper, and DIY section where Don bought a new drill from a very pleasant, and surprisingly well-informed, young male shop assistant.

"He was nice," said Rosemary. "Do you know him, you were chatting for ages?"

"I don't know him, but he recognised me from an accident I dealt with a couple of years back. He wants to join the job next year when he's a bit older. Would you believe it? I'm a role model!"

"He'll learn," said Rosemary with a grin.

After a light meal in the store's restaurant, Don and Rosemary decided to leave with their purchases and pop over the road to the nearby Odeon cinema, where the afternoon performance was about to begin.

Don had been a Police Cadet in Reading some years previously and had enjoyed the concession of free tickets to go to the pictures for the local police. It had been a godsend for a cash-strapped young man in those days, and Don had made full use of the facility. He had consequently become well known to many of the staff and got on very well with them.

However, most of the cinema's employees had moved on over the years, and, now he no longer worked at the local station, Don preferred to pay his way when going to the movies. Consequently, he was very pleasantly surprised when the cinema manager recognised him as he and Rosemary entered the picture house.

"Hello, young Don, nice to see you again." The manager shook his hand. "How are you these days?"

"I'm very well, thank you, Mr Jones. This is my wife, Rosemary."

"I'm pleased to meet you, Rosemary. Look, the film's about to start; you can leave your bags with Doreen in the kiosk. It'll save lugging them about. Here you are, take yourselves upstairs." He handed Don two tickets marked "complimentary" and gave a thumbs up to Doreen. He pointed at the bags the couple were carrying. Doreen smiled and nodded in reply.

The film was a light modern musical with a great soundtrack. Rosemary had been dying to see it since it first came out and she settled herself happily into the seat next to Don. As was usual with afternoon matinees, the cinema was almost empty, and the pair had a whole row to themselves.

During one particularly emotional scene, Don, who was in danger of dropping off to sleep, could feel his wife's hand tugging on his shoulder, gaining his attention. He looked at her, and she nodded towards a young couple sitting in the row in front of them.

Don couldn't see over the young man's shoulder but from his rhythmic jerking, and the hand movements of the giggling girl with him, it was obvious what they were up to.

Suddenly the scene was softly, but clearly, lit up by the beam from the usherette's torch – which clearly illuminated the man's exposed nether regions. The young lady gasped, covered her mouth with her hand, and removed the other one from her boyfriend's lap. The man, however, just grinned and poked his tongue out towards the usherette.

The young man's grin froze as he found himself staring at the badge on Don's warrant card, which the officer was holding in front of his face from behind. Don indicated with his thumb for the couple to exit to the aisle where the usherette stood back, ready to let them out and escort them from the premises.

Don began to stand up, ready to help, but the lady with the torch motioned him to remain seated. Don had met her many times in the past, and he relaxed back into his seat. He knew this lady was more than capable of sorting out the cheeky lovers without his assistance.

"How mean!" chided Rosemary. "Anyone would think you were never young."

"I had no choice," Don said. "There's no such thing as a free lunch you know – or a free cinema ticket."

The usherette was nowhere in sight when the film ended, and the pair were in good spirits when they eventually retrieved their shopping and made their way out of the cinema into the early evening sunshine. Don carried the heavier of their two bags in his right hand, and Rosemary held the other in her left. They linked their free arms together and walked down the street like a couple of teenage lovers.

It was too nice an evening to go straight home, so they decided to go for a stroll along Friar Street. The shops had, by that time of day, either closed or were just about to close. It didn't matter, Rosemary simply enjoyed looking in the windows. After a few hundred yards, however, her arm grew tired, so Don took both bags and Rosemary lightly held his left elbow with her right hand as they walked.

"I haven't seen the flowers in the Forbury yet this summer," said Rosemary. "Can we have a walk through before we go back to the car?"

The historic Forbury Gardens, and the adjacent Reading Abbey ruins, were a bit off their route back to Minster Street, but Don shrugged his shoulders and hefted the bags.

"Do I look like a donkey?" he asked with a grin.

"No, darling, you're Don Barton, not Don Key – but you'll just have to do."

They both laughed and continued walking along to the town hall, past the museum then down Valpy Street where the old Borough Police Station used to be located. At the end of the road, they crossed over the main street that led to the nearby railway station and went in through the entrance to the gardens.

The superbly maintained, ornate flower beds made a spectacular display as they walked along the pathway, and Rosemary was enthralled. By now, though, Don was growing weary from carrying the shopping and, at his suggestion, they decided to sit down on a bench facing the huge statue of a lion that dominated that area of Forbury Gardens.

"Did you know that's an Afghan lion?" said Don. "At least I think it is. The statue's a monument to the soldiers from the conflict in Afghanistan back in Queen Victoria's day. You know, the war Sherlock Holmes's Doctor Watson was supposed to have been in."

"Our teachers used to tell us stuff like that when we came here on school trips but …"

Rosemary's reply was cut short by the sound of shouting and a very loud bang coming from just inside the gate by which they had just used to enter.

The couple looked up to see a short, wiry man wearing an old-fashioned grey suit weaving his drunken way into the gardens. He was shouting at the top of his voice and carrying a wine bottle in each hand. He took a long swig from one of the bottles before throwing it onto the tarmac path where it shattered into a thousand pieces.

"What are you fucking looking at!" the man screamed at an elderly couple walking nearby. He started staggering towards them.

Don felt it was time to intervene. "Mind the bags, love," he said to Rosemary as he stood up and began making his way towards the drunk.

"Be careful, Don!" Rosemary pleaded. "You're not on duty, you know."

"Just stay there," Don told her over his shoulder as he drew close to the man.

Don opened his arms in a conciliatory gesture as he approached the man, and said, "All right, me old mate, calm down a bit and tell me what the problem is."

"Just who the fuck are you?" the man shouted.

"I'm a policeman, and you're going to get arrested if you don't quieten down a bit, so calm down, will you."

This seemed to enrage the man even further.

"What are you fucking staring at?" he yelled at the elderly couple, who had stopped walking and seemed frozen in their tracks.

The drunk threw his remaining bottle at the two old people, then he turned back to Don and raised his fists.

"Steady! Steady!" said Don, but the man lashed out with his right hand. Don sidestepped and grabbed the man's sleeve. He pulled the man towards him and neatly slipped his other arm around the man's forearm trapping him in an armlock.

The man twisted and pulled violently, causing them both to fall over onto the grass lawn at the side of the path. Fortunately, Don landed on top and was able to use his weight to hold the man down – with the armlock still in place.

Rosemary screamed and rushed over to where the men were struggling. She frantically looked all around and started calling for help.

The prisoner proved to be a lot stronger than he looked. Don had difficulty keeping him pinned down.

"Rosemary!" he shouted. "Get someone to phone the nick. I can't hold him much longer."

Rosemary, loathe to abandon her husband, shouted at the old couple to run and find a phone box. However, as it happened, their help wasn't needed. Two uniformed constables, helmets in hand appeared at the entrance and ran over to where Don was still lying on top of the man, trying to keep him down.

Rosemary shouted, "That's my husband, he's a policeman."

The officers got either side of Don and, having firmly gripped the prisoner, helped Don to lift him to his feet.

The drunk was no longer fighting but, as Don released his hold, the officers kept both the man's arms securely pinned behind his back. At this point, a police Ford Transit van arrived at the entrance to the gardens, and a hatless uniformed sergeant rushed up to the disturbance. Don recognised the "skipper" as one he had worked with in the past. Sergeant Mudders, a decent sort of bloke, as he recalled.

On seeing the sergeant, the prisoner began howling, "Ow! Arghh! Let me go! You're breaking my arm! Arghh! Please, you're really hurting me!"

To Don's amazement, Mudders said, "All right, lads, let him go."

The officers released their hold on the man who promptly drew back his fist and landed a right hook squarely on Don's jaw. Don staggered back as the two constables jumped back on the prisoner and wrestled him, again screaming and shouting, to the ground.

Once the drunk had been properly subdued and was safely locked away in the back of the Transit, the sergeant, somewhat embarrassed, went up to Don and checked he was all right and not badly injured.

"Look, Don," he said, "I'm really sorry. I didn't think he'd kick off like that, Bill doesn't normally attack the police. He'll be full of apologies in the morning."

"Do you know him then?" asked Don.

"Yeah, 'Wild Bill' we call him. He's a sad case. Ex-POW from the Burma Railway. Suffered really badly in the war.

Nicest bloke you could meet until he has a drink, then he becomes a demon."

"So, you thought it would be okay to let him loose?" said Don angrily, rubbing his chin.

"Well, you know what the press are like these days. Before you know it they'd have had themselves a great story about police brutality to a war hero."

"Yeah, but they've never had to deal with a violent drunk, have they? All very brave, these chaps, sitting behind their typewriters. No bloody idea of real life." Don was hopping mad.

"I don't blame you for being upset. I'd be the same if he'd thumped me. Anyway, Don, you don't need to do any more on it this evening. We'll let him sober up in the cells then bail him out. I'll do the paperwork, just send me a short statement through the internal dispatch – tomorrow will do. Okay?"

"Okay, Skip," said Don, finally calming down a bit. "I need to get Rosemary home anyway; she's pretty upset."

The sergeant shook hands and walked off. Don re-joined Rosemary by the wooden bench.

"Are you all right, love?" he asked.

"I'm fine," she said. "It's you I'm worried about. Are you okay?"

"I'll live," said Don, smiling. "Let's get back. You can cook me a nice dinner. Returning hero and all that."

"You really are a hero, Don, and I'm not joking. I just hope the public are properly grateful. I don't think they always know how much they owe you chaps."

"Well, one of them wasn't exactly grateful," said Don, picking up their bags from the seat where they'd left them. "My new drill's been nicked."

Instinctively, he scanned the area and saw what appeared to be a youth ducking behind some bushes a couple of hundred yards away. He glanced at Rosemary and decided to let it go. She's had enough for one day, he thought. Joe public doesn't know how easy he's got it!

It was six pm before they finally got home, and their good spirits of earlier in the day had pretty much returned. But they were both utterly exhausted.

"Whew, my feet are killing me!" said Rosemary, throwing her shoes in the corner before going to the sofa and collapsing in a heap.

For Don it felt good to see her this happy and smiling – just like her old self. We need more time like this together, he said to himself, but without the adventure.

"How are you feeling now?" said Rosemary.

"You know, it sounds stupid, but I'm more upset about the drill than the assault," said Don

"Yes, that is stupid!" she said. "A drill can be replaced, you can't!"

Don grinned. "I'm glad you realise that," he said. "And just to prove how indispensable I am, I'll cook the dinner. How's that?"

"Well, it's the least you can do after scaring the life out of me AND those late suppers I've made for you all week."

"I'd been working hard!" Don protested.

"Oh, and if you put a bottle wine in the fridge," she said, ignoring his remark, "it should just be chilled nicely by the time the spuds are bubbling."

"*Yes, milady,*" he replied, treating her to his best imitation of Lady Penelope's "Parker" from the TV show, *Thunderbirds*. "Oh, and by the way, your ladyship, there's a certain matter you started back there in the cinema that I think we should finish between us."

"I don't know what you mean, I'm sure," she giggled as she replied.

"I'll get that wine then," said Don.

A couple of hours later, while they were sitting cuddled together on the sofa watching television, the phone rang.

"Don? It's Dave here," Detective Sergeant Johnson liked to keep things as informal as possible. "Have you got an up-to-date passport?"

"Yeah, I've got one here," Don replied cautiously. "Why do you ask?"

"Strictly speaking, you don't need it where we're going, but the airlines like to see one."

"Are we going somewhere, then, Sarge?"

"We're off to the Emerald Isle, mate, first thing in the morning. I'll pick you up at six; we're already booked on the nine-o'clock flight to Dublin from Heathrow. Obviously in civvies, smartly dressed please – suit if possible – but don't bother packing a bag. We fly back at seven and should be home in time for last orders down the pub."

"But I'm day off tomorrow," protested Don.

"No sweat, the overtime's been authorised, all paid – a nice little pick-up for you!"

Don groaned inwardly; Rosemary had been looking forward to lunch at her parent's house on Sunday. This was not going to go down well.

"Can you tell me what's going on?" he asked.

"Right, strictly in confidence, Steven Hoskins has turned up. He walked into a Garda station this afternoon and said he knew we were looking for him. He's refusing to return to England but says he'll speak to us if we fly out to him. The lads in Dublin are arranging an interview for us, but they won't take any official action on our behalf without proper authority."

Don was fully aware that the spate of IRA bombings then taking place on the mainland had strained diplomatic relations between the two countries; however, it was well known that individual police forces would usually co-operate with each other as much as they could. It was strictly on an informal basis, but only if there were no political considerations – and the offence was serious enough.

"Why me, Sarge, surely you need another senior detective with you for something like this?"

"I would have thought that was obvious, Don. You're the only one who's met this Hoskins chap – I need to know I'm talking to the right person. I'd look a proper Charlie if I ended up talking to a ringer, now wouldn't I?"

"Okay, but you'll need to tell me what I can say to him. I don't want to go putting my foot in it, so to speak."

"I'm sure you wouldn't do that, Don, so don't worry about the interview. I'll give you a full briefing on the journey."

Of course, it made sense – and there was no denying the urgency. Under normal circumstances, Don would have found it an interesting experience and he would have been very keen to go. However, he felt terrible letting Rosemary down; the couple had decided to tell her folks all about their current difficulties and had been going to seek a bit of parental advice.

Diane had cast a long, dark shadow.

However, this was a murder enquiry, and the job came first, so Don knew better than to argue. He realised he really had no choice in the matter. Sergeant Johnson was putting it politely – but there was no doubt that his invitation to go on this enquiry was an order he dare not disobey.

If you can't take a joke, you shouldn't have joined – as the old saying went.

"Okay, skipper, I'll be ready at six. But I was supposed to be taking the missus out tomorrow – so don't be surprised if I've got a black eye when you pick me up."

CHAPTER SEVEN
HEATHROW AIRPORT

J ohnson arrived in a divisional CID car spot on six o'clock the next morning. The driver, George Cracknell, was a young DC who Don had worked with previously and with whom he got on well.

"Good morning, Don," said Johnson. "How did it go with Rosemary?"

"You can never tell with women," grinned Don. "Both she and her mum were surprisingly good about it, I had no grief at all. Rosemary understood how important this trip was. She's decided to have lunch at some village pub with one of her new friends from work, instead of seeing her folks. It's something she's been meaning to do for a while, so there was no drama."

"Good to hear it. Right then, if it's okay with you two, I'll sit in the back and go through some paperwork while you guys sit up front and have a chat. Just forget I'm here."

"Okay, sarge," said Don

"Look, Don, I'm serious, it's Dave, for today at least. I really don't want an IRA bullet in the back of my neck because of your rank-conscious Traffic bullshit. Okay?"

Johnson was smiling, but there was no doubting he meant what he said.

"Okay, er, Dave, no problem."

The journey to London along the M4 went surprisingly smoothly in the early morning traffic, and they arrived at Queens Building at Heathrow Airport just under an hour later. The two travellers bade Tim goodbye, and, under Johnson's directions, they made their way to the Special Branch office where they reported to the duty officer. The officer asked them to wait in a small anteroom, and a few minutes later, a very well-spoken and dapper young detective wearing an immaculate dark suit came in and introduced himself.

"Gentlemen, good morning, I'm James Partridge, how do you do." He shook hands with Don and Johnson. "Have you had breakfast? No? Then let's pop along to the canteen and have a quick chat before I take you to your flight."

The "quick chat" turned out to be a comprehensive lecture on the dos and don'ts of operating in Ireland in the existing political climate. With the ever-present threat of terrorism, police officers had to be especially vigilant. The canteen breakfast, however, was excellent.

"The IRA would have a field day if they could get their hands on a couple of British police officers conducting an investigation in the Republic," their host told them. "So, no talking to anyone other than the people you've gone to see. A sergeant named Rogan from the Garda Siochana will meet you at Dublin airport. He'll look after you while you're over there. He's a good man; we've dealt with him before, so take heed of any instructions he gives you. Oh, and don't be taken in by his somewhat laid-back attitude. He's as sharp as they come..." and so it went on.

Partridge stayed with the two officers until it was time to depart. He eventually took them through to Terminal One via a secure rear connecting corridor. He then escorted them all the way out onto the tarmac and over to the staircase that led to the door of the aeroplane.

"It only takes one phone call from the public area to put us in danger," Partridge explained. "It could be a fellow passenger, a cleaner, or anyone. There are IRA sympathisers everywhere. We take nothing for granted working here. Well, goodbye, gents, have a good trip." He handed Johnson a folded newspaper he'd picked up somewhere en route. He shook hands with the two men then turned smartly and marched back into the terminal.

Up to that point, Don had been quite ambivalent about the threat to his safety. After all, the troubles were focussed in the north of Ireland, and one rarely heard of problems in the south. However, watching Partridge walking away, Don felt suddenly exposed and vulnerable. As he followed Johnson onto the plane, he had the uncomfortable feeling that he would be very happy once this little adventure was safely behind him.

They were the last passengers to board the flight and, despite having economy class tickets, Don was pleasantly surprised to be directed to the first-class seats at the front of the aircraft, well apart from the other travellers. Don had never flown first class and was grateful for the fact that he didn't have to pay for the upgrade. How the other half lives! he thought.

They declined the offer of champagne from the elegantly dressed stewardess but, once airborne, they both ordered coffee. With two steaming cups on the folding tables in front of them, they lit up cigarettes and relaxed into the luxuriously upholstered seats.

"Now, it's time for us to have a chat," said Johnson as the cups were cleared away. He handed Don the newspaper he had been carrying. "Have a look at this."

Don noticed it was the *News of the World*.

"Shitty death!" spluttered Don as he looked at the banner

headline across the front page. His lighted cigarette fell from his mouth, and he had a frantic few seconds trying to retrieve it before he calmed sufficiently to look back at the newspaper. Johnson smiled to himself and continued looking out of the window.

LONDON SEX GODDESS BRUTALLY MURDERED

The article went on to say that an infamous dominatrix known to her clients as Mistress Stern was found battered to death the previous Tuesday morning. Her body had been found in some woods, near to her home in the village of Brompton in Berkshire.

There were photographs of a younger Susanne Hoskins, as well as a picture of her house, a shot of the scene of the murder, and some archive footage of what appeared to be a mediaeval dungeon, complete with whips, canes shackles, and other torture equipment.

"The paper did a number on her two years ago," explained Johnson, saving Don the trouble of reading the whole article. "One of their reporters pretended to be a punter and did a big story exposing her naughty goings-on. She and two other women were offering their professional services to masochistic males, mostly bankers and big company executives. All very discrete – and very expensive.

"Once we found that out, we got onto the Yard and, according to the Vice Squad chappies, she'd been on their radar for years. It turns out she'd been a very successful domme until the paper blew her cover. After the article appeared, her clients deserted her – hardly surprising. She lost a lot of business and eventually sold out to another sex worker. Last the squad knew, she'd retired to the country."

"Bloody Hell!" exclaimed Don. "I would never have guessed that. So could her murder be a session with a client that went wrong?"

"Who knows?" said Johnson. "But that's not all, there's these."

He extracted a brown envelope from the leather briefcase he had stowed under the seat in front of him. However, before he handed it over to Don, he had a good look around the immediate vicinity.

The photos inside were black and white images of two teenage boys. The shots were of excellent quality and obviously professionally produced. The lads in the pictures were completely naked and were posing in a variety of sexual positions. Nothing was left to the imagination.

Don was shocked. "How old are they, they look like kids?" he asked quietly.

"Probably thirteen or fourteen is the best guess, but until we find out who they are, we can't be sure. The Obscene Publications Unit have been aware of Hoskins for years, but they don't recognise these two."

"If they've known of him for years, why hasn't he been pulled?" asked Don.

"Well, up till now he's only photographed adults; proper models, porn actors, and the like. He's never been sussed as a kiddie-fiddler. If he was, his feet wouldn't have touched, ages back."

"The dirty bastard," said Don. The pictures had really turned his stomach, and he felt quite ill.

"Now listen, we're being careful who else we show these to. This is not to get out to the press, got that?" Johnson was deadly serious.

"Of course, but what has all this filth got to do with the murder?"

"Well, you weren't to know it, but one of the bedrooms in the Hoskins house had been set up as a photographic studio – complete with a double bed and expert lighting. We found these on an unexposed roll of film in a dark room they'd set up in the shed out the back. Obscene Pubs tell us Hoskins used to run a lucrative little side-line supplying homo pictures to dirty book shops in Soho."

"Used to?"

"There's the odd thing; they were sure he'd packed it all in around the time his wife gave up her dungeon. He was apparently going all respectable and was sticking to his day job as an advertising exec in the City. So, Master Hoskins has got a few questions to answer. But whether he will actually answer us is anybody's guess."

The weather had been fine and bright when they'd taken off in London, but the sky over Dublin had turned a steely-grey as they landed and, judging from the wet tarmac, it had recently rained. Following instructions from the flight attendant, the two men remained onboard the aircraft until the other passengers had alighted.

A tall, barrel-chested man in a blue suit was waiting for them at the foot of the steps as they eventually exited the plane. The big man had his arms folded over the red tie that hung down over his chest, and the expression on his face was cold and hard.

Don felt a knot in his stomach.

"Mister Johnson and Mister Barton, I presume," he said in a gravelly voice. He glared at the two English officers for a moment, then, suddenly, his face split into a huge smile, revealing his large white teeth. He roared with laughter and held out his hand.

"I'm Mike Rogan," he said as he shook hands. "You can call me Mike, or Michael if you prefer, but," he held up a warning finger, "whatever you do, don't call me Mick, I can't stand it." He roared with laughter again. "Don't look so worried, young Don, you're in safe hands with Mike Rogan, ask anyone."

CHAPTER EIGHT

DUBLIN

R ogan checked that the English officers had no luggage, other than the briefcase Johnson was carrying, so he led the way. They ignored the doorway and walked past the airside wall of the terminal to a quiet car park situated at the rear of the main buildings.

A thin, youngish-looking man in casual clothes was smoking and lounging against the side of a metallic blue, somewhat used-looking, Ford Cortina 1600E. He straightened up and trod out his cigarette as he saw the three men approaching.

"All quiet, Tim?" Rogan asked as they got nearer.

"I'm not sure, Mike," the man replied. "There's been a Transit van pass the other side of the fence a couple of times. It could just be workmen, but I can't be sure."

"Any markings, registration number?" asked Rogan.

"No, plain white workers' van, too far away to get a number plate."

"Well, it's probably nothing, but you'd best do a spot of dry cleaning on the way to the RV. You can never be too sure with these things."

Rogan turned back to his guests and said, "Don, you climb

in the front there and have a chat with Tim. Dave, you and I will squeeze in the back of this little motor and talk to each other about murder and suchlike."

Once aboard, the men were driven away from the terminal to where a uniformed police officer was standing by a tall wire gate set into the perimeter fence that surrounded the airport. The officer opened the gate as the car approached and nodded to the occupants as they drove out past him.

"A spot of dry cleaning, you say, Mike?" Tim called back to Rogan.

"Okay, but don't go too mad; we want to get there in one piece," the big man answered, then turning to Dave, explained, "It's what the Special Branch lads call it when they think they may be followed. We basically shake off any tail."

"Is it that bad?" asked Dave.

"As far as bombs and shootings go, there's nothing at all going on in the South," Rogan said, "but the IRA still have quite a presence down here – despite the organisation being illegal in this country. They keep their heads down most of the time, but we don't take any chances. Anyway, what can you tell me about this killing?"

"Well, basically, this man Hoskins' wife was found dead at the side of the road, about a mile from her home, near the entrance to a local wood. She'd received one very hard blow to the back of the head that cracked her skull, and she died from a bleed in the brain. When we went to look for her husband, he was missing and turned up over here a few days later."

"So, you think he might have done it?"

"We were fairly certain of it to start with, but now things have got a bit complicated." He handed Rogan the newspaper and photographs. The big man made no comment as he handed them back.

"Well, isn't it simple enough?" Rogan said. "All you have

to do is establish if Hoskins was here at the time of the killing."

"I wish it were that easy," Dave replied. "We have no way of knowing if he killed her then ran off to Ireland or was he already in the Republic when she died."

"But surely, if you have the time of death, all you need to establish is if he was already here when it happened."

"Yes, of course, we have the time of death, but it doesn't help a lot in this case. Whoever clobbered her hid her body in some bushes about fifty feet from the road, but what he didn't realise was that she was still alive, if only barely. The poor woman must have regained consciousness at some point then dragged herself over to the edge of the road. God only knows what she suffered, but we have no way of knowing how long it took her to expire."

"So, you have a time of death, but not the time of the actual assault? Tricky," Rogan mused.

The car had picked up some speed but slowed down as it entered the city. Don was very impressed at Tim's superb driving skills.

"Now, don't you boys be worried," shouted Rogan. "Tim here is the finest driver on the force. Hasn't he got medals and trophies all over the house from the races he's won? We'll be all right – just close your eyes and hang on!"

The next twenty minutes passed in a blur. Don was a highly qualified advanced car driver and motorcyclist, and he had attended some hair-raising training sessions in his time. However, he was lost in admiration for this Irish policeman as they drove through the back streets of Dublin. They hurtled along as though the town were deserted and they had the streets all to themselves.

They flew along the small streets from junction to junction, sometimes indicating a turn, sometimes not. Occasionally, they indicated one way then turned the other, and at every turn, Tim checked his mirror to see if anyone else had copied their manoeuvre.

Fortunately, Tim's skill in handling the car was matched by his knowledge of the city's road system, and they soon found themselves back out of town and negotiating the twisting lanes of the Irish countryside. Here, Tim was really in his element, and Don noticed that the speedometer on the car frequently showed them to be travelling at well over a hundred miles an hour, sometimes along roads barely wide enough to allow two cars to pass one another.

It was on one of these roads that they encountered the white Transit.

The van was approaching them at low speed between two rows of parked cars. With no room to pass both vehicles had to stop. Don could now clearly see the other driver, a thin young man with black wavy hair. He was wearing working clothes. A heavier, older man, similarly dressed, was sitting beside him, smoking a cigarette.

"Stay here," growled Rogan as he opened his car door.

Don looked up as Rogan passed him, and he noticed for the first time that the Irish policeman was armed with a revolver. It was tucked neatly away in a shoulder holster under the armpit of Rogan's suit. Don could feel his mouth go dry, but he made a conscious effort to appear calm.

The big detective strode straight up to the driver's side of the van and motioned for the window to be wound down. He then leant into the vehicle and spoke to the driver and his mate.

Don couldn't hear what was being said, but from the body language, it was obvious the two men were getting a roasting. Rogan finally stood back from the vehicle and motioned with his thumb back along the road in the direction the van had driven from.

"Right, now fuck off, the pair of you!"

This time Don could hear his colleague quite clearly.

Rogan got back into the Cortina and said, "Nothing to worry about. Sure, I know them two well enough. They just got curious when they clocked this so-called undercover police car at the airport. What a feckin' joke! It's time the commissioner forked out and got us some new kit."

"So, what did you tell them?" asked Johnson.

"I said they were interfering with a surveillance operation to catch a gang of bank robbers – and if they didn't clear off, they'd be looking at five years apiece for obstructing the police."

"Will they report back to anyone?" said Johnson.

"Them two fucking tearaways? Sure, they wouldn't know who to report to even if they did want to. No, they're too scared of the law to do anything that stupid."

"But suppose they call your bluff?" asked Don.

Rogan put a heavy hand on Don's shoulder. "Who's fuckin' bluffing?" he said quietly, then burst out laughing.

There were no more sightings of the van, and eventually, they arrived at the small seaside town of Skerries. Tim slowed down to a sedate 30mph as they negotiated the picturesque coastal road that led into the harbour. They arrived at an imposing (if rather dated) hotel and Tim pulled in through an arched entrance and parked in the small car park at the rear, well out of sight of the road.

"Hoskins has refused to be interviewed in a police station," said Rogan, "so we agreed with his solicitor to see him here. We've used this place before, and the owner is fully vetted. Besides which, he's married to my cousin." Rogan gave them a toothy grin.

"What about the brief?" asked Johnson.

"We know him quite well. Sure, Dublin's not that big you know, so you get to know them all in time. He's a sharp one but straight as a die. He'll do us no favours in the interview, but he's never been suspected of being a security risk. We should be okay."

Tim stayed with the car while Rogan led Don and Johnson in through a rear entrance and along a wood-panelled corridor to a small private function room. The room contained a number of round tables with wooden chairs, and there was a small bar that, to Don's disappointment, was currently locked up.

There were two men sitting at a table in the middle of the room, one of whom Don instantly recognised as Steve Hoskins. Hoskins was dressed in a dark suit sporting a black armband. Although the suit appeared expensive, the wearer looked dishevelled. He was unshaven, red-eyed and visibly startled when he looked up and saw Don.

"Hello, Mr Barton," he said. "I wasn't expecting to see the local village bobby out here. Are they running short of detectives in the Thames Valley?"

Don hadn't liked Hoskins when they had first met, and the little man did nothing to endear himself to him now. Don chose to ignore the facetious remark and looked over to Johnson. He gave the detective the briefest of nods to confirm that it was indeed Steve Hoskins who was here for the interview.

Rogan looked at the four men. "Right, gentlemen," he said loudly. "As we all know, this is an informal meeting in which the Garda Siochana has no official involvement. The two English officers have no authority here in the Republic, no-one is under arrest, and, Mr Hoskins, you are free to leave any time you chose. I'm sure, Mr Horan, you'll wish to have a few words before we start." He looked over to the thin-faced man in the business suit who sat next to Hoskins.

"Thank you, Sergeant Rogan, for making all that clear," Horan spoke clearly and precisely with the merest hint of a cultured Irish accent. "My client is anxious to be of whatever help he can to the British police in their endeavours to solve his wife's murder. He is adamant that he has no knowledge at all regarding this hideous crime; but, whereas he will freely answer all questions pertaining to his wife's death, he reserves the right to decline to answer any questions that are irrelevant to that death or that may be self-incriminatory on his part. I presume we will be taking notes?" He paused and, receiving an affirmative nod from Johnson, continued, "So, maybe the pace of the interview could reflect this fact?"

Johnson gave Horan his most engaging smile. "Only too happy to oblige, Mr Horan. My shorthand is a bit on the rusty side as well."

The two officers sat down opposite the lawyer and his client.

"While you get started, I'll see if I can find us all a cup of tea from somewhere," said Rogan. He wandered across the room and out of the door as Johnson began the interview.

Don recalled the short briefing on interview technique Johnson had given him on the flight:

"Always start by asking questions that your suspect has no reason not to answer," he'd said." That will get him into the habit of answering you truthfully and make it harder for him to clam up when you ask something more pointed. Sprinkle the questions you really want to ask into in the middle of several others, to which you, ideally, already know the answer. Be aware of any change in his demeanour with these questions – it may indicate he's started telling porkies." And so, on it went.

"Right, Mr Hoskins, if I could just begin by asking your full name, your date of birth, and your occupation." Hoskins described himself as a self-employed advertising executive with a small firm in the West End of London. Johnson asked him a few brief questions about this employment and Hoskins happily supplied the answers.

"Can you tell us, please, when was the last time you saw your wife?" Johnson asked eventually.

Without hesitation, Hoskins replied, "Yes, certainly. It was last Monday afternoon; she drove me to the airport to catch my flight over here." He stopped abruptly, his eye welled up, and he said in a small voice, "I can't believe I'll never see her again."

Fighting back the tears he looked over to Don. "You saw what we were like, Mr Barton. We loved each other. I could never do anything to hurt her. You have to believe me."

Johnson gave Don a discrete pre-arranged signal to ask, "What about this man she had an affair with, the one who wrote the letters?"

Hoskins gave Don a puzzled expression, then slowly smiled as though he'd just realised something.

"I wondered what she'd said to bring you to the house that night. So, she told you I'd found some love letters did she?" He gave a mirthless laugh. "That was one of the scenarios she used to employ in her professional life back in London – before she retired that is. She used to role-play the part of a cheated wife who then had to punish her husband for his infidelity."

"You mean her life as a prostitute?" asked Don. Johnson winced, inwardly at least.

Hoskins looked fit to explode. He slammed his fist on the table, stood up and loomed threateningly over Don. "She was NOT a prostitute!" he yelled. "After that disgraceful invasion of privacy by that rag of a newspaper, your own Vice Squad carried out a full investigation of Suzanne's business affairs – they even checked her tax returns. How many charges were brought? I ask you, how many charges? You tell him, Sergeant," he glared at Johnson, "I'll bet you know, even if he doesn't."

Johnson decided to pour oil on troubled waters. "No, Mr Hoskins, you're quite right; Mrs Hoskins had operated fully within the law. She was a sex worker but not a prostitute."

Hoskins sat back down, but Johnson wasn't about to let Hoskins score points without some reply. He took the photographs from his case and placed them slowly, one by one, face-up on the table. "What can you tell me about these?" he asked.

Hoskins sat back and looked pointedly away from the table. The solicitor, Horan, spoke up:

"As previously stated, my client reserves the right not to answer questions not directly connected to the death of his wife."

"So, you're saying that these pictures have nothing to do with Mrs Hoskins death?" said Johnson.

Before Hoskins could reply, Rogan reappeared at the door. He was walking in front of a squat man in a white linen jacket who was carrying a huge metal tray containing a teapot, milk sugar, and several cups and saucers. "I presume we'd all like a cup of tea?" Rogan asked loudly. The man in the white jacket put the tray down on a nearby table and left the room without speaking. Rogan began pouring the tea.

Everyone in the room visibly relaxed as the tea was served. Don noticed Hoskins' hand was shaking slightly as he drank. Hoskins looked over at the young officer and said, "I'm sorry, Mr Barton, I know you're just doing your job; I didn't mean to sound offensive. But you see, Suzanne took very great pains not to be classed as a prostitute. Nothing sexual ever occurred between her and her clients. The fact is that she was raped when she was thirteen and couldn't stand any form of intimate male contact."

"But you were married?" interjected Johnson.

"My relationship with my wife was one of mutual respect and support. We comforted one another, but there was no sexual intimacy, ever."

"Are you a homosexual?" asked Johnson. Horan began to speak, but Hoskins silenced him with a wave of his hand.

"No, it's all right." He looked back at Johnson. "I don't mind admitting it. But I do nothing outside the law in my private life. The days of criminalising people simply for the way they're made and the way they think is, thankfully, well behind us."

"Yes," agreed Johnson, "the 1967 act did legalise homosexual contact between consenting males – but only if it occurs in private and if there are no more than two adults, each over twenty-one, present. These photos clearly appear to breach those conditions."

Horan, who had been making notes during this exchange, spoke up, "May I suggest we stick to the case in hand, Sergeant? My client has agreed to speak to you about the death of his wife; any discussion regarding other matters is totally outside the agreed parameters of this interview."

Hoskins looked pointedly over to Johnson and said, "Is there anything else you wish to ask me, or may I leave?"

"I just need to know the reason you came here to Ireland at this moment in time." He looked over to Horan. "I think you'll agree that it is relevant to our enquiry to establish the whereabouts of the husband of a murder victim at the time of her death."

Hoskins went on to explain that he was Irish on his mother's side and that he had several close relatives still living in that country. His uncle had been taken seriously ill last Sunday and was not expected to live. The following evening Hoskins has taken a flight to Dublin, but he was too late, his uncle died before Hoskins could see him.

"I made several attempts to call home after I got here," he said. "I assumed Suzanne was with friends when she didn't answer. It wasn't until Friday I found out she had been killed. I knew you'd be looking for me, so I went straight to the police."

"Is that it, then, gentlemen?" asked Horan, making it clear he felt the interview had gone on long enough.

"Just one more question," said Don. "Where's your car, the Jag I saw in the drive the night I came to your house?"

Hoskins was visibly taken aback. "As far as I know," he said," it's at home where it should be. Is it not there, then?"

Johnson explained that the car was missing, and he asked if there was anywhere Suzanne could have left it, if she'd been using it. Hoskins insisted he had no idea of the whereabouts of the vehicle.

Horan left Don and Johnson one each of his business cards and said that any further contact should be through his office. He and Hoskins then left the hotel.

After they left, Rogan said to the two Englishmen, "Did you like that with the tea? I thought the time was ripe to come back in – and nothing calms people down like a nice cup of tea."

"So, you were listening outside all the time?" asked Don.

Rogan roared with laughter. "Of course I bloody was, young Donald! Did you really think I'd be leaving you lot alone to play in my backyard? Now, that wasn't going to happen, was it? Anyway, there's no way I'm letting you two go back to London without having a taste of some real Guinness. There's a little bar the lads use near here, and it serves the best porter you ever tasted. We'll try a couple then I'll get you back to the airport in good time for your plane."

"Oh, and by the way," Rogan looked at Johnson. "You wouldn't want to be caught going through customs with those pictures. It may be safer leaving them here."

"I thought you may say that," grinned Johnson, handing over the envelope. "I guess there are people you wish to show them to?"

"Your man's an Irishman on his mother's side. Should you request it, getting him sent back to England could be a problem. But this is Ireland, we might well understand someone murdering his wife, these things happen. But this stuff is something else again. One look at these and the Pope himself would sign the extradition papers!"

The drive back to Dublin was uneventful, and Rogan took

them to an ancient back street pub somewhere in the bowels of the city. He dismissed his driver with instructions to return and pick them all up at 5 pm. The publican recognised Rogan as they went in through the front door and he let them all into a discrete room at the rear of the premises. There was a handful of men in dark blue suits sitting around the room with drinks in front of them. Rogan acknowledged a couple of them before indicating a table for Don and Johnson to sit down.

"Right lads," he told them. "Your money is no good in here. You just have what you want, I'll sort it all out later. My governor's given strict instructions you're not to leave here sober."

"Won't they be closing at 2 o'clock, though?" asked Don.

Even Johnson joined in the laughter that burst out in the room.

"You've not been to Ireland before have you, Don?" was all Rogan would say on the subject.

The three men then proceeded to steadily drink the afternoon away. Rogan was full of stories that he frequently punctuated with raucous laughter. Like most Irish people, he had spent some of his time in the past working in England. However, most of his family were in America. He even had a brother in the New York City Police Department.

"Have you not been tempted to join him?" said Johnson.

"Ah, Sergeant Rogan of the NYPD, it does have a nice ring to it," Rogan mused. "I'd go in a shot, but Mary, the wife that is, has all her family here and she'd never leave them. Anyway, Dave, what did you make of your man, Hoskins?"

"I suppose he *might* have been telling the truth," Johnson replied slowly.

"Yes, he might," said Rogan. "And the price of Guinness *might* come down in the next budget."

The two men laughed. Don was perplexed. "If you

thought he was lying, why didn't you challenge him?" he asked Johnson.

It was Rogan who answered, "If it wasn't for lies, Don, you'd often not know where to look for the truth."

"Yes," Johnson added, "and by challenging a liar, you put him on his guard. In fact, you may even be helping him get his story straight. No, it's usually best to just let them run on."

Don looked at the two old detectives. "I've a lot to learn," he said.

"Sure, you're not doing too bad for a young feller," said Rogan. "We'll make a detective out of you, won't we, Dave?"

"You never know," Johnson replied. "Stranger things have happened."

They all laughed.

Don did his best to keep his alcohol consumption at a manageable level and, mindful of the briefing they'd had from Partridge, he was guarded in what information about himself that he revealed to his garrulous host. Johnson, on the other hand, seemed to simply absorb one pint after another with no apparent effect, nor any change to his demeanour. The afternoon sped past.

Don could still feel the effects of the Guinness as he walked through the Arrivals lounge at Heathrow. The journey back had been something of an anti-climax, and there had been no special treatment on the flight. Rogan had dropped them off outside the terminal building in Dublin saying, "You'll be fine now, lads. No-one will be bothering you leaving the country."

Throughout the journey, Johnson had been strangely quiet, as though deep in thought. Don wondered if the booze had got to him after all. However, as they walked through the terminal building, Johnson took his wallet from his inside pocket and pulled out two twenty-pound notes that he handed to Don.

"Here, Don," he said. "You go outside and get a taxi

home. I've got to check in with Special Branch and phone the governor back in Newbury. There's no sense in you hanging around. Get the driver to give you a receipt and bring it in to me in the Incident Room around two tomorrow afternoon. If there's any change, buy your wife a nice bunch of flowers – by way of an apology for spoiling her day off. We'll make up our notes together when you come in. Go on now, get cracking. I'll see you tomorrow."

Don shook hands with Johnson and went over to the taxi rank.

It was just over an hour later he was pulling up outside his police house in Brompton. To his surprise, the house was in darkness and the curtains hadn't been drawn.

He paid off the taxi and went indoors with a strange feeling of foreboding.

"Hello! Rose, I'm back," he called.

There was no reply.

The living room was empty, and it was obvious that there had been no work done in the kitchen. Don went up to their bedroom, and his worst fears were realised.

Rosemary had removed several items of personal clothing, and her suitcase was missing. A message had been written in red lipstick on the mirror above the dressing table:

HOW COULD YOU BE SO CRUEL!!! I NEVER WANT TO SEE YOU AGAIN!!!!

Don stared at the mirror for a full five minutes. The sense of foreboding he had been feeling on entering now gradually turned to one of dread. He knew Rosemary to be a level-headed woman, certainly not one given over to hysterical outbursts. What on earth could have occurred in the few short hours he'd been away to make her want to disappear and leave a message like this? Something had happened, that was obvious; but what was it? Don's mind raced as he mentally ran over everything that had taken place in the past few days, and he drew a blank. His conscience was clear, he had done nothing wrong. So what was going on?

There was only one thing for it. He needed to speak to Rosemary's mother. She had been incredibly supportive in bringing about the reconciliation after his transgression all those months ago – and it was to her that Rosemary had almost certainly turned to comfort this time. But would Mum be so understanding if she thought Don had strayed again?

There was only one way to find out.

He picked up the telephone and, with a trembling hand, dialled the number.

CHAPTER NINE
NEWBURY POLICE STATION

I t was Monday morning, and the Murder Incident Room was alive with activity. Uniformed and plainclothes officers, of all ranks and both sexes, were coming and going in a constant stream. They all looked busy, and they were all holding pieces of paper.

The permanent staff were sitting around a large oblong table. Some were sifting and indexing the results of enquiries that were coming into the room; others were completing pro-forma documents to raise "actions" that needed to be taken. A uniform sergeant was sitting at the head of the table. He was equipped with three large wire trays, each of which was filled to overflowing. The sergeant sifted and organised all the information that came into the room. This would later be passed to Detective Superintendent Merryweather, the officer in charge of the investigation.

The typing pool for the murder was situated just along the corridor from the main Incident Room, and it was here that Dave Johnson called into on his way to see the superintendent. There were four typists employed in the room, and the din caused by their machines meant that the door to the room had to remain shut.

Johnson opened the door and stepped back to allow a plume of cigarette smoke to waft past him. Typists were always cold, so even in summer, the windows of their office remained firmly closed. The senior typist, Violet (known as Vi) was seated just inside the door. From this position, she was able to supervise the other ladies as well as monitor all comings and goings. All work coming into the room initially came to her desk, and she allocated it to the others as appropriate.

Johnson was always impressed by the skill these women (or 'girls' as they were called) possessed. Although they each had their own preference, they were all proficient at audio as well as copy typing and could faithfully transcribe the most complicated of documents whilst holding a conversation – and smoking a cigarette.

However, being an exclusively female occupation, typists were notoriously underpaid. It actually wasn't unheard of for detectives, earning a small fortune on overtime and expenses, during an incident to have a whip round to give the girls a boost to their wages out of their own money.

Sitting at a small desk in the corner, a seventeen-year-old male police cadet was also allocated to the room. Teased and spoiled by the women in equal measure, his job was to take messages, run errands, do the photocopying – and fetch the tea.

The lad stood up as Johnson entered the room.

"Sit down!" shouted Vi. "He's only a sergeant."

Johnson grinned. "I can always rely on you to remind me of that, can't I, Vi?"

Dave and Violet had been friends for years. Her husband, George, was an inspector at the nearby town of Wantage. Vi loved to tease Johnson about the difference in rank.

"Well, Dave, it looks like you had a whale of a time in Ireland. George will be jealous."

"George has got nothing to be jealous of, with you to go home to, Vi."

"Don't listen to this silver-tongued rascal, Gordon," she said to the cadet. "He'd soon lead you astray."

However, she did enjoy the compliment.

"Did you get a chance to type up my notes, Vi?" said Johnson.

"I've done them with my own fair hand," she told him. "So don't go looking for mistakes or you'll get a kick somewhere you don't want it!"

"I wouldn't dare!" laughed Dave as he took a sheaf of papers from her. "Seriously, thanks, Vi, you're an angel. Once we put this job to bed, we'll have to get out for a meal together somewhere."

"Yes, definitely. George and I would like that."

The room, which had gone quiet during Johnson's conversation with Vi, exploded back into life as he left and closed the door behind him.

It was eleven o'clock before Dave Johnson was finally able to speak privately to Merryweather over a cup of coffee in the superintendent's office. Johnson gave a full account of the previous day's activities to his senior officer, who in turn listened intently to every detail of Johnson's report.

"So, basically, Guv, we're not really much further forward. Hoskins admitted nothing but his alibi. Even if it were possible for him prove it, still doesn't necessarily cover the time of the actual assault."

"Yes, but what do you think yourself, Dave? As you say, Hoskins is still very much in the frame, but did he do it?"

"I honestly don't know," Johnson replied. "He's certainly got a temper, we saw that ourselves. I also got the impression he was lying about his car. Finding that could be important."

"And, on top of all that, there's the business of the kiddy-porn," said Merryweather. "And have a look at this, it came back from Aldermaston first thing today." He handed

Johnson a form that the latter recognised as a forensic science laboratory report. It confirmed that a metal box sent to them for examination had proved positive for traces of both heroin and cocaine, indicating that the container had been used at some point to store a quantity of both these drugs.

"Where did the box come from?" Johnson asked. "I take it this is the box the dog handler discovered buried under a tree during the search of the area around the scene?" asked Johnson.

"That's the one. Are we supposed to believe it's a coincidence that a supply of dope was hidden near to the scene of a murder?"

"Well, a number of people use the woods, it's a bit of a lovers lane. What have Drug Squad got to say?"

"Nothing at the moment; I'm due at headquarters to speak to their governor later today. I'm not sure what to make of it. I somehow can't see Hoskins as a drug dealer. Not along with his other nefarious activities, but, then again, who knows?"

"Well, we know our victim wasn't a user," said Johnson. "The PM report showed no sign of any illegal drugs in her body. It would be odd if she were a supplier and not trying the stuff herself. It's probable Hoskins is a user though. He had that runny nose that coke sniffers often get."

"Yes, and talking of the post-mortem," said Merryweather. "What do you make of this nonsense about Hoskins never having had sex with his wife? The report clearly showed she was very sexually active – and quite recently too."

"Hoskins is as queer as a nine-bob-note, I'd stake my life on it. I'm inclined to believe him about the sex thing. But that doesn't mean he wasn't jealous of someone else shagging his missus. Maybe there's another body somewhere – perhaps a lover we haven't found yet."

"I bloody well hope not!" exploded the superintendent. "Look, Dave, we're getting nowhere fast with the one body we do have. But, just to be sure, I'm sending Jack and Charlie up to the Yard to work with the Vice Squad. We'll see if we can't scare up some of Suzanne's old clients. We're also doing background checks with both of the Hoskins' friends and families, but nothing has come up yet." Merryweather paused and stared hard at his colleague.

"So, what about young Barton then, Dave? Someone's been shagging Suzanne Hoskins and who's better placed than the local bobby to pop in from time to time while hubby's away?"

"I really don't think so," replied Johnson carefully. "I'd swear he was straight as a die. Either that or he's the coolest customer and the best actor I've ever come across."

"But we know he's a shagger, though, don't we? I mean, he even denied knowing Anne Wilson. Maybe he's got himself into another tangle. He could be shagging half the women in Berkshire for all we know."

"Anne Wilson I don't know about but, if you mean his being booted off Traffic, he's actually told me all about that," said Johnson. "According to him, it was a one-off. His job bike was in for a major service, and he'd been put on lates, driving the Accident Unit – you know, the Transit full of cones that runs up and down the motorway. It's the most boring job on Traffic and, on top of that, he'd been lumbered with having to take a probationer on attachment out with him. The probationer was a female who, as it happened, was having problems at home. Needless to say, she used Don as a shoulder to cry on."

"You mean she was a married woman?" interjected Merryweather. "I thought we were talking about some young, innocent girl."

"Oh no, in fact, those fools in the recruiting department had stretched the rules to get her into the job – desperate to show that the force is into modern thinking, I suppose. She's actually a couple of years older than Barton, and she was already onto her second husband. No kids though. Anyway, one night, instead of going home at midnight, the two of them went up the West End for a drink. They did the dirty deed in a lay-by on the way back. She goes home but, unfortunately for her, hubby was waiting up."

"Oh dear!" said Merryweather.

"Exactly. There was a blazing row, and she told him what had happened, threw it in his face, so to speak. Of course, he was on the blower next morning to complain and, before he knew it, Barton was on the nine o'clock bus to Brompton."

"I'm sorry, Dave," said Merryweather with a grim smile. "But you've just confirmed that our Mr Barton has a liking for attractive, older women. Hardly lets him off the hook, does it? I want you to stay close to him. If Barton is our mystery lover then sooner or later he'll let something slip – and there's nobody I trust more than you to be there to spot it, if and when it happens."

"So, you've no idea why she's run off?" asked Johnson.

Don wasn't sure why he trusted the older man, but in the past week he had come to view the detective as, if not exactly a friend, then certainly a mentor – someone he could talk to. Consequently, when the two of them met as arranged, he'd told Johnson about Rosemary leaving.

"No, I phoned her mum, who told me she'd be staying with them for a few days. Her mum just said Rosemary was upset and didn't want to talk to me." Don spread his hands in despair. "What am I to do, Dave? How am I supposed to sort things out when I don't even know what the problem is?"

Johnson was aware of the bond of trust that had developed between them, and he was anxious to maintain it. He knew he would have to tell Merryweather about this sooner or later, but he didn't want to give the superintendent even more cause to doubt Don if it could be avoided. He decided to give the young constable a bit of time to find an explanation.

"I'm no marriage counsellor, Don, but I have been in this job a bit longer than you. Take my advice and pull out all the stops to find out why she's gone – then shift heaven and earth to get her back. Meanwhile, let's keep this between ourselves. Oh, and I wouldn't let on to your colleagues if I were you – you know what gossips coppers are."

"Don't I bloody just!"

"Right, well try and put your troubles out of your mind for a bit – we've got work to do."

Don knew it was good advice, but he found it hard to concentrate while his mind was full of images of Rosemary. Everything he did reminded him of her.

No, he told himself. I must concentrate on the job.

The two men spent the next hour making up their official pocketbooks, detailing their discussions with Hoskins. They were aided by the shorthand notes Dave had taken at interview. Once complete, they each formally signed, timed, and dated each other's entries. The shorthand notebook itself was labelled up as an exhibit, before being placed into a clear plastic bag with a tamper-proof seal, ready to be handed to the uniform sergeant acting as Exhibits Officer for the incident.

"So, how's the investigation going then, Dave?" Don asked. "There's bugger-all information coming out of the Incident Room."

"No, and that's the way we're going to keep it – at least while Hoskins is on the loose."

"He's still a suspect then?"

"He's our only bloody suspect at the moment, but that could change any minute. There's a stack of enquiries in progress, mainly in the Met, but we've nothing to go on just yet. It's all these loose ends we don't like. There's nothing straightforward about this case at all. Oh, and, by the way, you're one of the few people who knows about them photos, so keep it dark."

"Is there anything I could be doing to help?"

Johnson thought for a moment then said, "Actually, there is. We still don't know who these two little Herberts are." He fished two photographs out of his briefcase and handed them to Don.

Don examined the pictures and said, "These are the faces of the two boys in the porn shots, aren't they?"

"Yes, the Photographic department were able to blow them up and cut them out of the originals, you could now show these to your maiden aunt without raising a blush. Hang onto them for a bit, see if you can find out who they are. There's no need to tell anyone why you're asking, but you could show them about a bit on your travels. Who knows, someone may recognise them."

"I did have one idea," said Don carefully. "Have you considered that they could be apprentice jockeys?"

Johnson leaned forward in his chair. "No, to the best of my knowledge, no-one has even suggested that. Go on."

"Well, when I first went to Brompton I was shocked to see what looked like twelve-year-old boys brazenly drinking in the local pub. Everyone thought it highly amusing when I challenged them. Some of these guys are in their mid-twenties, but you'd swear they were still at school."

"And they're apprentice jockeys?"

"Well, they're stable lads officially, but all stable lads dream of becoming Lester Piggott one day. They are tiny and very underdeveloped physically. They come from all over the place – a lot come from Ireland." He let the thought hang in the air for a few seconds. "There's a few top trainers that have stables in this area. Just a thought."

"A bloody good thought," said Johnson. "Leave the stables to us, I'll get an enquiry team on it – you concentrate on your local parishioners. You're to phone me every day from now on. I want to know everything that happens, got it?"

"How long for?"

"Until I say so, cocker, until I say so."

"Right-o, skipper, leave it to me." Don shook hands with Dave then headed back out to the car park where he'd left his patrol van.

He had an idea he wanted to test.

CHAPTER TEN
NEWBURY DISTRICT

D on drove back to his office and made a few discreet enquiries. He picked up the phone and dialled the Newbury number he'd just been given. The phone was answered after a few rings.

"Hello," a male voice came on the line.

"Is that Fred Weston, the former constable from Brompton?" Don inquired.

"Who wants to know?" came the guarded reply.

"It's Don Barton, the constable from Brompton, the present constable from Brompton."

"Are you indeed? Are you the one the villagers call the Olympic torch?"

"Pardon?"

"In the village, they say you never go out. Nobody's hardly seen you, except flashing by in that fancy van. You don't walk anywhere and don't even get down the pub from what I hear."

"I'm ex-Traffic."

Roars of laughter: "Of course! I should have known. You buggers never walk anywhere. Anyway, what do you want from a poor old pensioner like me?"

"I'd like a chat with you if I could, Fred. I need to pick your brains."

"About that murder, I suppose. I wondered if it'd occur to anyone to speak to me. Problem is, once you're out of the job, it's as though you never bloody existed." He paused. "Okay, mate, that's not a problem, it's hardly your fault the job's being run by amateurs. What sort of time do you want to call round?"

Don had no difficulty in following Fred's directions to his home, a semi-detached, red brick council house in Thatcham with a small parking lay-by at the front. The front garden was a gardener's dream, a blaze of colour, very well designed and beautifully maintained. Don walked up to the front door and rang the bell.

Fred Weston was as imposing as his garden. A tall, well-built man in his mid-fifties, he was wearing a white open-neck shirt and dark trousers. He answered the door with a broad smile, and his handshake could crush coconuts. According to Don's information, Fred was a veteran of the Korean War, where he had seen action as a gunner in the Royal Navy. He was universally respected, always placid – but not a man to cross.

"Come in, come in," boomed Fred. "The missus is out at bingo, so we've got the place to ourselves. She would have made you a cup of tea, but I can't be bothered." He led the way through to the kitchen where a bottle of whisky and two glasses stood on the table. "Take a pew, young Don, I'll be mother." He poured out two generous glasses, then sat facing his visitor.

"You've a nice place here, Fred," said Don. "Is it council?"

"Yes, but I had to fight for it. When you retire from the job, they have to officially kick you out of your police house, did you know that?" Don shook his head. "They take you to court and serve you an eviction notice. It has to be done – it's the rules. You can't blame the brass, they have to do it before the council will even look at re-housing you."

"I didn't know that," said Don, genuinely shocked. "I thought it was just automatic that you got a council house after you retired."

"No, it's quite humiliating, to be honest, but that's the way it is. Then, after I got the eviction notice, they tried putting me on the bloody Rostock Road estate! Would you believe it? Can you imagine an ex-copper living there? Every other resident is CRO!" Fred exploded, referring to the acronym for the Criminal Records Office.

"Don't bear thinking about," said Don taking a swig of his whisky. "Anyway, I need your help. Do you know these two?" He handed Fred the photos Johnson had given him earlier.

Fred looked long and hard at the pictures and said, "To be honest, Don, I've no idea at all who they are. I don't even recognise any family resemblance."

"Not to worry, it was worth a try. I was told you knew everybody in the village. Maybe they're from somewhere else."

"Well, I have been gone well over a year now, so they could be newcomers. There is one other person you could check with though."

"Oh yeah? Who's that then?"

"Her name's Emily Pritchard. She lost her husband in Korea, same time I was there. I didn't know him, but she and I became good friends. She's retired now, but she used to be the secretary at the local school. She was in post for decades, there's not a family in the district that she doesn't know, and she never forgets a thing. I've got her address here somewhere."

"Thanks, I'll definitely speak to her."

"Here you go." Fred wrote an address on the back of an

envelope which he handed to Don. "Tell her I sent you and that I said I'll be up to see her next week some time."

It was well after nine when Don finally drove back to Brompton. Fred had been a mine of local information, and Don had learnt more in a couple of hours of his company than he had in the whole of the previous six months working in the area. However, the two of them had demolished half the whisky bottle, and Don was praying that he was given no more jobs on the radio before he got home and booked off.

He also had to watch his driving. It was possibly true that some coppers would look after each other when it came to minor offences, but that was by no means certain – and no conceivable enactment of the Old Pals Act could save you if you crashed a job car whilst under the influence!

This time he was lucky. He made it home in one piece, and the whisky actually did him the favour of allowing him to sleep longer and deeper than he had done for days. Next morning, he booked on at ten and set out to meet the formidable sounding Mrs Pritchard.

The lady in question lived in a picture-postcard cottage in a quiet hamlet about eight miles from Brompton. There was something strikingly familiar about the layout of her front garden that caused Don to wonder just how close a friendship had existed between her and Fred Weston. Well, good luck to them, he thought, it's no-one's business but their own.

Emily was in her early sixties and appeared to be as fit as a flea. She was a handsome woman and gave the appearance of having been quite a beauty in her youth. Her manner was brisk and business-like, and she spoke with a cultured, but neutral, accent that, at the time, was known as BBC English.

"Well, Mr Barton, I've been expecting you. Mr Weston phoned me this morning and said you'd be popping in to see me."

"Yes, he tells me that you were a big help to him during his time as village constable in Brompton."

"My goodness, yes," she laughed. "Between us, I think we were responsible for half the male teenage population of the area getting thrashed in Mr Headley's office. He was the headmaster, you know."

Don laughed. "Yes, Fred told me about your arrangement. It sounded quite effective."

"Of course, Mr Headley's dead now, poor man, but in his day he was a force to be reckoned with. You should have seen some of those tough young thugs reduced to blubbering wrecks on the business end of Mr Headley's cane."

Emily smiled and sighed as she remembered seeing the sorry looking boys, bending over in their school trousers. Trousers that were stretched tight over upturned bottoms. Don felt that there was something more to Emily than met the eye. There's something quite wicked about this nice old lady, he thought.

"Those were good days," she said, confirming Don's thoughts. "I always felt Mr Weston had it right – not prosecuting the boys I mean. Six of the best then get on with your life, without a criminal record to hold you back."

"In the village, apparently they call me the Olympic Torch because I never go out, but PC Weston was the Gurkha," said Don.

"Really? How so?"

"He never took prisoners."

"I didn't know that." Mrs Pritchard obviously didn't appreciate the humour. "They're a strange lot in that village, always have been. Anyway, constable, how may I help you?"

Don showed her the photos. "I'm trying to identify these two lads. I was hoping you might recognise them."

Emily studied the pictures carefully before saying, "No, I'm quite sure I don't know these boys."

"So, you don't think they're local?"

"Positive. I have been retired for three years, but, even so, I would have known them when they were younger. If they were local lads, local to Brompton that is, I would certainly know them. As it is, I'm sorry I can't help you."

Don was disappointed but said: "Never mind, Mrs Pritchard, thanks for taking the time to look at them. However, if you do think of anything that may help me to identify them, I would be grateful if you could give me a ring at the office. I presume you know the number?"

"Of course I do. Like I say, I'm sorry I can't be more help. But, while you're here, I may have some other information you may find interesting. Have you had any reports of poachers recently?"

Don thought for a few moments. Poaching was an ever-present crime in the countryside with modern poachers stealing pheasants by the truckload or sometimes taking deer by clubbing them to death having first caught them in the beam of a powerful lamp. But Don could think of no recent complaints of this nature.

"Why do you ask?" he inquired.

"It's just that I saw two men skulking about Bluebell Wood with a rifle at four in the morning the day before that poor woman was killed."

Don nearly fell off his chair. "Are you sure of the time and date?" he said.

"Oh yes, quite sure. I'd been sitting up with an old friend who's dying of cancer, and it was definitely around four a.m. that I was driving home. I just got a glimpse of them ducking into the woods as I drove along the lane."

"And you think it was a rifle they had, not a shotgun?"

"It didn't look like a shotgun; it had a long, single barrel. I suppose it could have been an air rifle, but it seemed a bit too big to be one those things."

"Have you any idea who these men were?"

"Oh, I know exactly who they were!" she exclaimed. "I'd know the Churcher brothers anywhere. Two of the nastiest little hooligans I ever had the misfortune to meet. They used to cause Mr Weston no end of trouble – and no matter how many times Mr Headley caned them, they always found new mischief to get into."

"Are you willing to make a statement?"

"Of course," she said. "Anything to help put those two little horrors where they belong."

CHAPTER ELEVEN
HAMPSTEAD NORREYS SECTION

Don was suffering a crisis of indecision. He had returned to his office and knew he should update the murder team with his latest information, but the Incident Room had advised him that DS Johnson wasn't due in until later that day. Don didn't want to speak to anyone else on the enquiry about what he's heard, but he was equally anxious to follow up the lead Mrs Pritchard had given him.

Well, he reasoned, the information wasn't directly connected with the murder, was it? As well as that, it WAS part of his normal duty to follow up a poaching complaint. If he didn't talk about the murder and just focussed on the armed trespass issue, surely nobody could complain about that? Damn it, it was worth a punt, and who knew where it might lead?

Mrs Pritchard had told Don that she believed the Churcher brothers owned a van and ran a small odd job business from their mother's cottage on one of the large estates in the area. The house had been a tied cottage when their father had been alive, and his widow had been allowed to stay on and take a tenancy when her husband was killed in a farming accident. To the best of Mrs Pritchard's knowledge, the mother still worked in the school canteen and so was unlikely to be at home during the day.

This suited Don very well. If he could get hold of the young men on their own, he stood a far better chance of discovering something of importance than if an over-protective mother were present. He made up his mind and headed off to meet these notorious brothers.

The cottage itself was quite small, but it was set in a half-acre of land that afforded the luxury of a kitchen garden at the rear and a large gravel parking area to the side. Beyond the parking area was an outhouse that was too big to call a shed but not large enough to be termed a barn. There was a fairly recent model Ford Transit van parked on the gravel when Don arrived with a young man looking in through the open doors at the rear.

Don parked on the road and walked across the gravel. "Good morning, are you Frank?" he asked.

The man turned around and looked at Don. "No, he's indoors. What do you want him for?"

"You must be Alan then?"

The man nodded briefly. Don noticed that he was quite smartly dressed in flared jeans, black shoes, and a colourful shirt with a large collar. Nothing at all like a farm labourer or workman.

"It's actually both of you I want to talk to. I've had a report of poaching in the area."

"Poaching! Are you serious? Us! Never in the world. It's them bloody travellers you want to talk to if it's poachers you're after. Bloody stupid! Who says we've been poaching?"

"You were seen with a gun down by Bluebell Wood in the early hours of the morning last Monday week."

"Who saw us?"

"It's obvious who, innit?" came a voice from the house. Don turned around to see an equally well-dressed young man standing in the doorway, the two men were not identical, but they could easily have passed as twins.

"I told you he'd spotted us," the newcomer continued.

"Who, that copper?" said Alan. "He was too busy pumping up that bird in the back of his motor to be bothering with us."

"So, you admit you were there?" said Don. He was desperate to hear more about this copper in the car but didn't want to show his interest.

"Yeah, but we weren't poaching. We were after rabbits, and that's common land there, so we weren't doing anything wrong."

Don wondered what Anne Wilson would have to say about that, but he let it pass.

"Rabbiting at four in the morning?" he said.

"It's the best time this time of year – just before the sun comes up."

"Did you have a gun with you?"

"Yes, and we have a licence for it an' all," said Frank.

"A shotgun certificate?" asked Don.

"We don't have any bullet guns, so we don't need anything else."

"I was told it was a rifle you had with you."

Frank laughed. "No, it does look like one, though. Hang on, I'll fetch it."

He ducked back into the house and emerged a moment later carrying the weapon in question.

"It's a single barrel, four-ten long, full choke with a bolt action." Frank demonstrated the working of the bolt, and Don could see he was telling the truth.

"It's better than a twelve bore," said Alan. "Quieter, cheaper cartridges, and a much better killing gun for bunnies – not much cop for birds though. But that doesn't matter because we don't shoot birds because we're not poachers!"

"Did you speak to the man in the car?" asked Don.

The two young men laughed.

"He was at it so hard I thought the suspension on that old Triumph Herald of his was going to collapse."

"If you didn't speak to him, how do you know he was a copper?"

"Because he drinks up the Green Lion. The landlord is an old mate of his, or so we're told."

"What about the woman with him?"

"Could have been anyone," said Frank.

"Did you ever know a lady called Suzanne Hoskins?"

"The one what got murdered?" said Alan.

"We did a couple of small jobs for her husband a while ago, but we never really met her," added Frank.

"Could it have been her in the car?" asked Don

The men shrugged.

"S'pose so."

"Could have been anyone."

"Did you see anyone else in the woods?" asked Don. "Or anything I might be interested in?"

The young men shook their heads.

"Right, well, no going back to Bluebell Wood until I tell you it's okay. I'll be checking with the landowner, so you better be telling the truth about being allowed to shoot there."

The men just looked at him. Don debated with himself whether or not he should take a statement from these two, then he thought better of it. It would be for the best to speak to Johnson first, he decided. He nodded to the brothers then turned and walked away.

He was home and off duty at eight pm when Dave Johnson called him.

"Hiya, Don, they tell me you were after me earlier. Sorry, I wasn't in. I had some urgent jobs to do at home, then the dentist. So, what have you got for me?"

"It's about this mysterious lover of Suzanne Hoskins – has it occurred to anyone that it could be a police officer?"

Johnson went quiet for a moment. "No, Don, I don't think anyone has come up with that idea," he lied. "Why, what have you got to tell me?"

"Quite a lot actually, Dave. Pin your ears back and listen to this."

Merryweather was livid. He was beside himself with rage. He sat at his desk and glowered at Johnson who was standing nervously in front of him, twiddling his fingers.

"I don't believe you, Dave. I really fucking don't!"

"Sorry, Guv."

"Sorry? Is that all you've got to say for yourself? First, you neglect to inform me that Barton's been over the side again."

"We don't actually know that," interjected Johnson.

"Don't we? Don't we really? I suppose his missus has fucked off because he forgot to bring the washing in! Don't be so bloody soft. Of course he's been at it again, but then on top of that, you now tell me that he's trampled his muddy great size twelves right across the middle of a high-level Drugs Squad investigation. You were supposed to be keeping an eye on him for me to stop this sort of thing happening."

"Yeah, but in fairness, Boss, I didn't know about this drugs op either."

"No, Dave, you didn't, but if proper procedure had been followed, Barton would have spoken to you with this lead he'd got. Then you would have spoken to me before acting on it. At that point in time, I would have had a word in your shell-like, and Barton could have been reined in. Come on, man, you've been around long enough to know that there's a reason for the procedures. You're the last person I thought I'd have to explain that to."

"What can I say, Guv? I really am sorry. What is this drugs connection anyway?"

"HQ Drug Squad have been running an operation for the

past six months, and the Churcher brothers have appeared on their radar several times. The main junk comes into the country through Bristol then some of it gets distributed to small-time dealers like the Churchers at all-night parties in Swindon. They use their odd-job business as a cover for flogging the stuff to the middle-class twats who, thanks to the fucking motorway, now infest the villages of our green and pleasant land."

"Well, nothing Barton's done should compromise that, surely? I mean if he doesn't know anything, how he can blow the op?"

"Well, we know these little shits picked up a load of drugs Sunday night, and we presume they hid them in the woods."

"That's why they'd have been creeping around there with a gun?"

"Exactly, but now know that they're of interest to the police they will certainly wind their necks in – and any hope we had of them re-visiting that hidey-hole of theirs is long gone."

"Okay, I get it. But what about this Inspector Mollington?"

"I suppose it could have been him shagging Mrs Hoskins," Merryweather conceded. "But we've no direct proof of it. Obviously, we'll follow it up, but I'll do it personally. Mollington is a Bramshill flyer, and nobody'd going to thank us for fucking up a promising career like his on some wild goose chase."

"I'll make sure Barton keeps his mouth shut."

"You do that. Oh, and, Dave."

"Yes, Guv?"

"We've been friends a long time; I don't want that to change. You've let me down this time, but what gets said in this room stays in this room. Consider yourself bollocked, and that's an end to it."

"Thanks, Guv. But, by the way, I've just had a thought."

"Go on."

"Well, if the brothers picked up the drugs from Swindon and hid them in Bluebell Wood Sunday night, they must have had a damn good reason to go back and retrieve them so soon afterwards."

"Obviously, they were worried we'd find them."

"But if that's the case they must have known we were going to be searching there. Why would they think that if they didn't know something about the murder? If they didn't kill Mrs Hoskins themselves, they must have at least known her body was there."

Merryweather sat back and thought for a minute. "You know we'll make a detective of you yet, Johnson. All we've got to do now is prove it without letting them know we're onto their drugs dealings."

CHAPTER TWELVE
DIVISIONAL HEADQUARTERS

D ivision's area commander, Chief Superintendent
Mike Boxwell, looked at the collection of files
sitting on the desk in front of him and sighed. It
was just after 6 pm, most of his staff had already gone home,
but Boxwell had decided to stay on and work his way
through this small pile of annual appraisal reports that had
accumulated over the past few weeks.

It was a requirement of his post that, once a year, he (or his
deputy) spend a few minutes discussing career development
with each of the officers under his command. Following this
interview, the commander would append a few words of
wisdom, as well as his signature, to the bottom of each report
which went off to HQ for any necessary action and filing.

It was a task that Boxwell took seriously, he knew how
important these appraisals were to the men and women who
worked under him and he always fully briefed himself on
what had been written by their direct supervisors.

Boxwell himself, as an RAF sergeant, had flown
Mosquitoes during the war and, in the mid-forties, he had
gone on to become a police officer, initially with Oxford City
Police until it merged, following amalgamation, in 1968, with

the newly formed Thames Valley Constabulary. Most of his service had been as a detective on CID, working at all levels. Now, as the head of a rural division, he had risen through her ranks as far as he was going, and his career was drawing towards its close.

There was a knock at the door, and an old acquaintance, Phil Merryweather, entered.

"Hello, Phil." Boxwell leaned back in his seat and smiled. "Come in, I was wondering when you'd get around to seeing me."

"Sorry, mate, I've been meaning to call in, but you know what it's like. You've done enough of these jobs yourself as I recall."

"So, how's it going?" asked Boxwell as he walked over and opened the top drawer of a four-drawer filing cabinet.

"It's a bloody mess, to be honest. It should be a simple domestic murder, but there are all sorts of complications."

"Really?" Boxwell turned around with a bottle of malt whisky and two glasses in his hand. He placed the glasses on the top of the cabinet and poured a generous measure into each before returning the bottle to its hiding place.

"Mud in your eye, Phil." The two men drank the toast and put their half-empty glasses back on the desk.

"I only know the stuff DI Thompson has been bringing to the morning briefings, so what's the full picture?"

"As you know, the victim, Mrs Suzanne Hoskins, was found dead at the side of the road, and her husband did a runner to Ireland. Straightforward so far, but now the water gets muddy. Mr Hoskins has spoken to us and swears he last saw his wife when she drove him to the airport at which time she was alive and well."

"And you think he might be telling the truth?"

"Well, it wasn't exactly what you might call a conventional marriage. He's a homosexual porn merchant, and she was a retired (or so she said) high-class dominatrix from London. Hoskins says they never had sex, but her PM revealed she was actually very active in that department – and quite recently as well."

"One of her old client's, perhaps?"

"Yes, that's what we thought, but our enquiries in that direction are moving slowly to say the least. She was the subject of News of the World sting operation two years ago, and her activities were plastered all over the paper. It seems that most of her punters were from the upper echelons and they hastily withdrew to their country piles. Most of them pulled up the drawbridge and dropped the portcullis."

"Was she blackmailing anyone, do you think?"

"It's possible, but you know the establishment. They're protecting their own as usual."

"Hmm, yeah, but murder is a bit different to sleaze."

"Well, we've got two men working with Vice Squad at the Yard, but they keep running into dead ends when it comes to identifying old customers."

"Any family connection?"

"Suzanne's mum was a drunk, and the girl was raped by her step-father when she was thirteen. She was taken into care when her mum died, and she was brought up by foster parents."

"Anything there?"

"A very respectable middle-class couple. Both still alive, but only just. They were very good to Suzanne apparently, even sent her to private school. She left at eighteen and joined the sex industry, pandering to men with a craving for corporal punishment. She eventually ended up running a business of her own – which went south once the newspaper report appeared."

"And Mr Hoskins?"

"English father, Irish mother, most of his family are still over there. He went to university then went into advertising. At some point, he found he had a talent for photography and, through his gay contacts, was able to run a lucrative little side-line producing dirty pictures for a number of outlets in Soho. We found some kiddy-porn at his house along with a bedroom studio."

"So, he hadn't retired then?"

"Apparently not. Anyway, as far as we can see, his cover story holds water. He genuinely did have a funeral to go to in Dublin. We're still trying to I.D. the boys pictured in the photos we found but no luck so far, locally at least. Someone suggested they might be apprentice jockeys."

"Very unlikely," snorted Boxwell. "I know enough trainers on this patch to tell you that all these young riders are dead keen on making it big one day. If they were seen posing in porn mags and got identified, the Jockey Club would pull their licences quicker than that. They'd be out of racing for good. The risk would be just too great for the few quid they'd earn doing it."

"Yeah, that's pretty much what we've been told already. But those aren't the only complications."

"Go on."

"Well, traces of cocaine were found at the victim's house along with a number of fingerprints we can't yet identify. Also, we uncovered a hidey-hole nearby where drugs have recently been hidden."

"Was Mrs Hoskins an addict?"

"Not according to the post-mortem; we don't know about the husband, though. It's possible he's a user. If so, it raises another possibility."

"Yes?"

"The local officer, your man PC Barton, has discovered that two poachers were seen at the scene of the murder some hours before it happened. It turns out these men feature in a large-scale undercover Drugs Squad operation that's currently underway."

"And Drug Squad have asked you to back off?"

"Pretty much. Problem is that Barton has already been to see them."

"But surely that's not a problem. He can't possibly have knowledge of the drugs operation, can he?"

"No, and he doesn't know about the cocaine traces being found either."

"So, where's the problem?"

"These two young Herberts have told Barton they saw an off-duty police officer at the scene of the murder shagging an unknown female – who could turn out to have been our victim. The lovers were in the back of a car a few hours before the murder."

Boxwell went quiet for a minute. He was "old school" when it came to morality and got very depressed when police officers transgressed and let the side down.

"I suppose you know who it is?" he said eventually.

Merryweather explained in detail the facts as he knew them.

"So," said Boxwell, "et me get this straight. "We are told that someone, who two poachers say was a police officer, but don't know his name, was seen in a Triumph Herald having sex with an unknown and unseen woman – who may or may not have been Mrs Hoskins. PC Barton thinks the police officer MAY have been Inspector Mollington because he THINKS the inspector MAY own a similar vehicle. Is that about it?"

"I'm afraid so. It's a bit thin, to say the least, but we're going to have to follow up on it somehow. What can you tell me about Mollington?"

"He's not a graduate, but he's very bright. He passed the sergeants exam, first go, in the top two hundred nationally and got selected for the Special Course. He did his twelve months as a sergeant in Bracknell and got automatically promoted inspector and posted here a few weeks ago."

"I thought the flyers all went to busy main stations; no offence, Mike."

Boxwell laughed. "None taken, Phil. Actually, it was his own idea to come here. He wanted to be somewhere relatively quiet to give him time to write a paper on equal opportunities in the service – as part of his Open University degree course."

"Hmm, or maybe to be close to a girlfriend?"

"Well, either way, it's rumoured his dad is a close friend the chief constable. So anything we do has to be done right."

"Any suggestions?"

"I don't want to get involved with your murder, Phil. However, I suggest you leave this to me and let me approach Mollington from another angle. I'll make a few discreet enquiries first."

"I'm fine with that, it's probably just another red herring anyway. I really can't see a bright young prospect like Mollington risking throwing his career away for the sake of a retired tart from London. It just doesn't add up."

"What about PC Barton, will he keep it to himself, do you think? The last thing I need is a load of vicious rumours running round the place."

"I don't think he's stupid enough to start gobbing off, but I'll be honest, I'm not at all sure about young Barton. It well may be you have a wrong 'un on your hands there. Anyway, I've got Dave Johnson looking after him, and if anyone can keep the lid on, it's Dave."

"Absolutely, I worked with him back in the City days. You're right, they don't come much better than Johnson. Okay, Phil, give me a couple of days, and I'll get back to you."

"Thanks, Mike, for my part I'll do my best to keep you advised of any other developments."

"Right, well, thanks for dropping in, even if it was to bring bad news. I suppose I better back to these appraisals …"

CHAPTER THIRTEEN
CHURCHERS' COTTAGE

T here was nothing Alan Churcher liked better than to sit in the garden on a sunny day and read comics. As a boy, Alan had not been very popular at school, but he did have one special friend, a rather overweight and equally unpopular kid called Tony. Tony was in the same class as Alan, and his parents were fairly well off. He used to get comics delivered to his house each week, and he always passed them on to Alan once he had finished reading them.

Tony's family had emigrated to Australia when the boys were just fourteen, but Alan had kept all the comics in a pile under his bed. Although he was now twenty-two years of age, he still loved reading them when he got the chance.

His favourite was *The Eagle*, a real boy's paper, and Alan was happily sitting in his back garden, imagining himself flying through the cosmos with Dan Dare, when he heard the sound of tyres crunching on gravel. The noise was coming from the front of the family cottage and signalled that brother Frank was finally home. Frank, being two years his senior, had been Alan's father figure and mentor throughout most of the young man's life.

The boys' father had passed away when the boys were young, and their timid mother had been left with bringing the boys up on her own. She proved to be an admirable mother and had worked all hours to see that her sons were provided for, but she lacked firmness in her character.

The boys had not exactly run wild, but they had certainly been allowed to go increasingly further astray as the years passed. Since they had been grown up, she'd had very little control over them.

Alan's reverie was rudely interrupted by the sharp pain of a tennis ball hitting him on the back of the head.

"Oi, dozy bollocks! Get your nose out of that stupid comic. We've got stuff to talk about."

"Hey, Frank, that bloody hurt! Watch it, will you!"

"Serves you right for being a wimp. Those comics are for kids, not grown men. What do you think the mistress would have done if she'd caught you reading them?"

Both men were silent for a moment at the reference to Suzanne Hoskins. She had been a powerful influence in their lives, and now she was dead.

Their first meeting with her was seared into their memories:

"What are you doing in here?" Suzanne Hoskin's voice was as sharp as a whip. "You're supposed to be mending the tap in the kitchen, not sneaking around the bedrooms."

Steven Hoskins had arranged for the young odd-job men to come to the house and take care of a few routine maintenance matters. However, he'd had to go to London, so his wife was left to supervise the work alone. She'd given the men their instructions then gone out into the garden. Frank, however, had decided to have a little look around.

If Frank Churcher was the slightest bit startled or perturbed at being caught rummaging, instead of getting on with the work he was being paid to do, he made no show of it. He turned towards Suzanne and gave her a cheeky grin.

She's not bad for an old 'un, he thought to himself. Quite tasty, now he looked at her properly.

"Don't worry about the tap," he said. "My brother's taking care of it. I wanted to see what you got up to in here – it's not like any bedroom I've ever seen. It's more like some sort of studio. Are you a film star or an artist or something?"

Suzanne put her hands on her hips, and, standing with her legs slightly apart, fixed Frank with a glare. "It's none of your business, you cheeky little bastard," she hissed.

"I found this in the cupboard. The headmaster had one like it when I was at school." Frank held up a two-foot length of bamboo cane with a curved handle at one end. "Are you one of them women that gets money for beating up dirty old men?" he asked.

"I'm quite capable of hurting young men as well," she said menacingly.

His smile widened. "What sort of things do you do?"

Now it was her turn to smile.

"I can do all sorts of things," she said slowly. "Perhaps I'll show you."

"What? If I'm a good boy?"

"Maybe, but it's much more fun if you're a bad one."

She walked across the room and took the cane from Frank's unresisting hands. She held it in front of his face with the curved handle in her right hand whilst slowly running her left hand along its entire length. She finished the move with her index finger tapping the rounded tip. She flexed the cane a couple of times in front of the fascinated young man, then she turned to one side.

In a lightning-fast movement, she slammed the rod down with a sharp crack onto the end of the bed, causing a small cloud of dust to fly into the air.

"Were you often naughty at school?" she said sweetly.

His mouth had gone dry. "Sometimes," he croaked.

"I'm rather good at dealing with naughty boys," said Suzanne. "I think you're being naughty now."

She glanced down and, with the end of her cane, gently tapped the bulge that had appeared in the front of his tight jeans. "Boys like you need a mistress to keep them in order. How would you like me to be your mistress?"

Frank felt as though he were dreaming. "Oh, yes," he managed to say finally. "I think I might at that."

She held his gaze for a long moment.

He was totally transfixed by her eyes and didn't see the cane lash upward in a vicious arc. The bamboo went "thwack" as it made solid contact with the end of his penis. Even through the heavy denim of his jeans, the pain was excruciating. He let out a high-pitched yelp and clutched his bruised part with both hands.

Suzanne laughed as she watched him dancing around the room, holding himself.

"When you speak to me, you address me as Mistress," said Suzanne sharply. "Now take all your clothes off and bend over that chair."

"Can I fetch my brother first, please, mistress? We share everything. We always have and always will."

"Has he been naughty as well?"

"Oh yes, mistress, very naughty indeed."

"I don't want to talk about her," said Alan sullenly. "She was nothing but trouble when she was alive, and she's even more of pain in the arse now she's dead."

"What? Don't you miss her, then?"

"I miss the sex, she was good at that, but I don't miss the other stuff, no."

"Come on! You loved it!"

"I didn't, Frank, it was you that liked it, not me. I just did it to keep you happy."

"Anyway, forget about that. There's a bloke in Newbury will give us five hundred in cash for the Jag, no questions asked."

"What! It's worth loads more than that!"

"Yeah, but who's gonna give it us? We aint even got the logbook. Look, this geezer will put it through his books at five grand and give us a receipt. That way we can finally spend some of our drugs money without getting into bother if anybody asks where the dosh has come from. We could give Mum a bit of a treat, buy her something nice for a change."

"Yeah, but what if that copper comes back, what then?"

"He can't prove nothing. The car's legit, don't forget. It's not as though we nicked it, is it? Anyway, they're not even looking for it. It's not been on the telly or in the papers. We'd have seen something by now if the motor was hot."

Alan wasn't convinced but said, "I suppose so. If you say so, Frank. So, what have you done with the dosh and all the gear?"

"It's all somewhere nice and safe, don't you worry."

"Yeah, but where have you hidden it?"

"Like I said, somewhere safe."

"Half of that's mine, you know. I've a right to know where you put it."

"Yes, bruv, you have," said Frank patiently, "but I'm not telling you."

"What! Don't you trust me or summat?"

"Look, I know you aint gonna steal it, but I also know you can't keep your trap shut. So, if the law or anyone starts asking questions, you can't tell them nothing if you don't know nothing."

"I can keep my trap shut!" Alan was angry. "And I've a right to know where the stuff's hidden."

Frank wanted to thump his brother but decided to try to placate him instead.

"Tell you what, here's twenty quid."

"What's that for?"

"So you can take me to the pub and buy me a pint, dopey!"

The brothers looked at each other and burst out laughing.

"Come on," said Frank. "Put the comics away, the boozer's been open for ages."

CHAPTER FOURTEEN
BROMPTON POLICE OFFICE

D on considered himself a fairly pragmatic character, certainly not overly given to introspection or, heaven forbid, self-pity. But as he sat in his one-man office, staring at the pile of paper on his desk, the pangs of loneliness and isolation that had been his constant companions for the past few days were as real and tangible as the cup of tea that sat cold and unconsumed in front of him.

It was several days since he had heard anything from the murder incident room, and Rosemary was still refusing to speak to him, even on the telephone. To take his mind off his misery, Don had immersed himself in the routine of rural police work.

He had manfully tackled the trayful of document productions, accident statements, summonses, and warrants that had accumulated over the past couple of weeks, and his sergeant would be well pleased to see just how up to date Don was with his work. However, there was scant satisfaction in a job well done when that job was, itself, lacking in appeal.

A sharp knock at the door brought him out of his reverie, and Don was genuinely pleased to see Ian waiting at the door.

"They've put me on Area Car today," grinned the young officer. "So, I'm fully legit wandering off my own patch for a change, and I was wondering where to get a cup of tea."

"I'd better put the kettle on then," said Don. "Grab a pew, mate, and I'll be with you in two shakes of a…"

"No need to say it, just get a brew going."

Don went through the connecting door to his house and re-emerged a few minutes later with two steaming mugs in his hand. He saw Ian staring intently at one of the close-up photographs of the young boys that Don had inadvertently left out on the desk.

"I know this little fucker," said Ian. "Why have you got his picture?"

Don knew that knowledge of the pornographic pictures was still officially under wraps but felt there was no harm in trusting Ian. After all, Don had already shown the snaps, albeit without explanation, to a quite a number of other people.

"Do you know him then?" asked Don.

"Yes, he's one of the boys from Burridge House. You know, the children's home on my ground for kids who the courts say are in need of care, protection, or control. Not offenders, necessarily, but always on the verge of trouble. The councils in London send them out to the sticks to get them away from bad influences in the city."

"So, what about this one?"

"Well, I caught him trying to hitch a lift on the motorway a week or two back. He was on the slip road, and a motorist reported him as being suspicious."

"What did you do with him?"

"Well, he wasn't technically doing anything wrong, just trying to get home to London. So, I simply took him back to the home and let them deal with him."

"Right, forget that tea, you're taking me to Burridge House, let's move."

The journey in the despised Marina took about fifteen minutes and, despite Ian's constant questioning, Don kept his silence and said nothing. His head, however, was in a whirl. He knew that he shouldn't be making enquiries without Johnson's approval, and he knew there could be serious trouble but, damn it all, he was deeply involved in this case whatever CID had to say, and he had no intention of being marginalised and left out of things.

The door to Burridge House was answered by a jovial man of middle years wearing a well-worn suit that just about fitted around his ample midriff. Ian introduced him to Don as Mr Hodge.

"Please call me Gary," said the man. "I think we know each other well enough by now, Ian."

"Is there somewhere we can talk please, Gary?" asked Don. "It's a bit confidential and possibly very important."

The small reception room at the front of the building led into a much larger living area where a number of teenage boys were watching a very loud television set that was playing an advert for Golden Wonder crisps. On seeing the officers, the boys gave a rousing cheer – but they remained seated and didn't bother to get up from the armchairs and sofas that littered the room.

Gary led the way through this area into a small office and closed the door behind them.

"I'll get straight to the point, if I may, Gary," said Don. "Is this one of your boys?" He handed Gary the photo that Ian had picked out back in Brompton.

"Yes, that's Eric Mitchell," said Gary, without hesitation. "Has he been up to something?"

"I'd just like to have a word with him if I may," said Don.

"Not possible, I'm afraid."

"It could be very serious."

"Even so, I can't help you. Eric has been taken back into the system in London since his last escapade. God knows where he is now, and I very much doubt that his social worker will want to be much help. It's not the done thing any more, you know, to be taking sides with the law that is. You'll probably need a court order to speak to him. Sorry."

"So, he got kicked out just for trying to get back to the Smoke?" asked Ian. "I mean, it's not as though he gave me any trouble."

Gary looked decidedly uncomfortable. "Strictly off the record, you should have searched him, Ian. He had enough cocaine on him to seriously impress his old mates up the East End."

Ian turned bright red. "So where's the coke now?" he asked.

"Down the toilet, I'm afraid."

"Bloody Hell," said Don, half to himself.

"Don't be too upset," said Gary. "It's only white powder until it's been analysed. It could be anything. So, don't worry, none of us can get into any trouble."

"It's a bit more serious than that," said Don. "What about this lad, another one of yours?" He showed Gary the photo of the other boy.

"Yes, that's Alan Stretch. He's a shy, quiet lad, not tearaway material at all in my estimation. Mind you, we've had a lot of wet beds from him just lately – that's usually a sign they've been up to something."

"Can I have a word with him?"

"Well, it should be okay. But I'll have to be present while you question him, *and* I'll have to stop the interview if I feel Alan needs protecting. I have to take this *loco parentis* thing seriously you know."

"I've no intention of upsetting him," said Don, "and, if I'm right, we may well be protecting him from harm rather than trying to harm him."

Gary disappeared into the building and returned a few

minutes later accompanied by a thin, pale-faced youth with long lank hair. The boy was snivelling and immediately burst into tears when he saw the officers. Gary put a kindly, supporting arm around the young man's shoulders.

Don looked up at the boy and smiled. "There's no need to be upset, Alan," he said. "My name's Don, and this is my friend Ian, we're both here to help you. You know what this is about, don't you?"

The boy nodded miserably.

"It wasn't me," he said. "It was Eric. He said he'd beat me up if I didn't go with him. I didn't even get any of the stuff they gave him."

"Who gave him the drugs, was it the couple at the house – the ones taking the pictures?"

By now Gary and Ian were looking totally perplexed, but Alan didn't seem to notice.

"No, it was the two with the van," Alan said. "They picked us up and took us to the house, then left us there."

"With the man and the lady?"

"No, she came later and shouted at us. She called us names and made the man drive us back here in his Jag."

"What about the two men in the van, do you know who they are?"

"No, but Eric knew them. I was never told their names." He paused and screwed up his face, then: "Well, actually, one of them is probably called Alan, same as me. Eric called over to me one time, and the bloke answered thinking Eric was talking to him. I hardly saw the other one, I never spoke to him at all."

Don realised that it was time to contact Johnson.

"Alan, I'm going to ask you to repeat all this to a friend of mine called Dave. He's a detective, but he's a really nice chap. You'll like him." Then to Gary, "Have you a phone I can use? I really need to call this in immediately. Oh, and we'll need to stay with Alan until Dave gets here. Any chance of a cup of tea while we're waiting?"

"I'd better make it for you myself," said Gary with a grin. "Unless you like it with worms in it…"

CHAPTER FIFTEEN
ROUTINE ENQUIRIES

D on was on duty at ten the following morning and, as he opened the dispatches that had been dropped off at his office by the Area Car, he reflected on the previous evening's events.

To Don's great relief, Dave Johnson had been delighted with the way the two uniformed officers had handled enquiries at Burridge House. On receiving the phone call, the detective had sped out to the children's home and an hour later was in possession of a comprehensive statement from young Alan Mitchell. Dave had then arranged a full medical examination and agreed with Gary that the boy should be given support and supervision – as well as sorting out some counselling for the lad.

Don and Ian were, by now, chomping at the bit to race round to the Churcher's cottage and bring the two brothers in for questioning. Johnson had to restrain their enthusiasm.

"Look, lads," he said, "you've both done a great job until now, let's not spoil it by charging like a bull at a gate and risk screwing it all up. The superintendent will need to be brought up to speed, for one thing. Calm decisions will need to be taken. We'll need to get warrants organised, line up a search team, get forensics on board, photographer, all sorts of things. So, bugger off now and get your pocketbooks made up. Oh, and…"

"I know," said Don, "keep our gobs shut."

"You're learning."

Well, he may well have been learning, but that didn't help with Don's excitement and impatience. As he sorted through the pile of enquiries on the desk, his mind was racing as he contemplated what was going to happen next. He liked and trusted Johnson, but it wouldn't be the first time that the credit due to the uniformed officers was pinched by CID – and he wasn't about to let his and Ian's involvement be relegated to a footnote on the murder file.

He needed some fresh air. He picked up a handful of summonses from his "In" tray and decided to go out and serve them. It wasn't a job he liked. Finding people at home was bad enough, but even when he did catch them in, the recipients usually made it clear that they didn't particularly enjoy having their day ruined.

For once, Don's van was running like a dream, and he gave it a quick clean before taking it out. He slid behind the wheel and slackened his seat belt so that he could reach across to the handset on his VHF radio. Lower performance police vehicles had yet to be equipped with the new inertia reel style of seatbelt, so the strap lay slack on Don's lap.

His first call was to a remote farmhouse near the village of Allworth. The summons was for a minor speeding offence, and the farmer harangued Don for ten minutes about the inconvenience of having to go to court, and why couldn't Don just take the fine from him now?

Don finally got away and was still chuckling as he drove down the dirt track that led to the country lane. The lane connected with a twisty, narrow road that weaved through isolated countryside towards the village of Compton. There was one car approaching from the left, and Don stopped at the end of the track to let it go by.

Don didn't immediately recognise the blue Jaguar XJ6 as it sped past him, but there was no mistaking the identity of the driver who stared at him, open-mouthed, from the side window of the vehicle.

Don pulled out to give chase and, as he did so, he flicked the switch that activated the rotating blue light on the roof of the van. He accelerated in pursuit, and both vehicles were soon travelling at speeds well over 60 mph – and it was obvious that the Churcher brother at the wheel of the XJ6 had no intention of stopping.

On the face of it, there should have been no contest. The Jaguar XJ6, with its superb 4.2-litre V6 engine, was capable of propelling the car to speeds of well over 120 mph. The rest of the car's engineering fully supported this power – and the vehicle's road-holding and braking capabilities were comparable with the very best that the top European car brands had to offer.

Against this, Don was driving a light, commercial Ford van. The van was capable, flat out, of around 75 mph and held equipment such as cones and road signs that were loosely stored in the back. However, the Mark 1 Escort was a tough little vehicle with a robust 1100 cc engine. The gears had been configured to maximise the vehicle's load-carrying ability, but it also gave it plenty of torque and good acceleration when the van was lightly loaded.

However, it was a classic tortoise-versus-hare scenario and, had they been travelling on a wide main road, the performance saloon car would have been easily enough to have seen off its pursuer.

But, they weren't on a main road.

They were hurtling along a twisting, winding little country lane – and Don was a police-trained and highly proficient advanced driver.

Nonetheless, from the outset, the Jag rapidly pulled away from the police vehicle.

Don picked up his radio handset. "Foxtrot Golf Five Zero for HT. I'm in pursuit of a vehicle that has failed to stop on the Aldworth to Compton road about one mile north of Aldworth village." He reeled off the index number of the Jag and advised the controller that the car was believed to be subject of crime.

"Sorry, Five Zero, there are no units showing in your vicinity. I'll try on another channel to get a Traffic mobile to assist you. Please keep the commentary coming. You have priority."

By the time they reached the first set of sharp bends, the saloon car was already a good 200 yards ahead of Don. But, looking ahead, he could see that the Jag was going far too fast on its approach to the first element, a sharp left-hander. Don wasn't surprised at all when he saw the brake lights showing angrily – and he could see the car rapidly losing speed as it hit the apex of the bend. The momentum of the heavy saloon car caused it to lurch violently over to the wrong side of the road and, as it exited the bend, it was out of position to negotiate the sharp right-hand curve that was now looming in front of it.

Meanwhile, Don had correctly read the road ahead, and he'd eased off his accelerator in good time before reaching the end of the straight. This allowed him to double de-clutch and perform a smooth change down into third gear without losing too much speed. He was now able to maintain his position and balance through the challenging, twisty stretch of road. Unlike the Jag, his vehicle was under full control. Don seized the opportunity and began to close the gap between them.

The van was only equipped with a rather feeble blue light, and it didn't have any audible signalling instruments, such as two-tone horns or a siren. So, he flashed his headlamps and thumped the horn button in an effort to get the Churchers to pull over.

Frank Churcher was having none of it. He managed to regain sufficient control of his vehicle to survive the series of bends. As the road opened up ahead of him, he once again used the power of the Jaguar to pull away from his pursuer.

Back on a straight stretch of road, and with his quarry getting away, Don picked up his radio handset and updated his control room.

"Foxtrot Golf Five Zero, am still in pursuit of the stolen Jag on the Compton road out of Aldworth. The driver has repeatedly failed to stop. We are currently passing the Bull Public House, speed in excess of six-zero mph. Jag approaching another series of bends. I can see the target vehicle braking in front of me. The driver does not appear to have full control, over."

"Five Zero, from the Control Room Inspector, do not, repeat, do not make any further attempts to stop the vehicle. Maintain observation from a safe distance for as long as you safely can. Is that understood, over?"

"You're breaking badly, HT, please repeat, over," said Don, not wishing to acknowledge an instruction he had no intention of obeying.

As they came up to the next series of sharp bends, Don could see another vehicle approaching them on the other side of the road. Churcher had either not seen this vehicle or, more likely, decided to ignore it. He swung the Jag wildly over to the right in an attempt to go wide into the left-hand bend now in front of him. However, this inadvertently placed his vehicle directly into the path of the oncoming car, putting them both in danger.

At the last moment, the other driver panicked and swerved his car to his nearside in an attempt to avoid a head-on collision. His car mounted the grass verge then fishtailed on the dry grass before bouncing and slipping back onto the carriageway.

Don, as he flew past, was relieved to see that the car and its occupants appeared undamaged by their near-miss. He took another quick look in his rear-view mirror and was reassured to see that there was no urgent need for him to stop and give any assistance.

The journey through the next series of bends was almost a repeat performance of the one that had gone before. Once more, the powerful, but heavy, Jaguar lurched terrifyingly from side to side, and again Don's little van was able to close in on its quarry.

"HT for Foxtrot Gold Five Zero, you are to abandon, repeat, abandon this pursuit. Did you copy, over." The controller's voice was becoming more urgent.

"You're still breaking badly, HT. Say again, over."

The line between advanced driving and dangerous driving is, at best, a slim one. The main difference is that the advanced driver should, at all times, be in full control of his vehicle. This includes always being able to stop within the distance he can see to be clear ahead of him.

And it was now that Don made his fatal mistake.

As the road again opened up into a long straight, Don was determined to keep the distance between him and the Jaguar as short as possible. So, as both vehicles exited from of the last of the bends, Don was right up behind the Jag – but his little van dangerously inside its own braking distance.

Without warning, Churcher fully applied the Jag's brakes, and the big car screeched to a sudden halt in the middle of the road with smoke billowing from its tyres.

Don felt panic rising as he realised a collision was inevitable, but he only had a split second to brace himself.

He stood as hard as he could on his footbrake. There was a squeal as the tyres on the light van lost traction with the road almost immediately. The police vehicle slid along the tarmac and continued its forward motion at an alarming rate.

It was as though everything went into slow motion, and the crunching sound of the coming together of the two vehicles was something Don would remember in his dreams for years to come.

The impact crumpled the front of the van like paper as it slammed into the much more substantial saloon car. Unfortunately, the slack in his seat belt failed to keep Don secure, and he was thrown violently forward, causing him to hit his head on the steering wheel.

There was no sensation of pain, but everything went black as he passed out.

Don had no idea how long he'd been out – and pain wasn't far away as he fought back to consciousness. He now experienced the worst headache he had ever known.

As he regained full consciousness, he slowly realised that he was lying across the back seat of a moving car.

Without warning, he was violently sick.

"You dirty bastard!" came a voice from beside him. "That went all over my new jeans."

Don opened his eyes to a blurred and misty world, he started to sit up but was told, "You stay right there, mate." He compliantly lay back on the seat, but very soon he was feeling decidedly nauseous.

He had no choice. He had to get upright. Thankfully, nobody prevented him sitting up.

As his senses slowly returned, he made out that he was in the back of Jaguar. The car was being driven by Frank Churcher, whose brother, Alan, was in the back seat, sitting next to Don.

Alan was holding the family's .410 shotgun across his lap – with his hand across the trigger guard.

CHAPTER SIXTEEN
KIDNAPPED

D on's head was throbbing with pain, but he could feel his strength slowly returning as his vision cleared.

The brothers may have looked similar to one another, but their demeanours couldn't have been more different. Alan, sitting next to Don, was grinning and jovial, as though enjoying a private joke. His brother, Frank, who was driving the car, was, on the other hand, apparently in an angry rage. He kept hitting the dashboard of the car with his open hand and repeated the word "fuck" over and again.

Don looked at Alan and said, "Don't you think you two are in enough trouble without kidnapping a police officer? Why don't you just pull over and let me out?"

Frank hit the dashboard again and shouted, "We are NOT in any trouble. We've done nothing wrong, and we'll let you out when we bloody well get there."

"What? You don't think killing Mrs Hoskins and stealing this car is doing anything wrong?"

For some reason, Alan thought this was hugely funny. He burst out laughing and said, "What? Us? You think we killed the mistress? We wouldn't do that, would we, bruv?"

"No, we bloody wouldn't, and we didn't nick this motor neither!" shouted Frank. "And now you've fucked it right up with that bloody van. It'll cost a fortune to get that back end fixed. I hope you've got insurance on that police car of yours."

"If you've done nothing wrong, why didn't you stop when I signalled you?" said Don.

"I tried to bloody stop, and you crashed into the back of me."

"That makes it your fault, don't it?" said Alan, to Don, with a grin.

Realising that this nonsense was getting him nowhere, Don changed the subject. "So, where do you think you're taking me now?" he asked.

Frank turned around in his seat and said, "Just sit still, you'll see where we're going when we get there."

He turned back to face the road and shouted, "Oh, Shit!"

A tractor that had been approaching them had started turning right across their path into a field. Frank swerved to his offside to go past it, but suddenly realised that the tractor was actually drawing a trailer – and consequently both sides of the road were now blocked. He slammed his foot on the brakes as hard as he could in an attempt to stop before the car hit the tractor.

Nothing happened.

The pedal went straight to the floor with no resistance at all. Frank frantically pumped the brake, but by the time it finally operated, the car had shot behind the trailer and collided with the high grass banking at the side of the road.

The car mounted the bank, went up onto its nearside wheels, carried on forward, then rolled over onto its roof. It then bounced back onto four wheels before continuing its corkscrew motion. The badly damaged vehicle slid on its side on the tarmac and finally came to rest lying on its offside with its wheels still spinning.

After a few seconds the engine cut out, but the warning light on the dashboard showed that car's ignition was still live – and Don could hear an ominous dripping sound coming from the front end of the car.

Suddenly Don smelt petrol and, at the same time, realised he was lying sideways across Alan who was unconscious and lying under him in the back of the car. Don looked forward and saw that Frank was pinned to the front seat, trapped by the collapsed roof of the Jag.

His head and neck were at a strange angle, his sightless eyes were open and staring.

Drip, drip, drip. Petrol? Don knew he absolutely had to get out of the car – and fast! He first reached upwards and tried to push and turn the handle – but the door and its mechanism were buckled and jammed.

He frantically looked around him and saw that the shotgun had been thrown loose between the seats. He grabbed the fore end of the weapon and used the barrel to hit upward in an attempt to smash the side window.

It was hopeless. He simply didn't have enough room to get a swing at the glass. Then he had a brainwave. He wriggled round and placed the muzzle of the gun against the glass. He squeezed the trigger.

Click. Nothing happened.

He could now detect the acrid smell of burning wires, and the dripping was getting louder. Try as he might, he just couldn't stretch forward far enough to reach the ignition key in order to break the circuit.

He resumed hitting the window with the gun and, finally, after what seemed an age, he heard the sound of someone banging around outside the car.

"Can you stand?" came a man's voice. "You need to get out of there, mate – and bloody quick!"

Don twisted his head around and saw a face looking down at him through the side window of the car. The man was gesticulating and shouting whilst heaving on the door handle.

"It's stuck, I can't open it," the man shouted in panic. "The car's on fire. I've got to get you out of there."

"Smash the glass!" shouted Don. "Smash the bloody glass!"

The man looked dubious but, after a moment, yelled. "Okay, cover your face!"

He raised his fist and repeatedly hammered hard down on the window, but the toughened glass refused to break. Time and again, the man repeated the effort, but it was no use. Eventually, Don could see the man frantically looking around. He then disappeared before returning a few seconds later with a large brick in his hand.

Using both hands, the stranger lifted the brick high above his head and smashed it down as hard as he could. Don covered his eyes with his hands as the heavy brick fragmented the glass that now showered his head with hundreds of small glass crystals.

Ignoring the broken shards of glass at the edge of the window, the rescuer reached into the vehicle. The glass cut viciously into his unprotected hands and arms, but with superhuman effort, he pulled Don up through the broken window then onto the grass verge.

The two men now heard Alan Churcher screaming in terror from inside the car. They quickly staggered back to the vehicle and between them managed to pull the frantically thrashing young man to safety.

"My brother's in there!" Alan screamed. "We've got to get him out!"

As Alan began to stumble back to the car, the men could see a line of burning fuel running backwards along the upturned underside of the car toward the petrol tank.

Don, who'd seen too many car fires in his time, knew exactly what was about to happen. He grabbed Alan's shoulders from behind and jerked him back, throwing him none too gently onto the ground. Just then they heard a loud whoosh, and the tank exploded.

In a matter of moments, the car was well and truly ablaze, radiating fierce heat and sending plumes of black smoke high into the midday sky.

Ignoring the still screaming Alan, Don staggered to the middle of the road and sat down.

His head began to swim; the world went out of focus. Don tried to fight it, but he knew he was losing consciousness. He heard a buzzing in his ears and, for the second time that day, he had no choice but to allow the warm, cosy darkness to overcome him.

T he first thing he was aware of as he came out of the darkness was the muffled sound of voices. But it was cosy where he was, and Don didn't want to wake up. He was reluctant to leave the warmth and the comfort that the darkness provided. He felt safe in its embrace, like being back in the womb. However, try as he might, the warm sleep was slipping from his grasp, and consciousness was not to be denied.

As the sensations of touch and sound slowly returned, Don reluctantly abandoned his cosy haven and opened his eyes to re-join the real world.

"Ah, looks like you're back with us, young Don," came a familiar voice. Don realised he was lying in a bed and staring up at the smiling face of Dave Johnson. "Nice to have you back, you had us worried for a while."

"Where am I?" croaked Don through parched lips.

"Here, mate, have a sip of this." Dave held a glass of water to Dons lips. "Don't try to move too much, I'm told you may find it painful."

"I'm in hospital then?"

"Newbury District. You've got a room all to yourself. VIP treatment no less."

"Newbury? That's good," said Don weakly. "If it was too serious, they'd have taken me to Reading or Oxford. So, I suppose I've been lucky. How long have I been here?"

"Couple of days, that's all. Your mate Ian's been in with you most of the time. I only got here an hour ago."

Memories of the accident flooded back, and Don said, "How's Alan Churcher? I know his brother's dead, but I didn't see how badly Alan was hurt in the crash. Also, there was a guy who helped us."

"The man who helped you was the tractor driver. He was just treated for cuts to his hands and sent home. As for Alan, don't worry about him. He's safely banged up in the cells. The magistrates have given us a three-day lie-down while we sort out the charges."

"Has he admitted the murder?"

"Look, Don, I'll tell you everything, but I need your statement first. I'm sure you understand. I can take it down in shorthand and get it typed up for you to sign when you're feeling a bit better. Are you okay with that?"

"Yeah, no problem. Where should I begin?"

For the next hour, Dave Johnson sat by the bedside and asked questions. He scribbled away in his notebook throughout the interview. Don did his best to remember everything that was done or said from the time he first spotted the Jag.

"I can't understand how the accident happened," said Don. "I know we were motoring, but we weren't going so fast that we shouldn't have been able to stop."

"I can answer that, funny enough," said Dave. "Believe it or not, the vehicle examiner has figured it all out."

"What, from that burned out wreck?" said Don incredulously.

"Apparently, it's happened to a few of these new Jags. The problem is to do with the fact that it has disc brakes all round. When he drove off from the accident with your van, it seems Churcher didn't fully release the handbrake. According to the examiner, you only have to leave it on by one notch for the discs at the back to get red hot from the friction. If the wrong type of brake fluid has been put into the system, it can boil and cause a thing called vapour lock. When you apply the footbrake, the vapour compresses, and the brakes simply don't work."

"And that's what happened?"

"Yes, so it would appear. The examiner found the handbrake setting then checked with the local garage in Brompton, the firm who last serviced the car. They've coughed to using standard fluid when they adjusted the brakes – according to them they didn't know about the problem."

"Okay, but what about the murder? Has Alan put his hands up?"

"Not exactly. He reckons that for some time he and his brother have been giving Mrs Hoskins a good seeing-to. It happened whenever hubby was away. Pretty wild, some of it. Running naked in the woods, canes and whips, that sort of thing.

"The morning she was killed, the three of them (Alan, Frank and Suzanne that is) are playing a game in Bluebell Wood when hubby turns up in his Jag and catches them at it. Bloody great row follows, and she storms off. Hubby picks up a stone and whacks her on the back of the head."

"So, Hoskins is guilty after all?" said Don.

"I don't think so. It doesn't add up. Alan reckons the brothers helped Hoskins hide the body – and in return for that, and driving him to the airport, sold them the Jag for the princely sum of one pound."

"What! That's ridiculous."

"Absolutely, it's a load of cobblers. Alan reckons Hoskins even gave them a receipt – no sign of it, of course."

"Because it never existed! What does he say happened to it?"

"He reckons Frank had it and it must have burn in the wreck. All very convenient, as indeed is having someone who's safely across the Irish Sea to put the blame on."

"So, what are we charging him with?"

"Well, as his fingerprints are all over the Hoskins house we feel pretty confident charging him with murder, as well as stealing the car – oh yes, and kidnapping you, of course."

"Is he saying anything about that?"

"He says his brother wasn't used to driving automatics and hammered the footbrake with his left foot trying to de-clutch – hence the sudden stop that caused you to crash into the back of them."

"Has he said what they were going to do with me?"

"He reckons they were scared you were badly hurt, so they decided to take you to the doctor's surgery in Chieveley. According to him, that's where they were taking you. He totally denies any intention to kidnap you."

"Bullshitting little bastard!"

"That's what we think as well."

"What about the drugs and the kiddie porn?"

"All that's subject to further enquiries at the moment. We'll see about them later."

Dave smiled and packed his notebook into his briefcase. He walked over to the door and opened it.

"Right, I'm off back to the nick," he said, "but, before coming here, I made a quick call on someone and straightened a few things out. You've got a visitor."

"Come in, Mrs Barton," he called out of the room.

As she walked in through the door, Rosemary took a long look at her husband lying in the hospital bed, his head swathed in bandages. With tears in her eyes, she walked over to him and took his trembling hand in hers. Don looked up at her, completely stunned. A powerful wave of emotion overcame him. Unable to control his feelings, he began crying himself.

"I'll leave you two to have a good weep," said Johnson from the open door. "Catch you both later!" And off he went.

For what seemed an age, Don and Rose just stared at one another, neither able to speak without welling up and choking back tears. Don's grip on his wife's hand, even in his weakened state, was so strong it left Rosemary in no doubt that he wasn't planning on letting her go anytime soon.

Finally, he was able to ask her about being there.

"Sergeant Johnson came and saw me this morning over at Mum's house. He must have got her address from somewhere. He told me what happened to you. He's a really nice man, isn't he, like a favourite, wise old uncle?"

Don laughed. "Well, I'm not sure about that, but he is a pretty decent bloke, I suppose. Mind you, he's the sharpest detective I've ever known – and I've met a few!"

"Well, Mum likes him. She even made him a cup of tea."

"Crikey, he must have really turned the charm on!"

"That's not fair, she's always nice to people."

"Only joking. Look, Dave mentioned something about straightening a few things out. I still don't know what it was that needed straightening – and that's the truth, Rose, honest."

Rosemary blushed and went quiet for a moment.

Finally, she said, "Right, I'll tell you what happened."

"I wish you would. I've been beside myself."

"Do you remember that day you went off to Ireland?"

"The day you left me. How could I forget?"

"Well, you know I was going for lunch with Jenny. We decided to go to The Green Lion over on the Wantage road. Jenny had heard it was under new management and that the food was brilliant."

"Oh yeah, I know the place."

"Anyway, we drove over in her car, and we were just walking into the pub when another car pulled into the car park, and guess who got out of it."

"I've no idea."

"Only that fucking bitch of a policewoman!"

"What! Not Diane?" Don was shocked. It wasn't at all like Rosemary to use profanity.

"I recognised her straight away from that time you brought her home for a meal break. Well, she took one seriously guilty look at me then jumped back in her car and was out of there like a scalded cat."

"Bloody hell, Rose! As God's my witness, I have no idea what she was doing there."

"No, I know that now that Mr Johnson's told me what was going on. But at the time, I was sure she was there to meet you."

"How could I have been meeting her? Even if I hadn't been going to Ireland, I'd have been at your parent's house with you."

"Come off it, Don. How many times have you let me down at the last minute because you were called in to work? You could easily have had a 'surprise' phone call then packed me safely off to Mum's leaving you clear to get up to all sorts."

"So, what's Dave said to you to make you change your mind about it?"

"I've no idea how, but he seemed to know exactly what she was up to – and it was nothing to do with you. But she actually *was* meeting up with a married man, another policeman. Dave wouldn't tell me who he was, but it seems he used to be her sergeant over at Bracknell when she first joined."

Don had a lightbulb moment. "I think I know who she

was meeting," he said quietly. "Can you remember what car was she driving?"

"A green one, a Morris or something, you know, the one up from the Mini."

"Could it have been an Austin 1300?"

"Yeah, that could be the one."

Don went silent as it dawned on him just what a complete fool he'd made of himself. It wasn't Mrs Hoskins that Mollington had been shagging in Bluebell Wood that night; it was Diane.

Of course, it all made sense now. Mollington had turned up at Newbury just after he got promoted and transferred from Bracknell. He must have been Diane's shift sergeant back at his old nick. Now, it would seem that he had been having an affair with her even back then. It came as a shock to realise this must have already been going on the same time Don had flattered himself that it was he who had been the answer to a poor maiden's prayer, the glamourous white knight on a shiny motorcycle.

So, he'd had no need to be worried about meeting her at Ascot after all. It was apparent now that there was no danger of Diane having fallen for him. Actually, thinking back to the attention she was enjoying from all those young men in the meal tent, it made him wonder how many other lovers had been taken in. To Diane, Don was no more than a notch on her bedpost, a bit of fun, something on the side – a casual conquest.

Overcome with guilt and shame, Don looked up at the face of the wife he had nearly lost, the woman whose love he had so casually taken for granted – then callously betrayed. She smiled down at him.

This time, when the tears came, they didn't stop.

CHAPTER EIGHTEEN
AWAITING TRIAL

With Alan Churcher charged with murder and remanded in custody, the Incident Room became basically a file preparation unit. Enquiries were still coming in and had to be actioned (there were always loose ends to be tidied up), but active investigation of the murder had all but ceased.

There was a mountain of painstakingly tedious paperwork for the officers, typists, and civilian workers to get through. The task appeared never-ending.

However, slowly but surely, a file of evidence came together.

The file was ultimately sent to the Director of Public Prosecutions who authorised proceedings to continue and for the case to be brought to trial.

The committal proceedings were held at Newbury Magistrates Court where the examining justices had all the statements read out to them and all the physical, or "real," evidence produced and logged. The magistrates agreed that there was a case to be answered, and the matter was committed for trial at the Crown Court in Reading.

While all this was taking place, Don continued to make a

good recovery from his injuries. A week after his reconciliation with Rosemary, he was discharged from hospital to convalesce at home. The football season had started again in August, and he was soon fit enough to manage a couple of visits to Elm Park with his father-in-law to see Reading play.

"The Royals," as they were known to their fans, were both men's favourite team and were, once again, setting out in their attempt to gain promotion from the Third Division.

Rosemary had settled back into work and seemed content. However, both she and Don knew that for the first time, there was something missing in their relationship. Something had been lost and, if they couldn't recover it, things would never be the same again between them. It wasn't that they weren't both making the effort, but, for the present, true happiness remained a distant memory.

Don recovered in a remarkably short period of time, and he resumed duties as soon as he was able.

He had been back to work for just over a fortnight when he received his witness notice to attend the trial of Alan Churcher. In the same dispatch, there was a similar notice to be personally served on one of the witnesses: Miss Anne Wilson, the landowner who had found Suzanne's body.

The following day, Thursday, Don was working the four pm to midnight shift. It was a dull grey day with the threat of rain, and temperatures were more suited to April than September. Shortly after seven in the evening, he drove his van to Miss Wilson's country residence. He parked on the gravel driveway of the large house and, having alighted from the vehicle, he walked up to the front door and pulled on the chain of the old-fashioned doorbell.

There was no reply to his ring, so Don walked to the side of the building to see if there were any lights showing at the rear. The house was a large two-story red-brick pile, late Victorian and set in just over half an acre of ground. The gravel drive ran all around the outside of the premises, and Don noticed that the gardens were mostly given over to grass with a few trees. The overall impression, enhanced by the dull autumn twilight, was one of neglect.

"Who are you? What do you want?" a female voice shouted.

Don hadn't heard the front door opening, but when he turned around, he saw that Miss Wilson had emerged from the house and was now standing on the driveway glaring at him. She was holding a double-barrelled shotgun across her body.

"Oh, it's you, the cowboy policeman," she said. She broke the gun and removed two cartridges.

"Don't worry," she continued. "It's only dust shot, stings like mad but it wouldn't kill you. I have to be careful, being here on my own. You never know who's creeping round."

"I've got to give you this," said Don, trying to ignore the shotgun. He took the witness notice out of his summons pocket and approached her with it in his hand. She turned her back and walked into the house before placing the gun against a convenient wall. Don followed her into the hallway.

Anne switched on the light and studied the document Don handed her.

Don couldn't help but notice that she was very attractive. Dark-haired, slim but with a good figure, she was wearing a black silk blouse, a fashionably short pencil-thin skirt, and dark, low-heeled shoes. A thoroughly modern, smart young woman.

"It says I have to attend the court and give evidence, but there's no date on it," she said. "The policeman who took my statement said I wouldn't have to attend the trial."

"No, it's very unlikely that you'll be called in person, but until the defence formally accepts service of your statement we have to assume you'll be required to testify. As for the date, it hasn't been set yet. Before we can do that, I need to know if there are any days that need to be avoided, holidays and such."

"I'll need to check my diary; you'd better come in and sit down. Would you like a cup of coffee? I was just going to have some."

Don was in no rush that evening, and the control room knew where he was if they needed him. He also felt that the incident with the horse had got him off to a bad start with this woman, and he wanted to improve their relationship. Beside which, as a member of the local gentry, she could prove to be a useful contact to have in the area.

"Yes, thank you, I'd love a cup."

She led him into a large reception room where there were two sofas positioned opposite one another separated by a wooden, highly polished coffee table. Don sat on one of the sofas while Anne disappeared off to the kitchen to prepare the drinks.

Don sat back and took the opportunity to look around him. The walls were oak-panelled and gave the room something of a forbidding appearance. The leaded windows, which provided a view to the front of the house, were barred shut, and there was an imposing stone fireplace set into the opposite wall. The log fire had been set but not lit.

It had obviously been some years since the building had received any serious attention. Electric lights had been fitted at some time around the walls. However, despite being switched on, they were of low wattage and did little to alleviate the overall gloomy aspect.

Anne returned carrying a metal tray containing a coffee pot, cream, a sugar bowl and a small plate of biscuits. She set the tray down on the table in front of Don. She then produced two coasters onto which she placed the cups and saucers.

"Cream and sugar?" she said, pouring the coffee. It was the first time Don had seen her smile.

As she leant across him, Don got a whiff of perfume. It

was elegant and expensive – and he was sure she hadn't been wearing it earlier when she'd invited him in.

Having poured the coffee, Anne walked over to a writing desk at the far end of the room and returned carrying a large red, leather-bound diary. She sat down on the end of the sofa and switched on a reading lamp that was conveniently situated on a small table beside her.

She donned a pair of black-rimmed reading glasses, crossed her long, shapely legs, and slowly turned the pages of the diary.

"How far ahead should I be looking?" she asked.

"Well, certainly three months, six to be on the safe side."

"Hmm, this is no good, I'm hopeless at recording appointments. I'll need to speak to Mr Baines, my estate manager. He knows better than I do where I'm going to be at any time." She snapped the diary shut.

"It must be a very large estate to warrant employing a manager," said Don.

"Sixteen hundred acres, or thereabouts," she said. "There are six tenant farmers and an assortment of other small businesses – and cottages, of course."

"And Bluebell Wood?"

Anne sighed. "Yes, and Bluebell Wood. My father bought that bit of land intending to start a logging business. If you go deep enough into the woods, you'll find the footings for a sawmill. My dad was dead keen to get that going, but it all fell by the wayside when he got ill."

"What are the woods used for now?" asked Don.

Anne gave a disgusted little grunt and said, "A lovers' lane mostly. The public are supposed to stick to the footpaths and bridleways, but they rarely do. I'm constantly chasing trespassers away."

"So, it's not common land then? People shouldn't be shooting on it, for example?"

"If you're referring to the two Churcher brothers, they're

actually okay being there. They've been taking rabbits on our land for years. I know they were a couple of tearaways, but for some reason, Dad liked them. 'Loveable rogues' he called them."

"And you, what did you think of them?"

"They were creepy, made my flesh crawl." She shuddered at the memory. "They were always leering at me. I wouldn't like to imagine what they were thinking, the dirty little sods. Ugh! Disgusting!"

"Yes, an odd pair, that's for sure. Hopefully, you won't have to worry about them again. With Frank dead and Alan in prison, I mean."

"Yes, I know you shouldn't speak ill of the dead, but I can't say that I'll miss them."

Anne's frostiness seemed to have melted somewhat, so Don decided to press ahead and carry on chatting.

"It must have come as a shock for you, finding Mrs Hoskins body in the woods that day?"

"Well, the dogs found it actually. They stood and barked but wouldn't go near it. Poor woman, I know she was a prostitute, but nobody deserves that to happen to them." She paused for a moment. "I hope they throw the book at that Alan Churcher. Lock him away, I say."

"Tell me, Miss Wilson, do you manage the whole estate from here?"

"In the old days, everything was run from right here in the house, but some years ago we converted an old, rather large, summer house into an office. It's down at the far end of the rear lawn. It has its own vehicle access to the road which helps a lot."

"A summer house. Is it big enough?"

"It does get a bit cramped sometimes, but it's better than having people traipsing all over this place."

"So, it's just you and Mr Baines?"

"Well, it used to be my father and I. Mum died when I was

twelve, then Daddy developed Alzheimer's – just as I was finishing at university. It took six years to kill him. By the end, he was so bad he was in need of constant care. I basically grew into the role of running the estate."

"How long has your father been gone?" asked Don.

"Just over a year now."

"So, you're living here all by yourself?"

"Well, there's Bruno and Satan, my two German shepherds. I have to keep them locked up out the back – ever since they bit the postman. Your predecessor, Mr Weston, said it was either keep them chained or have them put down."

Trust Fred to come up with a solution that didn't involve paperwork, thought Don. The story also brought Emily Pritchard to his mind. Another lady living alone in the countryside. Don wondered if Anne would become just like her as the years progressed.

"I presume running the estate takes a lot of time and effort?"

"You mean for a young woman on her own?" The frostiness was returning.

"I didn't say that," Don protested.

"You didn't need to. I could ask you what a smart young constable like Don Barton is doing working as a village bobby."

Don could feel his cheeks burning and prayed that Anne didn't notice.

"Touché," he said with a grin. "You got me there."

"Well, not that it's any of your business, but I was engaged to be married once," Anne told him. "It was while I was away at uni. He said he loved me, but obviously not quite enough. Not enough to want to help me look after my father that is. He said I should have Daddy put in a nursing home."

"Not something you were prepared to consider, I presume?"

"No, I wasn't! *This* was Daddy's home. He didn't send me

away when Mummy died, and I wasn't going to abandon him when he needed me." She was beginning to get upset and wiped a tear from her eye as she spoke.

"Look, I'm really sorry. I didn't mean to upset you." Don was beginning to feel uncomfortable.

Anne took a couple of seconds to regain her composure.

"Sorry about that," she said finally. "I still haven't got over it all. Anyway, we had no idea how long Dad would need nursing, and Raymond, that was my fiancée's name, wasn't ready to deal with all the issues."

"So, off he went," she added bitterly. "Good riddance."

At least I know where the low opinion of men stems from, thought Don.

"Right, let me make that call," she said briskly and stood up. She walked into the hall where Don had noticed an old-fashioned black Bakelite telephone on a side table at the foot of the stairs.

"Hello, Mrs Baines? It's Anne…Yes, fine, thank you …Is Ed there? I need him to check his diary for me…Oh, is he? Right … No, don't do that, it's not that urgent. I'll speak to him tomorrow… Thanks, Mrs Baines, bye for now."

"He's out at a darts match," she said, returning to the reception room. "He won't be home until late. I'll have to get those dates for you tomorrow if that's okay?"

"No problem at all. I can telephone for them if you like."

She paused, then looked at him. "It would be nicer if you could call round, if you have the time that is. It's just a change to have someone my own age group to talk to. Someone from outside the world of agriculture."

She saw him hesitate.

"Are you married, Mr Barton?"

"Call me Don, please. Yes, I'm married to Rosemary."

Was that a flicker of disappointment he saw cross her face?

"Well, you can tell Rosemary not to worry. I promise not

to eat you. Men are so definitely off the menu for me these days!"

Don laughed. "I'll be round about the same time tomorrow if that's okay?"

"I'll have the coffee ready."

"Until then, Miss Wilson. Goodbye." He stood up to leave.

"Oh, Don…"

"Yes?"

"You can call me Anne."

"Goodbye, Anne."

It took Don a lot of effort to concentrate on his driving as he left the house. To be sure, Anne Wilson was a very attractive woman, but why had he felt himself so irresistibly drawn to her? Could he actually be in danger of falling for someone he had only met twice, and then only briefly?

To make things worse, he felt sure that the feeling of attraction was mutual. There was that perfume for one thing. She had definitely not been wearing it when he first arrived at the house. Then there was her insistence that he return in person for those dates.

So why was he even thinking the unthinkable? Was he actually considering betraying Rosemary's fragile trust? The trust he'd recently fought so hard to regain.

The mental turmoil continued as he got home and booked off duty.

No, I don't need to go there, he said to himself. That's what telephones are for.

However, on the other hand, surely there was no harm in going back and simply chatting, was there? After all, nothing was going to happen, was it?

So, was he going to tell Rosemary about the encounter?

No, he didn't think so.

After all, why should he? There was no need if nothing was going to happen, was there?

"You're quiet tonight, love. What's wrong?" Rosemary's question roused him from his contemplation.

"Er, nothing. Just thinking about the job."

"Tell me," she said, sliding beside him on the sofa.

"I'd rather kiss you."

She giggled. "What's stopping you?"

It had just started to rain the following evening, and the little police van crunched onto the gravel. Anne was waiting by the open front door as Don climbed from the vehicle. She was wearing a silver-coloured silk dressing gown and open-toed slippers.

"I was hoping you'd come," she smiled. "I was just going to take a shower. Would you care to join me?"

She looked at him and laughed.

"Your face! I don't mean join me in the shower, you idiot. I meant join me for coffee. I can take a shower later. After you've gone," she added pointedly.

Don wasn't sure whether he was disappointed or relieved.

CHAPTER NINETEEN
AN EARLY VISITOR

I t was Rosemary who heard the doorbell chiming. She had always been a lighter sleeper than Don, and the slightest sound was apt to wake her. She looked at the clock on the bedside table and saw it was five-thirty in the morning.

She gave Don a dig in the ribs, but he just grunted and rolled over, dead to the world.

"Bloody man!" she said to herself as she slipped out of bed. She went out of the room to a window on the landing that overlooked the front door.

The woman who had rung the bell looked up as she noticed the curtain twitch and beckoned Rosemary to come down and let her in.

A couple of minutes later, Rosemary, none too gently, shook her husband awake.

"Don, wake up," she said.

Don was coming to very slowly and somewhat reluctantly.

"What is it, what's the matter?" He was still more than half asleep, and his voice was slurred as he drifted between two worlds.

"There's a woman downstairs," his wife said, somewhat more sharply than she intended. "She has a boy with her. I think he's a bit simple."

Don was finally waking up. "What do you mean, simple?" he said.

"You know, not all there. A bit slow."

"Where are they then?" Don was now fully awake but a bit grumpy.

"I've put them in the office. They're waiting for you there, so get up will you!"

Don slowly got out of bed and began dressing.

"Hurry up, will you, Don!" Rosemary was getting agitated. "They've been waiting ages."

Five minutes later, still somewhat blurry-eyed, Don entered his office where a middle-aged woman and a teenage boy were sitting waiting for him.

"Sorry to get you up so early," the woman said, "but I don't want him being late for school and I don't know how long you'll want him for."

Don noticed that she spoke with a pronounced Berkshire accent and had the look of a local country woman. The boy, a stocky youth, wearing the uniform of the local village high school, was about fifteen years of age and was staring morosely at his feet.

"So, how can I help you?" asked Don.

"Well, I want you to tell him he won't get into trouble," the woman said. "He's terrified you're going to take him off to prison."

"Why would I take you to prison, son?" Don asked the boy.

The lad continued to look down and shuffled uncomfortably in his seat.

"I dunno," he said truculently, "I aint even done nothing."

"Tell the man what you told me," his mother said. "You won't get into trouble, Danny, I promise, will he, constable?"

"I don't know," said Don, becoming frustrated. "What exactly has he done?"

"Well, he hasn't done anything, has he?" the woman said. "He only saw things. You can't go to jail for just seeing things can you? Tell him he won't get into trouble."

"What did you see, Danny?" Don used the name the woman had called the lad by. "You don't normally get into bother just for seeing things."

The young man looked up "What, even if it's a lady with no clothes on?" he almost shouted.

"Where did you see a lady with no clothes on?" Don asked him.

"Well, he's doing his Duke of Edinburgh Award," the boy's mother said, as though that explained everything.

"Okay," said Don patiently. "And?"

"Well, it involves a lot of camping out, so I bought him a new tent, and he wanted to try it. I said he could camp out in Bluebell Wood. It's an easy walk from our cottage, and I didn't think Miss Anne would mind. We've known her family for years."

Don was beginning to get interested. It was two weeks since his visit to Anne Wilson, and the whole issue of the murder seemed to have receded into the background.

"When was this?" he asked the boy.

"Well, we think it was the night of the murder. That's why we thought we'd better come and see you."

"Danny, are you saying you saw a naked lady in Bluebell Wood the night of the murder?"

"Yes, but I didn't mean to," the boy replied. "She was just there. I didn't know she was going to be there, did I?"

With an effort, Don controlled his frustration. He could see the boy was trying his best, but he just didn't seem to want to get to the point. On the other hand, Don knew there was a good chance the frightened young man would clam up entirely if he got upset.

"Danny, stop worrying, mate. You're not in any trouble, I promise. Just tell me what you saw."

The boy visibly calmed down. "You're sure I'm not in trouble?" he said.

"Completely sure, Danny. What makes you think you did anything wrong?"

"It's his dad's fault," Mum interjected. "He caught Danny watching his sister take a bath and gave him a right leathering. Told the boy he would go blind and end up in prison. Scared the lad half to death he did."

"Well, nothing bad's going to happen to you here, Danny, as long as you tell the truth that is. So, tell me everything that happened." Don put his hand reassuringly on the boy's shoulder as he spoke to him.

"Well, I hiked down to the wood and found a quiet place to put my tent up. It was a nice flat bit under a tree with some bushes all around. I ate my supper, and when it got dark, I got into my sleeping bag and went to sleep."

"I packed his supper for him," Mum said. "Just some cold cuts, cake, and such. He's got a little Primus, but we don't let him use it when he's on his own. He's not ready for that yet."

"Oh, Mum!" said Danny plaintively.

"Weren't you scared all by yourself in the woods?" asked Don.

"No, not really. I had my torch, and it was a full moon, so there was lots of light. Oh, and Freddie was with me."

"That's his teddy," said Mum.

"Right," said Don. "So, what happened?"

"Well, I was fast asleep then I heard all this shouting and wailing, and it woke me up."

"What sort of time was that?" asked Don.

"Danny can't tell the time yet, he's learning," said Mum.

"But you know it was late?" asked Don.

"Yeah, the moon was really high."

"So, what did you see?"

"Well, there was this clearing just the other side of the bushes, and a lady was sort of dancing around in the middle. She looked just like a fairy but older."

"And she had no clothes on?"

Danny looked panic-stricken.

"Danny, love, it's all right, the policeman said so."

"That's right, Danny, I promise you're not in any trouble. Just tell me what you saw."

Danny stole a glance at his mum and said, "Well, these two demons appeared and started prancing about."

"Demons?" said Don.

"That's what they looked like. They were wearing masks, but I knew who they were."

"And who were they?"

"They were the two men who are always hanging around outside our school selling wacky baccy to the older kids."

"Do you know their names?"

"No, one's called Frank, I think. They've got a van."

Now Don was very interested.

"What about the lady, did you recognise her?"

"Not until he saw her picture in the paper," said Mum.

"Have these men ever tried to sell you anything?"

Danny laughed. "Not likely! I'm not stupid, am I? You have to be a right twit to buy stuff from them."

"Good lad," said Don. "So, tell me what happened in the woods."

"Well, they all danced around a bit, then they started sexing one another on the grass."

"So, what did you do?"

"I got scared that they'd see me, so I packed up my tent and sneaked out of the woods."

"Then what?"

"I started to walk home, but one of the demons jumped out on me from behind a tree."

"That must have been scary."

"It was, he wet himself," said Mum.

"Mum!" Danny protested.

"It's nothing to be ashamed of, darling, anybody would have done the same, wouldn't they, constable?"

"Absolutely!" Don agreed. "Anyone would have been terrified. So, what happened, Danny?"

"It was Frank, I think. He got me by the throat and pushed me up against a tree. Then he got this big knife out and said he'd cut me if I told anyone what I'd seen. He said he'd kill my mum as well."

"The cheeky devil!" said Mum. "I'd like to see him try!"

"So, what happened next, Danny?"

"I just went home."

"I was surprised to see him in his bed the next morning," said Mum. "He told me he got scared out there in the woods by himself and came home. It wasn't until ages later when we saw the picture in the paper and he started crying that I found out what really happened."

"So, what do you think they were up to, dancing naked in the woods, I mean?"

"I've no idea, I'm sure!" said Mum defensively. "Our family's C of E. Always has been."

"Okay, no offence intended," said Don, puzzled by her reference to religion. "Going back to the night in woods for a minute, Danny, did you see any vehicles in the area or nearby maybe?"

"Yeah, Frank's van was parked on the gravel."

"Was there any other vehicle there, a car, for instance?"

"No, just the van. That's all I saw."

"What about other people, was there anyone else there?"

"No, just the fairy and the demons."

"You're sure about that?"

"Oh yes, I'm sure."

Don decided he'd heard enough; it was time to get some of this down in writing.

"Right," he said. "Thank you very much for bringing your son in, Mrs…?"

"Jackman," said Mum. "Mrs Mavis Jackman. People call me Mave."

"Well, Mave, we really could have done with knowing about this a lot sooner. The case goes to trial in just under four weeks, so I'm going to need a statement from you both if that's okay?"

"Will Danny have to go to court then?"

"Yes, but only as a witness," he turned to the boy. "There's nothing to be scared of, you just tell the court exactly the same as you tell me. I'll write it down for you now, but in court, it will be easy; someone will ask you questions, and you just answer them."

Don took the Jackmans' full contact details then wrote down a description of both Mavis and her son before writing down a lengthy statement from each of them. Mavis had to read everything over to her son, who it transpired had only rudimentary reading and writing skills.

"You'll probably get a visit from a friend of mine," Don said once everything had been signed. "He's a detective called Dave. He's a really nice man, you'll like him. He'll almost certainly have some more questions for you, but don't worry, Danny, you are definitely not in any trouble. got that?"

The boy nodded but didn't look totally convinced.

Just over an hour later Don was on his way to Newbury to show Johnson the statement he'd just taken. However, it was still early, and it was quite feasible that the detective may not have been in. So, Don decided to make a slight detour and visit someone else. Someone he was sure would be up, however early it was.

Emily Pritchard was busily clearing away her breakfast dishes when Don turned up on her doorstep.

"Hello, Mr Barton" she said. "I wasn't expecting to see you."

"Call me Don, please. I was hoping you could help me with a bit of local background if it's not too much trouble."

"Nothing's too much trouble when it comes to helping the police. Would you like a cup of tea?"

She made a pot of tea from her old copper kettle that was still hot and standing on the hob. Having poured two cups, she then sat down with her guest at the kitchen table to discuss the reason for the officer's visit.

Don realised he was probably breaking the rules of secrecy, but nonetheless, he told her about his early morning visitors and asked her opinion of what had been said to him.

"Hmm, well, it could be just erotic sex," she said, "but, of course, you know that already."

"It is the most likely explanation," said Don. "However, there could be more to it. There's been some funny goings-on in the area just recently, graves being desecrated and suchlike."

"And you think I can help you?"

"I'll be honest, I don't know why, but I have a feeling that you may have some understanding about these things."

"It intrigues me why you should think so, but I'll do my best for you. From the description the young man gave you, I think it could be some form of skyclad ritual," she said.

"Skyclad?"

"Naked, the pagans call it skyclad."

"And there are pagans living around here? Surely not."

"This is a very old area, Don," said Emily. "There have been pagans here for centuries. Christianity had all but died out in this country at the time of the Conquest. That was why the pope gave his blessing to William invading England in 1066."

"But that's ancient history!" Don protested.

"Some of the local families have been here since Saxon

times, maybe even earlier. There are a great many who clung to the old beliefs through the generations – and there are signs that their numbers are growing again."

"What, we're in danger of getting overrun with Devil worshippers?"

"The Devil is a Christian entity," Emily retorted, "and has nothing whatever to do with it. The folk we're talking about are more into worshipping nature – and the deities of the streams and forests; much like the ancient Greeks, in fact."

"Do you know any of them? The worshippers I mean, not the deities?"

"Well, the one that I did hear about was the now-deceased Mr Churcher senior, the boys' father. He was held in very high regard by some of the older families. It was even rumoured he was some sort of shaman or priest or something."

"So, could the two lads be responsible for the recent thefts in the graveyards."

"Certainly not!" said Emily. "That's the work of city louts who've been reading too much popular fiction and are out here at night seeking thrills. Perverted little sods! No, the Churcher boys will surely know the true rituals. They will have recruited the woman to help them access the spirits of the woods. Getting her to dance naked and go through the rites would be very much their cup of tea." She paused for effect then said: "On the other hand, they probably just wanted sex."

"Well, thanks once again, it's all a mystery to me. But ever little helps," said Don getting ready to leave. "Oh, and thanks for the cuppa. It was a rare treat to have a proper cup of tea for a change, it was just like my mum used to make. My wife only uses teabags, they're okay but not quite the same thing."

"Has she been gone long, your mum, I mean?"

"Just over three years, breast cancer."

"As long as you keep her in your heart, she will always be with you, you know that, don't you?"

"Thanks, Emily, yes, I do know that."

"Well, I'm sure she's very proud of you. Call in any time you like. I don't get anywhere nearly enough visitors."

Don promised that he would do that, and Emily watched as he left and drove off in his little van. She sat back down at the table, and her tabby cat jumped up onto her lap and purred as she stroked him.

"Well, what did you make of our visitor, Mr Crabtree?" said Emily. "I hope I didn't say too much – but I'm glad he liked the tea."

She looked deeply into the bottom of Don's cup, empty now save for the tealeaves that had gathered at the bottom.

The cat purred and mewed.

"Yes," said Emily. "Of course I noticed his aura. His soul may be young, but his heart is pure. I just hope it will be strong enough for the trials that lie ahead of him. There is much pain coming his way. I fear it will soon be catching up with him. He will need all the love he can get."

The cat purred.

"Don't be ridiculous, Crabtree! I'm far too old for all that nonsense."

Don found Johnson sitting alone in the station canteen drinking coffee and eating a bacon sandwich. He got himself a cup of tea and went over to join the detective.

"Good morning, Don," said Johnson. "Come and join me. Is that a statement you're clutching, is it for me?"

"Don't you want to finish your breakfast," asked Don, smiling.

"You cheeky sod! Give it here."

Don handed over the statement he'd taken from Danny

and explained the circumstances; he also mentioned his visit to Emily.

To Don's surprise, Johnson nodded his approval.

"A useful contact, that Miss Pritchard," he said. "You want to keep in with her."

Don sipped his tea as his colleague slowly read through the statement.

When Johnson had finished reading, he said, "What did you make of this lad, Danny?"

"He's a bit slow, borderline ESN his mum says – but not bad enough to have to go to a special school."

"You know I hate that term," said Johnson passionately. "Educationally Sub-Normal, ESN; as if the people who dream up these labels have some God-given right to define normality. We've got Littlemore Hospital up my way. Largest mental home in the country – except half of them shouldn't even be there."

"You feel strongly about this, don't you, Dave?"

"I do actually. I know I'd rather have young Danny fighting beside me in the jungle – especially if it came to a choice between him and one of these head-shrinkers. However, I digress, tell me more about Danny."

"Well, despite his, er, issues, he's a nice enough lad. Never been in trouble and he has enough sense to have contempt for drug dealers– and users for that matter."

"So, you don't think he's making this all up?"

"No, I'm sure of it. He's not the type."

"Well, if that's the case, this is just what the doctor ordered. It nicely corroborates some of the verbal admissions Churcher gave me as well as backing up his written statement. Well done, Don, the boss will be impressed."

"Are you going to retake the statement?"

Johnson shrugged. "I don't see the need; this is really good work on your part. I don't think you've missed anything at all. So, like I say, well done."

Don was feeling very pleased with himself as he watched Johnson leave the canteen, then he noticed that his tea had gone cold. For some reason it bothered him, as though it were some sort of omen.

"Don't be stupid, Don," he said to himself. "The statement was sound, Dave was happy, what could possibly be wrong?"

CHAPTER TWENTY
READING CROWN COURT

The first day of the trial had begun badly. Rosemary had cut her hand whilst making breakfast and the bleeding didn't seem to want to stop. Don's first aid skills were questionable at the best of times, but that day they seemed to have deserted him completely.

"If you'd drown in the bath," he quipped, "I could give you the kiss of life. I was brilliant at that as a cadet."

"I bet you were!" said Rosemary, not at all amused. "Was Dianne there with you?" She held a rolled-up tea towel against her damaged hand and pressed hard with her thumb. After a few minutes her efforts were rewarded, and the bleeding finally stopped. Don applied a plaster to the cut.

"Oh, and by the way," she said as he got into his van ready to drive off.

"Yes?"

"I didn't mean that about Diane. You can save the kiss of life until you get home."

Don made his way to Reading along the A4. At the far end of Prospect Park, he turned left into Liebenrood Road. He was making good progress heading towards the Crown Court in

Tilehurst Road when he suffered yet another delay. A van had collided with a car at the entrance to the park. Nobody was hurt but the drivers were both making allegation against each other. Don calmed them down but then had to wait a good fifteen minutes for a local unit to arrive and take control of the scene.

The two young policewomen that turned up were for some reason unfriendly and rather surly. They obviously didn't like dealing with road accidents, and they made Don feel as though the whole thing was his fault.

The encounter left a bad taste in Don's mouth and he was running late when he eventually pulled off Tilehurst Road and drove through the gateway of Artillery House. This ex-wartime military base had in recent years been refurbished and converted to courtrooms in an effort to relieve the pressure on the historic Crown Court building that for centuries had stood by the Forbury Gardens in Reading town centre.

He knew he should have come earlier! All the spaces allocated to police vehicles had been taken and cars crammed the small public car park. Don drove up and down, in and out, back and forth for a good fifteen minutes before he finally spotted someone driving out of a space in the public sector.

Then, ignoring a shout from a jobsworth in a black overcoat, he shot into the vacated space and abandoned his vehicle..

Checking, for the umpteenth time that he had the correct pocket notebook with him, he brushed the fag ash from the tunic of his freshly pressed uniform and began making his way towards the main entrance.

His route took him past the outside entrance to the holding cells – just as a prison van pulled into the parking bay. Don watched as the back doors of the van opened and was shocked to see Alan Churcher, wearing handcuffs and flanked by two solid looking prison officers, stepping out onto the tarmac.

Seeing Don, the young man became possessed with rage and tried to break free from his escort.

"You fucking, murdering bastard!" he screamed. "Let go of me, you cunts! I'm going to fucking kill him. He let my brother burn to death, wouldn't let me save him. He's going to die!"

Churcher continued struggling and shouting as the prison officers bundled him through the door of the cell block. However, before they got him inside, Don heard him scream, "I won't be in here forever. I'll burn your fucking house down with you in it! See if I don't!"

A little shaken, Don carried on and finally went into the court building, where he gave his details to the Crown Court Liaison Officer stationed inside the door.

"Nobody's going to want you for hours yet," said the liaison officer. "They haven't even sworn in the jury and there's a stack of pre-trial submissions to get though before any witnesses are going to be called. Why not nip over to the restaurant and get yourself a cup of tea? I'll call you if you're needed."

Even the severity of the barrister's black and white outfit could not disguise the fact that Davina Cooper was a strikingly attractive woman. She was tall and slender with luxurious natural blonde hair. However, she was obliged to keep her hair short. This was to accommodate the powdered wig she was required to wear whilst presenting evidence in court. The rules at the time were that the wig should cover all of a barrister's natural hair.

However, nothing could disguise her bright green eyes. Eyes that gave her a cat-like appearance, an appearance that was further enhanced by the fluidity of her movements.

Despite the fact that women had been getting called to the bar since 1919, a female barrister in a major criminal case was, even in the 1970s, still something of a rarity. To go with her good looks, Davina also had a mind that was sharp and incisive – as several of her past opponents had discovered to their cost.

Davina was completely ruthless in court. The warm smile that so easily charmed the judge and members of the jury became the sharp toothed grin of the tiger facing its prey as she launched into the cross-examination of some hapless witness.

Davina was a born competitor. She did not like to lose cases.

Davina entered the custody area and gave up her briefcase for inspection. Satisfied with the contents, the gaoler in charge of the cell passage led her to one of the holding cells and opened the inspection hatch.

"Officer, can you explain why Mr Churcher is sitting in handcuffs?" Davina demanded.

"It's in case he becomes violent, ma'am. He's already tried to attack a policeman out in the yard."

"Well, he's not in the yard now and there are no policemen present. So, kindly remove the bracelets. I refuse to confer with my client whilst he's in chains."

The gaoler gave her a dubious look.

"I can get an order from the judge, if you prefer," Davina continued.

Reluctantly the prison officer opened the cell door. He went over to the prisoner and unscrewed then removed the heavy, old-fashioned cuffs.

Having checked that his presence was not required whilst Davina exercised her right to private consultation, the officer then left the cell and locked the door behind him.

"When you're ready to leave, just press the button on the wall," he told Davina through the hatch.

Davina stood back and took a close look at her client.

She had to admit he was a handsome specimen. Tall, dark curly hair, well-built and possessed of rugged good looks. He could have passed for a film star – until he opened his mouth.

"Is my mum here?" he asked in a broad Berkshire accent. "Only she promised to bring me some fags."

"I haven't seen her, but I'll check when I leave," she promised. "Now, stand up and let me get a proper look at you. The impression you make on the jury is more important than you'd ever believe possible."

Churcher stood up and faced Davina for inspection.

"The suit is fine," she told him, "but you'll have to change that shirt and tie. I've brought these for you to put on instead."

Davina handed him a plain white shirt and a faded red tie that she produced from her briefcase and which he placed on the bed behind him. Churcher took off his trendy, bright orange shirt and the floral tie he had been wearing.

Watching him flex his finely muscled torso gave Davina an uncalled-for twinge of excitement. She had to remind herself that not only was she a professional lawyer, but she was also engaged to be married and shouldn't be admiring young men, however attractive they were.

Sadly, like so many beautiful things, Davina's day in the sun was destined to be brief. The eminent QC she was due to marry the following year would expect his wife to give up her career and stay at home to look after him. Her role would then consist of running the house and caring for the children they said they wanted, the grandchildren that both sets of their own parents so desperately craved.

None-the-less, on seeing his freshly scrubbed appearance, Davina permitted herself the pleasure of imagining Alan Churcher taking his morning shower; and she couldn't stop herself wondering what it would be like to be caressed by those big, strong young hands.

Enough of this nonsense, she told herself firmly, back to business.

"That's better," she said as he knotted his tie.

Churcher no longer looked like a sharp operator in trendy clothes. Now, he was more like a country yokel trying to make a good impression in his nice suit – and getting it hopelessly wrong. Perfect.

"Well, Alan, there's been some good progress since I visited you in prison last week. All reference to drugs has been redacted, but the judge knows you're helping the police catch the real villains so that's a good thing. It's also been accepted that the case against you for child pornography is wafer thin, the prosecution are not going to try to ahead with it."

"What does redacted mean?"

"It means they're not going to use it against you."

"Yeah, but what about the murder that I didn't do?"

"Well we've also made it quite clear that we don't accept Hoskins' written statement – so there's no case to answer regarding stealing the car. All in all, it's a good result with over half the charges against you dropped at the outset."

"But they still think I've killed the mistress."

"Yes, and they're hanging onto that nonsense about you kidnapping the policeman. Anyway, I think we stand a good chance of getting you off those charges as well. But only if we work at it. Let's start by having another look at this first statement of yours."

She handed Churcher a photocopy of a handwritten statement.

I, Alan Churcher, wish to make a statement. I want someone to write down what I say. I have been told that I need not say anything unless I wish to do so and that what I say may be given in evidence.

Signed: Alan Churcher

Davina paused and looked at her client. "Tell me, did they really advise you of all your rights?"

"No, the detective just said I should make a statement. He said it would look better in court if I showed I was co-operating. So, I just signed what he wrote."

"That's about usual," said Davina. "Okay, let's go on."

Me and my brother, Frank, own a van and we make a living doing odd jobs for people in the local area. About a year ago we met a man we called Mr H in one of the local pubs and we started doing work for him at his cottage. We used to go there at least once every week to do the garden and some maintenance in the house. Mr H was hardly ever there but his wife, Mrs H, was. After a couple of visits, she started having sex with Frank, then a while later they got me to join in as well. She had these canes like they used to use in school, and she liked to play these kinky games with us. Then she would give us boys a "good hiding" as she called it. She would pretend to be a teacher and we had to call her "The Mistress". She used to refer to Mr H as "The Headmaster."

Davina looked up at Churcher. There was something wrong here. Alan just didn't look the sort.

"Tell me about this caning stuff," she said. "Did you really enjoy it? I often saw boys being caned when I was at school and it looked like a thoroughly wretched experience. I'm sure they didn't like it one bit."

Churcher looked his barrister in the eye and said emphatically, "I hated it! I only did it to please Frank. He was always into it, even when we were boys. He said thinking about it helped him wank."

"Did you always do what Frank told you?"

"Pretty much. He was always the boss like."

"Hmm, interesting. Let's move on."

We mostly had sex at her house but sometimes we went to Bluebell Wood, where there's a hidden clearing, and then we would do it in the open. She was a fair bit older than us, but she was really good at sex and not bad looking, so we kept going back for more. We never gave her any money – in fact she still paid us for the work we did in the house. One morning at about four o'clock we were just going out rabbiting when she phoned us. She was very excited and angry and said she had to see us right away and that the headmaster was away in Ireland. So, we drove over to her house in the van. When we got there, she said Mr H had driven to Wales to get the ferry to Ireland. She said we were very naughty boys and she was going to give us both a good thrashing.

"Right, Alan, this is important. I presume the 'naughtiness' she referred to was bringing the boys to the house to be photographed?"

"Yeah, except we never done it."

Davina studied him for a brief while. With her experienced eye she could easily spot all the little tell-tale signs of someone telling lies. The fiddling with the hands, the lack of eye contact, the glances to the door and window as though looking for a means of escape. It all added up. But would the jury notice? Best take no chances.

"I'm going to give you two pieces of advice," she told him. "Firstly, if we do call you to give evidence and you get asked anything about those boys, just don't answer. They're bringing no charges against you on that point, so they can't question you on it. So, stay silent and I'll fire in an objection. Got it?"

"Whatever you say, miss. I'm completely in your hands. What's the second bit of advice?"

"Never play poker."

She wanted to go to the wood, so we took her, and we all got naked in the clearing. We then played some caning games and when she got tired beating us she laid down on the grass and we both had sex with her, then we got dressed.

"Who had sex with her first, you or Frank?"

"Frank always went first. He said it was his right because he saw her before me. Anyway, he'd got really horny watching her cane me. The mistress laughed when she saw him really hard and said they shouldn't waste it."

"And were you aroused as well?"

"Yeah, a bit, enough to do what I had to."

"But none of it was your idea?"

"To be honest, I'd have preferred to have gone rabbiting with Frank. If we'd done that then none of this would have happened." He brushed away a tear.

When we got back to the van we saw Mr H sitting in his Jag. He was parked next to us and was really upset and angry. He said he had got as far as Oxford then turned back when he heard about strikes at Holyhead on the car radio. It turned out he had seen us drive into the wood as he was going home, and he'd been watching us from the bushes. He called the mistress a whore and a slut and she called him a limp dick faggot and some other names. He grabbed her by the wrists, and she kneed him in the balls. She got him a good one and he doubled up for a few minutes. She just laughed at him and called him some more names then she turned around to walk off. Mr H lost his temper and picked up a big stone. He ran up behind her and hit her on the back of the head as hard as he could.

"It's this part of your story that will come under most attack in court, Alan. Before I decide whether to put you in the box I need to know how well you can answer some hard questions, okay?"

"Yeah, of course."

"Well, they are bound to allege that you are making it all up and that Mr H wasn't there at all. I know you've not been charged with rape, but it won't stop them making the jury wonder."

"Everything I've said in that statement is true. I swear it!" This time the body language didn't alter. Davina inwardly sighed in relief.

"So, can you explain how it was that you didn't hear Mr Hoskins drive up?"

"Simple. The clearing is a fair bit into the woods. You can't hear down to the road at all."

"Okay, let's talk about the fight. Where were you two when they were arguing?"

"We were just stood there."

"You didn't say anything? Either of you?"

"We thought it was funny, we were just laughing. Especially when she kneed him."

"Oh yes, that knee. I can see why Sergeant Johnson wanted that in the statement."

Davina's mind went briefly back to her days as a student. As one of a very small group of females at law school, she had received a fair bit of unwanted attention from the boys. She recalled how one of the more boorish young men had tried to grope her on the dancefloor at an end of term ball – and got the full benefit of her right knee for his trouble.

"How hard did she knee him?" Davina asked.

"The same as she used to do to me and Frank when we played games. She always did it as hard as she could – what she called full power."

Thinking back to the hapless law student, Davina hadn't kneed him anywhere near as hard as she could. Nevertheless, he'd had to hobble back to his room where he'd spent the next twenty-four hours lying on his back with his legs apart.

"So, how will you explain to the jury how Hoskins, having just been kicked really hard in the testicles, still had the strength to pick up a large rock, then hit his wife with enough force to kill her?"

Churcher chewed his lip and thought for a second before replying,

"Well, it's funny when you get hit there," he said. "It always hurts like hell – but sometimes when she did it you'd be down like a sack of spuds, then other times you got over it quite fast. It wasn't so much how hard she did it, more if she got you just right. She called it hitting the 'sweet spot.' She used to get all randy when she hit it. Sometimes, she got so wet.."

Davina held up her hand to stop him.

"I think I get the point," she said. "I rather suspect the

judge won't appreciate too much of that sort of detail. We just better hope you convince the jury, that's all."

"Well, it's all true. That's exactly how it happened."

"Right, let's move on."

She fell down and blood was coming from the back of her head. We all went over to her and could see she was dead. Her eyes were open, and she wasn't breathing. Mr H got very agitated and said we had to help him. We said no way, but he gave us a big wad of twenty-pound notes from his wallet. We said it wasn't enough, so he said he's give us his car and that it was worth a couple of grand. We said OK. He wrote out a receipt for the car and gave it to Frank. We then hid the mistress's body in some bushes. We were going to come back later and either bury it or dump it down a well or something. Mr H said nobody would miss her or report her missing so we didn't have to worry. Frank then drove him to Heathrow airport to get a flight to Dublin and I drove the Jag to an old barn we know and waited for him to come back. I had no idea the mistress was alive when we left her. I wish now that we had helped her and I'm really sorry for what we did. SIGNED: Alan Churcher

I have read the above statement and I have been told I can correct, alter or add anything I wish. This statement is true. I have made it of my own free will. SIGNED Alan Churcher

Davina chewed her lip for a moment. In her short career she'd already seen dozens of statements like this. She had rarely seen one that, as a genuine confession, was worth the paper it was written on. However, they were next to impossible to get thrown out, and juries notoriously refused to believe the police were less than scrupulously fair in their dealings with suspect.

"You do realise that without this statement they've got nothing on you at all? If you are ever in trouble again, never, ever make a statement until you've seen a lawyer," she said finally.

"But I didn't have a solicitor I could call out, and they said I had to get on with it."

"I bet they did! This Sergeant Johnson is a shrewd one to be sure. He made certain that the stuff about the kinky sex was in there. Very clever." She paused and thought for a moment.

"So, hiding the body and helping Hoskins was mostly Frank's idea?" she continued.

At this last remark, Churcher's eyes welled up and he started to sob. "It seems wrong talking about him," he said. "I don't want to put all the blame on him. He's not here to stick up for himself."

If only he could have saved the tears for the jury! "I understand," said Davina, "but you've got your mum to think about. She needs you home. You can't do Frank any harm now, so just tell the truth."

At the mention of his mum, Churcher brightened up. "I don't suppose you've got any fags, have you?" he asked.

"Sorry, I don't smoke," she replied. "Anyway, let's take a look at this second statement, shall we? I'm looking forward to getting PC Barton in the witness box. I'll enjoy challenging his evidence."

"Yeah, let's get the bastard!" Churcher grinned.

"Oh, and one more thing," Davina spoke sharply. "Don't think I haven't noticed what you've been up to while I've been talking to you. Take your hands out of your pockets and stop playing with yourself. If the jury see you doing that, they'll throw the book at you."

CHAPTER TWENTY-ONE
IN THE WITNESS BOX

Don decided to forgo the tea the liaison officer had suggested and instead took himself into the nearby police waiting room. Finding a corner seat, he studied the copy of his statement that he had brought with him – and on which he was sure to get questioned. With nothing better to do he spent the next hour trying his best to smoke enough fags to fill the giant ashtray that sat on a large polished table in the middle of the room.

Three cigarettes later he heard a familiar voice in the corridor outside. He looked up and a moment later the door opened. A very smartly dressed Dave Johnson entered the room. His face lit up when he saw Don and, having shaken hands, the two men decided that a cup of tea was now a very good idea. They informed the liaison officer of their intention and made their way over to the old Nissan hut that had been converted into a restaurant. Tea in hand, they found a quiet corner table where they could converse in private.

It turned out that Johnson's nice car was in for repair and he had travelled to court by train and bus. Puffing from his exertions, he was grateful to put down the large briefcase he was carrying that contained papers relating to the case.

"The legal boys have already got all the important stuff," he explained. "This is mostly antecedents and other rubbish that the judge may possibly ask for. He probably won't though. Anyway, how are things with you and the lovely Rosemary?"

"Better than ever," beamed Don. "We're even hoping to start a family as soon as we can. I really owe you one there, Dave, I won't forget it."

"I was glad to be of assistance, think nothing of it."

"Yeah, well, I'm still grateful to you. Anyway, this case of ours has lost a bit of weight hasn't it? Murder, kidnap, and car theft, that's it. Nothing about drugs, kiddy porn, or the stack of motoring offences."

"Strictly off the record, Don, the Drugs Squad have done a deal with your mate Alan Churcher. In exchange for immunity he's singing like a canary and giving them untold help with getting the goods on some large-scale dealers – and even one or two importers."

"But what about the two young boys in the photos, surely we're not dropping that case, are we?

"Sorry, mate, but in the end we couldn't go anywhere on the pornography. Social services felt it wasn't in the boys' long-term interests to go to court. They wouldn't let us anywhere near Eric and, on their insistence, Alan's statement was withdrawn."

"Christ! Whose bloody side are they on? And the motoring offences?"

"No luck there either – don't forget Alan Churcher was only a passenger. Besides which, even if the driver lived, we'd have had problems going for him. At no point in the chase did you give Churcher an approved signal to stop – which wouldn't have been legal anyway as you didn't have your hat on. AND, as far as the crash is concerned, you drove into the back of them. If we'd gone for it and Churcher made a counter-allegation, we'd have had to go after both drivers –

including you."

Don was just about to protest when they spotted the liaison officer entering the restaurant. He beckoned the two officers to come outside and then led them back to the police office. A barrister wearing a black gown and white powdered wig was seated at the table with a sheaf of papers fanned out on the brightly polished surface before him.

The barrister, a middle-aged, thickset man wearing glasses, stood up and smiled before shaking hands with the two officers.

"Leslie Smith QC," he said by way of introduction. "I'll be presenting the case for you. Are we okay using first names?"

"Yes, of course," said Johnson. "I'm Dave, this is Don."

"Well, I'm very pleased to meet you both, but I'm afraid I have some bad news for you."

"Bad news?" said Don.

"Yes, the judge is James Miller, a red judge, so you address him as My Lord, or simply Sir. Anyway, he's has read the file quite thoroughly and has already made up his mind about the case. Apparently he is Lord of the Manor somewhere out the sticks and, as far as he's concerned, what we have here is a couple of salt-of-the-earth young rustics who've been seduced and corrupted by the glamour of a big city harlot."

"Well, these good old country boys have a very profitable line in drugs dealing and they have also facilitated child sex offences!" said Don heatedly.

"The way he sees it, Alan Churcher, who has no previous convictions, is as much a victim as anyone. He has suffered the loss of his beloved brother as an indirect result of a perverted sex game that this woman came up with, a game that went badly wrong for them. We're going to have our work cut out, I'm afraid."

Johnson, who had remained silent during the exchange, now decided it was time to get involved in the conversation. "So, how are we going to play it?" he asked.

"Once we have a jury empanelled we'll get the pre-trial submissions out of the way. Then, once we get the actual trial going we'll begin with a description of the area, introduce the local photographs, et cetera. Then Miss Wilson's statement, which has been accepted by the defence, will be read to the jury. The plan drawer's statement comes next, followed by our first live witness, the police photographer, who will explain the album of photographs to the court and answer any questions. Has anybody seen him, by the way?"

"He's been delayed," said Johnson. "Car trouble."

"No matter, there's no way we'll get to him before tomorrow. So, if you're in contact with him, tell him to scrub it for today. We're not doing too well with our witnesses are we?"

"How do you mean?"

"The liaison officer tells me Mrs Jackman has had to take her son to the hospital, suspected fractured arm. It seems he fell of his bike going to school."

"Is he going to be all right?"

"She's going to let us know, but hopefully he'll be here tomorrow."

Smith made a note on his pad, then looked up and said, "So tomorrow, after the photographer, we'll read the dog handler's statement and get the murder weapon, the stone, introduced."

"So, you're not calling the dog handler in person?" said Don. "That's a bit odd."

"The defence have no issue with the stone being the cause of the initial injury. Surprising, but there it is. However, we will be calling Dr Steptoe, the pathologist. Now, his evidence is very important, so I expect him to be in the box for a while. I've not come across him before, do you know him, Dave?"

"Yes, he's very much old school from what I recall of him. He knows his stuff but he can come across as a bit bumptious."

Smith looked thoughtful for a second. "Well, we need him to be convincing," he said finally. "There are issues surrounding the actual cause of death that the defence will want to exploit, if we give them the chance."

Johnson shrugged.

"Right, then we can call Danny Jackman. That's always assuming he's here. If he's still absent it will be your turn, Don. No direct evidence concerning the murder itself, but the Jaguar car and the kidnap charge are your part in this jigsaw. Then finally, Dave, you get to have your say. I hope you're ready for a grilling?"

Johnson smiled. "Don't worry. I've done this a few times. I know what to expect."

"Well, don't get complacent. I've seen this young lady barrister before. She's probably the brightest new star to grace our profession in years. Good looks, charm – and a razor-sharp intellect. She's good, trust me."

"All I can do is tell the truth," said Johnson. Smith smiled.

"Right, Don," he said. "Let's have a final run through your statement, shall we?"

As Smith had predicted, it was the next morning before the court was ready to hear live evidence.

The forensic pathologist was in the witness box for over two hours.

Professor James Steptoe was the quintessential scientist. He was in his early sixties, silver haired and well over six feet tall. Like many tall men, he stood and walked with a slight stoop. It was without question that he was possessed of a brilliant mind, but it was painfully obvious to those that met him that he totally lacked dress sense.

For his appearance in court, he was wearing light blue trousers and brown shoes. His close-checked green cotton shirt clashed with his red tie, and the bowl of his pipe protruded prominently from the top pocket of his Harris tweed jacket.

His wife, Angel, an aging free spirit from the hippy generation, had assured him he "looked fine" when he left home that morning. However, James was fully aware of the eccentricity of his appearance and felt uncomfortable. He fervently wished he could have worn his habitual white lab coat instead of all this "formal attire," as he put it.

Like many in his profession, Steptoe did not believe in the concept of absolute truth. If it looked like cheese, smelt like cheese, tasted like cheese, and came in a wrapper labelled cheese, then it was *in all probability* cheese. He would never say: "That's cheese, no doubt about it."

Davina had never met Steptoe, but she had done her homework on him. Her research revealed that he was an honest and thoughtful witness – but his character was more suited to delivering a lecture than giving evidence in court. He was not used to his opinions being questioned, and he had a reputation for getting rattled if anyone had the temerity to challenge his findings.

It was here that Davina could see a weakness, a chink in his armour, something her sharp mind could exploit to her advantage.

She smiled sweetly as Steptoe stepped into the box and took the oath.

During his examination-in-chief, Steptoe confirmed that he had attended the scene of the homicide and examined the body of Mrs Hoskins *in situ* prior to having it removed to Newbury mortuary where he had conducted a full post-mortem examination.

He explained that when he first saw Suzanne, she was lying, fully clothed, in a shallow ditch a few yards from the side of the road. She was lying on her front; her right arm was outstretched, and her eyes and her mouth were open.

Photographs of the body were shown to the jury. As they

were being passed around two, of the female jurors began to cry, and one of the men looked as though he was about to faint. Davina was also given copies of the pictures which she showed to the defendant. Churcher could not bring himself to look at them and turned his head away.

Steptoe went on to say that one of the deceased's shoes was missing from her foot but subsequently discovered in some bushes twenty-five yards from where the body was found. There was clear evidence that Suzanne had dragged herself from these bushes towards the road – before expiring.

"Can we be absolutely sure that it was she who dragged herself to that position and that she wasn't moved there by some other means?" Smith asked the witness.

"That is what the evidence suggests, yes."

Davina, who was taking notes, underlined this answer.

Professor Steptoe went on to give details of the post-mortem examination. Photographs of the procedure were produced and handed to the judge. At his suggestion, it was agreed by all parties that it wasn't necessary to risk upsetting the jury by bringing them into evidence.

"Your verbal explanation of the results of your examination will suffice, thank you, Professor," the judge told Steptoe.

It transpired that Mrs Hoskins had suffered a traumatic injury to the back of her head that had massively fractured her skull and caused internal bleeding on the brain. This bleeding eventually resulted in her death, a minimum of one and a maximum of four hours later.

The witness, the jury, and the defendant were shown a large, jagged piece of flint. Yes, the pathologist concurred, this was indeed the one found near the scene. The stone bore traces of Suzanne's blood, and the contours of the stone were an exact match for the damage to her skull.

The professor concluded his evidence with testimony that examination of the internal organs had revealed that Mrs

Hoskins had indulged in sexual intercourse immediately prior to her death. Two distinct sets of semen were present in her vagina and, whilst certainly each was from different men, they both were of the same blood group as the defendant. Steptoe refused to speculate as to the exact timescale of events but agreed that it was a possibility that sex could have taken place after the assault.

The witness had been in the box for over an hour, so the judge ordered a fifteen-minute adjournment before permitting cross-examination by the defence. Davina used this break to prepare her notes.

"Remind us, Professor Steptoe," Davina said once the trial resumed, "exactly how Mrs Hoskins was dressed when you examined her body."

"As I said, she was fully dressed, wearing a light cardigan, a summer frock, underwear, and one shoe."

"And was her underwear correctly fastened and all in the right place?"

"Yes."

"And, in particular, her panties. They were worn correctly: snugly fitted, not inside out or the wrong way around?"

"Yes, that is correct."

"Not damaged."

"No, I cut them off with scissors at the mortuary. They seemed fine to me."

The judge decided it was time to intervene. "I fail to see where this line of questioning is taking us, Miss Cooper."

"My lord, during this witness's testimony, he stated that it was impossible to determine if sexual intercourse had taken place whilst Mrs Hoskins was still conscious. I am merely seeking to establish that the preponderance of evidence indicates that she was indeed fully conscious and most likely a willing partner to the activity – as is my client's contention."

"Hmm, I don't see why you couldn't have simply said so.

Well, Professor, is that a reasonable conclusion to draw from the evidence?

"Yes, my lord. Obviously, one can't be sure, but that possibility is certainly supported by the evidence."

"Thank you, professor. Pray continue, Miss Cooper."

"I'm obliged to your lordship. Now, professor, could you explain to the jury what exactly is meant by the term 'unconscious state.'"

Steptoe looked completely nonplussed. "Erm, well, its lack of awareness, lack of consciousness, you know, totally out of it."

"Many people think of it as being asleep, is that correct?"

"Oh no, it's nothing like being asleep. Far deeper, much more profound. For one thing, you don't snore when you're unconscious."

A titter of laughter went around the courtroom. Davina gave the witness an indulgent smile.

"So, breathing becomes very shallow?"

"Yes."

"Imperceptible?"

"Possibly."

"So," she said, "in this more profound state, do one's eyes stay open, for example?"

"Yes, frequently that is the case."

"Is it not a fact, professor, that there are countless examples of people being presumed dead who are, in actuality, simply unconscious?"

"As you say, countless examples. That's why death should only ever be certified by a qualified medical practitioner."

"So, when my client says he was sure the lady was dead before he helped move her, he could well be telling the truth?"

"He should have had her checked properly."

"But, in his own mind, he could very well be telling the truth?"

"Objection," Smith was on his feet. "The witness is being asked to hypothesise on what was in the defendant's mind."

"Sustained. Stick to facts that the witness can answer, please, Miss Cooper."

"I apologise, my lord."

"Now, professor," she continued, "to go back to your earlier testimony. As I recall, my learned friend asked if you could be absolutely certain that Mrs Hoskins, having come around, dragged herself to the side of the road. And your answer was:"

Davina consulted her notes, "*That is what the evidence suggests.* A somewhat ambiguous answer is it not?"

"Well, obviously, I can't be absolutely certain."

"Are we to infer then, *Professor Steptoe,*" Davina's voice rose an octave, "that, maybe, just maybe, some other party could have moved her body? Indeed, could Mrs Hoskins have, in fact, already been dead when this move occurred?"

"I don't think that's very likely…"

"Is it not a possibility that my client had no part at all in bringing about her death, that he was merely guilty of moving her body *post mortem*?"

"As I say, it's very unlikely."

"Nevertheless, is what I suggest a possibility, yes or no?"

"Well, yes, but…"

"Thank you, professor. No further questions."

The court rose for lunch at twelve-thirty. Danny had still not turned up, but his mum had phoned in and said he would definitely attend the next day. It was far from ideal, but Smith, having passed a message to the judge, decided Don should go into the box. This was despite the protocol that police evidence was normally presented only once all the civilian evidence had been heard.

There was the familiar knot in Don's stomach as he took the oath and confirmed his identity. He handed the bible back to the usher and took his pocketbook from the breast pocket of his tunic.

Leslie Smith stood up and said to the judge, "My lord, may the officer refresh his memory from his official notebook?"

The judge spoke to Don: "When were these notes made, officer?"

"These were notes made as soon as possible after the events, my lord."

The judge looked back to Smith. "I understand that some of these notes would have been made several days after the events in question. Is that not so?"

"That is correct, my lord. PC Barton was in hospital recovering from his injuries and unable to write up his notes for several days."

The judge looked over at Davina. "Does the defence have any objection?"

Davina stood up; Smith sat down. "No, my lord. My client is content for the officer to use his notebook."

All eyes now turned to the dock where Churcher was sitting, scowling, between the two prison officers.

Content wasn't the term the judge would have used to describe the defendant's demeanour. However, all he said was, "Proceed."

Smith now led Don through his evidence, starting with his sighting of the two men in the car, the first accident, his journey with the two brothers, and concluding with a description of the second, fatal accident.

Davina had sat quietly taking notes and allowed this narrative to run without interruption. However, when she stood up, Don felt the tension rising. The court fell totally silent.

"PC Barton, may I begin by congratulating you on making such a full recovery from this unfortunate accident." She emphasised the word accident. "However, there are one or two details in your account that I'm sure will be of concern to the jury."

She smiled at the jury of eight women and four men. Feeling that women were less likely than men to feel sympathy for a professional sex worker, Davina had used the challenges available to her to engineer this ratio. She was pleased with the result.

"Now you say you recognised this car, having seen it previously?"

"Yes, ma'am." Don had not, at this point, been required to give details of his first meeting with Suzanne. Such evidence was deemed hearsay as Churcher wasn't present to hear what had been said.

However, under cross-examination, the hearsay rule did not apply. The defence could also ask what are called leading questions, i.e. those where the fact is spelt out and simply confirmed or denied by a yes or no answer.

"Could you explain to the court the circumstances whereby you saw this vehicle?"

Don went through the details of his first, and only, meeting with Steve and Suzanne Hoskins.

"And what was said at the time about the car?" Davina asked him

"I don't understand. Nothing was said about the car."

"So, you've no idea whether the car still belonged to the Hoskinses? I mean, was it up for sale? Maybe it had already been sold?"

"Objection!" Smith was on his feet, and Davina sat down. "My learned friend is badgering the witness."

"Is this line of questioning taking us anywhere?" asked the judge.

Davina stood back up. "Indeed, it is, my lord. I am seeking to establish that the officer's decision to stop my client and his brother was based on an honestly held, but false, assumption of ownership of the vehicle in question. That being the case,

KEVIN FITZPATRICK

there was actually no reason for the Churcher brothers to have caused the accident nor to kidnap the policeman."

The judge looked dubious. It was obvious to him that Davina was trying to exploit Steven Hoskins failure to provide any evidence about the Jaguar car. She was within her rights, but James Miller did not like to see a jury misdirected by young lawyers who were sometimes too smart for their own good.

"I presume you intend introducing evidence of this change of ownership?" he asked.

"Mr Churcher will be stating as much, my lord."

"I think we can safely proceed on the assumption that the officer has no knowledge of this car being sold. Pray continue with your examination."

"Thank you, my lord. Now, officer, if I may turn to the domestic dispute between the deceased and her husband. There was evidence of violence at the premises, is that not so?"

"Towards property, yes, not people."

"Oh, so you had Mrs Hoskins medically examined, did you?"

"No, but…"

"You're not a doctor, are you?"

"She told me she wasn't injured."

"And you just took her word for it?"

"Yes, ma'am," Don looked, and felt, crestfallen.

"So, in the middle of the night, you went off and left this poor lady at the mercy of a violent and abusive husband, no medical exam, no support, no ongoing plan of action. The fact is, you didn't make a proper job of it at all. You treated it as just another nuisance domestic, not worthy of your attention. Is that not right, *Mister* Barton?"

"It wasn't like that." But when Davina glanced over at the jury she noted, with satisfaction, that they obviously thought it was exactly like that.

Davina was on a roll. "Right, let's talk about this so-called kidnapping," she said.

Davina emphasised the words "so-called" and gave another meaningful look to the jury.

"Let's start from the beginning, shall we?" she began. "You saw the Churcher brothers driving the Jaguar car and, having jumped to the conclusion that they had stolen it, you decided to give chase, is that correct?"

"I decided to stop the vehicle to find out what they were up to, yes."

"So, you chased after it?"

"Well, I followed it and put my blue light on to get it to stop."

"In your statement," she appeared to consult a sheaf of papers, "you say that you were driving a *marked police vehicle*. Describe this vehicle."

"Well, it was a blue and white Ford Escort van—"

"A van!" Another glance to the jury." You were driving a little van? Is that the type of vehicle the Thames Valley Police normally use for traffic enforcement?"

"Well, no but…"

"So, a normal driver would not be expecting to be stopped by this type of police vehicle, is that not so?"

"Not usually, maybe but…"

"And how were you dressed, officer?"

"In full uniform, just as I am now."

"Did you have your hat on?"

"No, it was beside me on the seat."

"As an ex-Traffic officer, I assume you are aware of the requirement for a policeman to be in full uniform to stop a vehicle – including a hat?"

"Objection, my lord!" Smith stood up; Davina sat down. "The defendant has not been charged with any motoring offences. The officer is being questioned over evidence that hasn't been presented."

"Indeed, Miss Cooper, I fail to see where this is leading us," said the judge.

Davina stood up. "My lord, the basic facts of this case are, by and large, not in dispute. However, the interpretation of those facts is very much in contention. I am seeking to establish, with the cooperation of the witness, that a much more likely explanation exists for why the Jaguar failed to stop, how the initial accident happened, and how it was that the officer ended up being transported by the defendant."

"Very well, but please try and stick to the point. Continue."

Davina could not have been more pleased with herself. With his objection, Smith had handed her a golden opportunity to plant seeds of doubt in the minds of the jurors.

"So, incorrectly dressed and driving an inappropriate vehicle, you have raced after my client and his brother in an effort to stop them. I put it to you, officer, that my client's assertion that the brothers had no idea initially that you were following them is perfectly reasonable."

"No! They made off at speed."

"Mr Barton, they were taking a recently acquired, high-performance car for a spin in the country. You would hardly expect them to be driving sedately, now would you?"

"Well, as far as I was concerned, they were trying to get away from me."

"As far as you *were* concerned! But now, with the benefit of hindsight, do you agree that it is possible that the men were, in fact, unaware of your presence and simply driving fast?"

"That's not how it seemed to me."

"But it is *possible*, isn't it?"

Don went silent for a moment.

"Come along, officer," said the judge. "Counsel for the defence has asked you a perfectly straightforward question. Is it a possibility, however remote, that the men did not know you were trying to stop them?"

"I suppose it has to be a possibility, my lord, but…"

"Thank you, constable!" said Davina. "We're finally getting somewhere."

Don looked annoyed, but somewhat crestfallen, and Davina became concerned that some of the jurors might be feeling some sympathy with him.

"Now, as to the actual accident," she continued. "If the deceased, Mr Churcher, suddenly became aware that he was being followed by a police officer. In fact, one who he suddenly realised was trying to stop him, it isn't surprising that he panicked and hit his brakes, is it?"

"Objection!"

"Sustained, you are asking the witness to hypothesise the thoughts of another person. Pray confine your questions to the witness's own thoughts and actions."

"Apologies, my lord," said Davina, then to Don, "Is it not the case that your driving into the back of the Jaguar car could have been a simple accident, yes or no?"

"Yes, but…"

"Thank you, and as a result of this accident you suffered a nasty concussion, is that correct?"

"Yes."

"In fact, you were knocked unconscious?"

"Yes, I was."

"So, when you came around, your thoughts were confused?"

"To start with yes, but…"

"And it was while you were in this state of delirium that you imagined you were being kidnapped?"

"Objection!"

"Sustained." The judge gave Davina a pointed look.

Davina changed tack. "Officer, why did you assume you were being kidnapped?"

"Well, they had a gun for one thing."

"Ah yes, the gun. A legally held shotgun that Mr Churcher says they had with them to shoot rabbits. Did either of the men actually threaten you with the gun?"

"Not in so many words maybe…"

"Was it pointed at you?"

"Not directly, no, but…"

"No, indeed! The fact is, that once again you jumped to a conclusion. You do rather a lot of that, don't you? My client's claim that they were looking after you following the accident and were taking you to the doctor's surgery is perfectly reasonable. In fact, it makes perfect sense, is that not so?"

"I think I know the difference between being given a lift to the doctors and being kidnapped!" Don was furious.

Davina held up her hand. "Under normal circumstances, of course, you do. But these were not normal circumstances were they? In fact, given your state of mind following the excitement of the car chase and the nasty blow on the head – not to mention your penchant for jumping to conclusions."

"Objection!"

"Will this take much longer, Miss Cooper?" The judge looked at his watch.

"No, my lord, I'm nearly there. I would just like to ask a couple of questions about the tragic accident in which my client lost his brother."

Up to this point, Alan Church had been silently enjoying watching the policeman being taken to task by his barrister, but now he jumped to his feet and shouted, "Yes, you murdering bastard, tell them how you let my brother burn to death!"

There was a brief scuffle as the prison officers forced him back into his seat. The judge looked over to him.

"I will not tolerate outbursts of that nature in my court," said the judge.

Alan, who was by now quietly weeping and sobbing, simply nodded his head in compliance.

"Continue, Miss Cooper," the judge said.

"If we could turn now to the matter of the second accident. There is no dispute, once again, as to the facts; however, there is one point I would like to clarify. officer. Why did you feel it appropriate not to attempt to rescue Frank Churcher?"

"It was too dangerous. The car was about to explode, and in any case, Frank Churcher was already dead."

"But you've already told us you have no medical training, how could you be sure?"

"It seemed obvious."

"More jumping to conclusions?"

"Objection!"

"Sustained. I won't warn you again, Miss Cooper."

"Apologies, my lord. However, Mr Barton, can we be quite clear about this. You felt justified leaving Mrs Hoskins to her fate on the night of the domestic dispute, and you felt it was acceptable, given the circumstances, to abandon Mr Churcher to a burning car."

"Given the circumstances at the time, yes."

"Thank you, officer. I have no further questions, my lord."

The judge took a long look at his watch then spoke to Smith, the prosecutor.

"I presume you will have a number of points to raise with this witness during re-examination?"

"Indeed so, my lord."

"It has been a long day for the jury, and I am minded to ask you to leave that until tomorrow, if there are no objections?"

"No, my lord."

"None, my lord."

"Constable Barton, I will remind you that you are under oath and you are not to discuss your evidence with anyone other than your counsel, Mr Smith. Is that clearly understood?"

"Yes, my lord."

"In that case, we will adjourn until ten o'clock tomorrow morning."

The court usher stepped forward. "Court will rise!" he said.

CHAPTER TWENTY-TWO
THE CASE CONTINUES

Don was feeling dejected as he drove home from the court. Whatever idiot had coined the phrase "dumb blonde" had never come across Davina Cooper, that was for sure! Don fully realised that the attractive young barrister had run rings round him in the witness box.

"She had me by the balls from the minute she started," he told Rosemary over dinner. His wife had cooked him a delicious spaghetti Bolognese and bought a bottle of Yugoslav Riesling to wash it down with, but even that couldn't lift his mood. "She even had me doubting my own testimony by the time she was finished. She is one clever lady," he added.

"When will men ever start taking women seriously?" said Rosemary. "She obviously has to be good to survive in such a male-dominated world. So, what happens now?"

"Tomorrow I'll go back into the box, and our barrister will question me to re-examine my evidence. He's allowed to clear up any ambiguities and so on, but we're not allowed to bring anything new out. Then it's Dave Johnson's turn; basically the whole case rests on his interviews with young Churcher."

"Well, in that case, you've nothing to worry about. I really can't see any young brief getting the better of Dave, however slick she may be."

"You really rate him, don't you?"

"Don, he's the best friend we've had in a long time. Yes, I do rate him."

On arrival at court the next morning, Don was instructed to report to the police office where Johnson was waiting for him together with the barrister, Mr Smith. Danny Jackman, dressed in his school uniform, was also in the room together with his mother.

Smith was in a buoyant mood. "Good morning, Don," he said. "I've just been chatting to young Danny here, and I've decided to put him straight into the box. Unless you have any strong objections, I feel we are best served by forging ahead. That means I won't bother with re-examination as far as you are concerned. Is that all right with you?"

Don was actually quite relieved. "Whatever you say, sir," he replied. "We in your hands."

"Excellent, that's settled then."

Danny pleasantly surprised everyone by giving his evidence clearly and confidently with no apparent trace of nerves. Smith led him through his statement virtually line by line and, as each question was posed, the boy looked directly at him and replied in strong, clear tones, albeit tinged with a strong Berkshire accent.

In conclusion, Smith asked, "Danny, you say you recognised the demons from having seen them before." He held up a warning hand. "We don't need the circumstances." Smith had been advised to make no mention of drugs during the trial. "A simple yes or no will suffice."

"Yes."

"Do you see that man in the court today?"

"Yes."

"Can you point him out, please?"

"That's him, there." Danny indicated Churcher who, in

return, scowled at the boy making him visibly quake with fear.

"No, further questions, My Lord." Smith sat down.

Davina, who had sat through the testimony without raising any objections, smiled indulgently in Danny's direction.

Don, who was sitting in the gallery next to Mavis Jackman, was growing concerned. After his experience giving evidence the day before, he knew only too well that this very attractive lady barrister's beauty was like that of the tiger, smiling before devouring its prey.

"Danny," she said as she began her cross-examination, "am I right in assuming that you are someone who is fond of nature?"

"I like animals, if that's what you mean, Miss."

"You've been brought up in the countryside?"

"Yes, Miss."

"So, you know all about the seasons, when to plant, when to harvest, that sort of thing?"

"Miss Cooper," the judge interjected, "I trust this line of questioning is taking us somewhere?"

"Indeed it is, My Lord," Davina replied. "If I could crave the court's indulgence for just another few minutes, it will all become clear."

The judge nodded his assent, and Davina turned back to Danny. "So, Danny, do you know about the phases of the moon?"

"Yeah, of course I do," the boy replied. "Everyone does."

"No, not everyone, Danny, only clever country folk like you. Some city people know nothing about the moon other than the fact it's in the sky."

Danny snorted derision.

"So, you definitely know when it's a full moon, like you described in your evidence?"

"A full moon's a full moon. It can't be anything else."

"And you are certain you saw the lady dancing in the light of a full moon?"

"Yes, Miss, definitely."

"Do you like stories, Danny?"

"Sometimes," the boy answered cautiously.

"Do you sometimes make up stories?"

"Miss Cooper!" The judge was angry. "If you intend to accuse the witness of telling lies, perhaps you could be a bit more direct and simply put it to him."

"Well, Danny, are you telling lies?"

"No, I'm not!" shouted Danny. "Look!" he said and poked his tongue out. "It goes black when you tell lies, and it's not black, is it?"

"Do you recognise this, Danny?" Davina held up a white paper booklet. "It's called *Old Moore's Almanac*."

"Yeah, my dad's got one. He's always looking at it."

"My Lord," Davina spoke to the judge, "I've taken the liberty of acquiring some extra copies." She indicated a pile of almanacs on her desk. "May I show them to the court?"

"Proceed."

The usher passed a copy to judge, then another to Danny, another to Smith, and finally gave one to the foreman of the jury.

"I've indicated the appropriate passage," said Davina, "and it clearly shows that on the night of the murder, there was no full moon. The previous one happened several days before the night in question, and the next was nearly three weeks later."

"Danny," she continued, "I put it to you that you've made all this up. You weren't there at all on the night Mrs Hoskins died, were you? It's all lies, isn't it?"

Danny burst into tears. "No, no, it's true, isn't it, Mum? Tell them!" he looked pleadingly towards his mum who sat ashen-faced in the gallery.

A murmur ran around the courtroom, and the judge tapped his gavel to call for order.

"Have you finished questioning the witness?" he asked Davina.

"Yes, my lord."

"Mr Smith?"

Smith was totally taken aback. "My lord, there's obviously an anomaly in the evidence that will have to be cleared up by the police. May I suggest a twenty-four-hour adjournment to allow us to investigate further?"

"Have you any objection, Miss Cooper?"

"No, my lord."

"In that case, we'll adjourn to eleven am tomorrow at which point I would like to see both counsel in my chambers."

When the usher called the court to rise, Danny's mum glared at Don then rushed forward to comfort her son. Don walked out into the lobby where he found Johnson pacing up and down, wondering what on earth was going on.

When Don had explained to Johnson what had happened, the detective said, "Christ! What a cock-up! Where's the boy now?"

Don looked around, but the Jackmans were nowhere to be seen. He ran to the exit door just in time to see Mavis and her son pulling out onto Tilehurst Road in the family Land Rover.

"Right," said Johnson when Don got back to him. "I'll speak to the superintendent. It's probably best if you bugger off home. I'll talk to you later."

Don went home, booked off duty and changed out of uniform. To cheer him up, Rosemary cooked him a nice dinner, and the two of them had just settled down in front of the television to watch *Crossroads* when the front doorbell rang. Rosemary got up to answer the door.

"Don, it's Dave here to see you," she said, leading DS Johnson into the living room.

"Sorry to bother you both," Johnson said. "Can we chat, Don?"

"I've told Rosemary what happened today," Don said. "So it's okay talk in front of her."

Johnson smiled at Rosemary. "Well, you won't be surprised to hear the governor's not exactly delighted at today's fiasco. The bollockings will start tomorrow at the Chief Constable's daily briefing – unless, that is, we can come up with some answers asap."

"Dave, I honestly don't know what to say. I would have sworn Danny was telling the truth. You saw him today, what did you think?"

"For what it's worth, I agree with you, but I can't see how he can be. I need to talk to him and find out what's going on. But to be honest, mate, it's a bit embarrassing. I've been trying to get to see him all afternoon, but I'm buggered if I can find the bloody house!"

Despite the seriousness of the situation, Don laughed. "That's always happening around here," he said. "The fact is, I haven't got a clue myself, I've never been to his address, I only saw him here in the office. Tell you what though, I'll give Emily Pritchard a bell and see if she can give us some directions."

Johnson was happily drinking tea and chatting to Rosemary when Don came back from his office. The young officer was holding a scrap of paper and looking amused.

"Right, I'm pretty sure I know where it is, but I reckon I better come with you, it's a bit complicated."

"Well, if you don't mind, Don, that would be great. Stay as you are, though, look fine. You can drive my motor if you like."

Don took Johnson's Cortina out of the village and across to the nearby common where he turned off the road and began driving along some unmade roads through Forestry Commission land towards some distant pastures where two ancient cottages stood side by side at the foot of a low hill. He pulled up outside one of the cottages and looked triumphantly over to his passenger.

"Bloody hell, Don! I'd never have found this place. Are you sure you can get us back out of here without getting lost?"

Before Don could reply, the door of the cottage opened, and a man strode out towards them. The man was not especially tall but was powerfully built. He was the quintessential farm labourer. He was wearing moleskin trousers with working boots, and the sleeves of his red check shirt were rolled up, revealing the knotted muscles of his forearms.

Don noticed the heavy leather belt that held up the man's trousers and wondered if that was the source of young Danny's terror of punishment.

Dave was out of the car in an instant. "Mr Jackman?" he enquired. "I'm Detective Sergeant Johnson from the murder investigation team. I take it you've heard what happened in court today?"

"Yes, Mave told me." Jackman sounded less than pleased. "I suppose you better come in."

He led the two policemen to the front of his cottage where he stopped and turned before opening the door.

"Look," he said quietly, "my Danny's a good boy, but a bit slow. I wouldn't take too much notice of anything he says to you, if you know what I mean. He doesn't really tell lies – but he's not always all there."

"Thanks for that," said Johnson reassuringly. "We'll certainly keep that in mind."

The men entered the cottage and nearly gagged at the strong smell of freshly cooked rabbit. The front door led into an open-plan kitchen with a concrete floor, and there was a large wooden table in the centre of the room. Danny was seated at a smaller table operating a metal contraption with a long handle. There was a basket of used shotgun cartridges by his foot and another row of cartridges lined up in front of him.

"He's reloading spent cartridges for me," said Dad by way of explanation. "My boss has a regular shoot on his land, and we tidy up after them. I get to keep the used shells as payment. Our Danny's not much at schoolwork, but he's really good with his hands."

"And his eyes, the dirty little pervert!" The men turned to see an attractive girl of about seventeen coming down the stairs that led to the upper story of the cottage. "He's been going through my stuff again," she continued.

Jackman's expression darkened. "Is that true, boy?" he asked menacingly.

"The policemen don't want to hear all our troubles, do you, Mr Barton?" This time it was Mavis Jackman who spoke as she joined the company from a back room.

"We just want a word with Danny about his evidence today," said Johnson. "If that's all right with you, Mr Jackman?"

"I suppose it has to be," said Jackman grudgingly. "Just remember what I told you."

"We won't keep you long. It's just about this question of timing that came up in court today. We need to go back over a couple of details. Mrs Jackman, when did Danny first tell you about the dancers in the woods?"

"Only a couple of days before I went to the police office," the woman replied. "We explained to Mr Barton why Danny took so long telling me."

She stole an accusing glance at her husband who retorted, "We keep ourselves to ourselves around here. It never pays to get involved with these Londoners."

"Yes, I understand that." (I'm glad *you* do! thought Don.)

"But, Danny," Johnson addressed the boy directly, "when did you first realise that the lady you saw dancing was the one who got killed?"

"Straight away, when I saw her picture in the paper," the boy said.

"Which newspaper was that?" Johnson enquired.

"The local paper, the *Newbury Weekly News*," Mavis answered for her son.

"Have you still got it?"

"As a matter of fact, we probably have," said Jackman indicating a large pile of newspapers standing beside the unlit fireplace. "We save them for the winter to light the fire with."

It took several minutes to locate the edition in question and, sure enough, the front page featured a full-face photograph of Suzanne Hoskins. The picture had obviously been taken some years previously, and Don guessed it was a file copy, probably furnished by the *News of the World* photo library.

"So, you get the paper every week?" said Johnson. "I'm surprised the paperboy can find you all the way out here."

"Well, we don't get it delivered," said Jackman. "My boss at the farm gets it every week, and he gives it to me when he's finished with it. It's a week out of date, but that doesn't matter. I mean it costs me nothing, and we mostly use it for the fire anyway."

"Yes, but I knew about that when Danny showed me," said Mrs Jackman. "That's how I knew it was the night of the murder. Danny said he saw the picture right away, so I knocked a week off the date and realised it must have been the same night."

"Just a minute," said Mr Jackman. "Show me that paper again."

Johnson handed it over, and Jackman stared at it for a full minute or so.

KEVIN FITZPATRICK

"I actually bought this paper," he said finally. "The boss was away on holiday, and all the blokes at work were on about the murder, so I picked this up at the village shop."

The colour drained out of Mrs Jackman's face, and she grasped the back of a chair for support.

"Oh, bloody hell, you did and all. I totally forgot that," she said. "Oh bugger! It looks like I've been leading you all up the garden path. Oh God, I am so sorry, it was my fault entirely. Danny can't read so he wouldn't have known. Oh dear, what can I say?"

"Please don't worry, Mrs Jackman," said Johnson, giving her a warm, friendly smile. "There's no real harm done as long as you're sure of what you're telling me."

"Yes, I am sure now. Oh dear, what have I done?"

"Look we're just pleased to get it all sorted out. You still did the right thing coming forward. We'll just grab a quick statement off each of you to cover the anomaly then we'll leave you in peace."

"Will we have to go back to court in the morning?"

"Not unless we send for you. I'll give you a ring once the judge decides what to do."

"Will Danny get into trouble?"

"No, not now we know it was an honest mistake. God, the jails would be full of witnesses if everyone who got something wrong were to get prosecuted."

Mave gave him a grateful smile. "Make the tea, love," she said to her daughter. "I think we could all do with one."

The girl scowled but nevertheless walked over to the kettle to do as she'd been bid.

It was getting late when the two policemen finally drove back to Don's house in Brompton.

"Fancy a quick drink before going back?" said Don.

"No thanks, mate. Another time though. I best get back; it's been a long day – and I'm not as confident as you driving around these country roads at night. Thanks for coming out though, I'd never have found that place by myself."

"I'm just happy that the error got sorted before it caused a problem. I didn't like that Jackman chap though, did you?"

"An honest, country, working man is my assessment. But I wouldn't fancy being in poor Danny's shoes tonight if that sister of his carries on telling tales."

"You're right there! That leather belt is the stuff nightmares are made from. It's no wonder we've got so many perverts in this country with dads like Jackman around."

"I'm afraid so. Anyway, I'm off, we can chat tomorrow."

"Thanks, Dave. I'll see you in court."

Don watched as Johnson drove off before going indoors. As he entered his home, he had the sudden realisation of how lucky he was to be going back for an evening of love and warmth with Rosemary – unlike poor Danny who he'd had to abandon to the tender mercies of his leather-belted father.

CHAPTER TWENTY-THREE
THE VERDICT

J ohnson and another man were sitting at the big table waiting in the police office at the Crown Court when Don arrived the next day.

"Good morning, Don," said Johnson. "Have you met Superintendent Merryweather?"

"Er, no. Good morning, Sir."

"Sit down and shut up, Barton. I'll tell you when I want you to speak."

The superintendent obviously didn't bother with niceties. So, feeling a bit like a naughty schoolboy, Don did as he was told and sat down next to Johnson.

"The Chief Constable is spitting feathers over this cock-up of yours," Merryweather continued. "And I'm here to get it sorted before we all end up with egg on our faces. To be honest, Barton, it's not you I blame." He glared pointedly at Johnson. "An experienced detective should have interviewed that boy and checked every aspect of his statement long before it ever went on the file, let alone ended up here in court."

His haranguing of the two men was abruptly curtailed when the barrister, Smith, breezed into the room.

Sensing the tense atmosphere, he said, "Sorry, gents, have I interrupted something?"

"No, Mr Smith, these two were just getting a well-deserved bollocking, but we can forget that for the moment. What have you got to tell us?"

"The good news is that the judge has accepted the Jackmans' explanation and young Danny is off the hook as far as telling lies is concerned."

"And the bad news?" asked Merryweather.

"Well, it was agreed that this evidence should never have been given. Of course, it's too late to withdraw it now and the jury are in danger of being prejudiced towards the defendant. Consequently, the judge offered to order a retrial."

"With all the expense and trouble that would cause," said Merryweather, conscious of the cost of a murder investigation. "All over the death of a London tart. I know it shouldn't matter, but not everybody will see it that way."

"Quite. However, the defence have offered an alternative. If we agree to drop the murder and kidnap charges, they'll submit a plea of guilty to involuntary manslaughter."

"What!" shouted Don. "Drop the kidnap? That was one of the most traumatic events of my life. I think I'm lucky to even still be alive."

"There's also the matter of this officer's claim for criminal injuries." To the young officer's surprise, Merryweather actually seemed to be taking Don's side in this.

"The judge was mindful of that and suggested that the charge could be left on the file but not proceeded with. The defence were reluctant at first but did eventually agree to it."

Don fell silent. He did indeed have a claim with CICB – perhaps this was the judge's way of ensuring a good settlement.

"How does the judge feel about the plea?" asked Johnson.

"To be honest, I suspect it was mostly his idea. A sentence of three years has been mentioned."

KEVIN FITZPATRICK

"That's rubbish!" said Don, fuming once again. "Those two little sods have stolen a car, been swanning about the countryside flogging hard drugs, procuring youngsters for the purposes of child pornography, ending up with killing an innocent member of the public – and we're talking three years! Seriously?"

"If we could have brought evidence of their criminality, it might have been a different story. But, as it is, we don't even have the deceased's husband here to help us. No, I'm sorry, gentlemen, but I think we have no choice other than to accept. What say you, Superintendent?"

Merryweather actually smiled. "I think that's the best all-round solution, Mr Smith. Tell the judge we're happy to accept."

Don was about to protest once again, but Merryweather silenced him with a warning look.

"I'll leave you to get on with your bollockings then." Smith exited the room as breezily as he'd entered.

Merryweather turned to Johnson. "Right Dave, I'll get back to HQ and give the Chief the good news. He'll be well pleased to get this whole thing finally put to bed without more resources being wasted. As to you, young man," he turned to Don who was still silently fuming, "you can think yourself lucky to get off so lightly – but I'd watch my step from now on if I were you."

With that, and without a backward glance, he strode out, leaving the two men alone in the room.

"Don, at the end of the day, it's a clear-up," said Johnson. "And your compo claim still stands a chance, so look on the bright side. Okay?"

Of course it wasn't okay, but Don merely nodded.

"Right," Johnson was back to his breezy self. "We may as well go in and hear the sentence."

• • •

"Court will rise!" called the usher, and everybody stood up. The judge took his seat, and the rest of the room sat down, ready to witness the final act in this drama. The reporters on the press bench opened their notebooks and awaited the verdict with pens poised.

"The defendant will rise."

Churcher stood up in the dock and gripped the rail in front of him. There were tears running down his cheeks.

Davina had also been busy that morning. She had decided not to call Churcher and had instead chosen to make a statement on his behalf. Don was expecting to be verbally castigated in her remarks but, to his surprise, Davina had given him a friendly smile on entering the courtroom, and her statement had spared him any serious admonishment.

In fact, she was almost complimentary, describing him as an open and honest officer whose judgement had been clouded due to the severity of his head injury. She offered sympathy for his position but felt it wrong that Alan Churcher should in any way be made to suffer for it.

She made great play of the fact that Hoskins had failed to return to the UK and re-iterated her client's contention that it was Hoskins who had struck the fatal blow.

"My lord, my client acknowledges the fact that he was wrong to assist Hoskins after the event. He strongly and consistently maintains that he had no idea whatsoever that the lady could still be alive when he helped to hide her body. However, having heard the medical evidence, he is now full of remorse and he regrets that he didn't do more to help her. He wishes the court to know that he had a great deal of affection for Mrs Hoskins and would have never knowingly done anything to harm her."

Davina went on to explain that Alan had lost his beloved brother in the course of these events and that his poor widowed mother now had no-one else left in the world to look out for her.

Davina was a gifted speaker, and the courtroom hung on her every word.

The judge looked up from his notes and fixed Churcher with a steady and serious look.

"Mr Churcher," he began, "you have pleaded guilty to the extremely serious offence of manslaughter, and it is the duty of this court to pass sentence upon you."

Churcher shuffled his feet and appeared uncomfortable.

"The taking of human life is a reprehensible crime and one that in most circumstances calls for the most severe penalties. However," he continued, "The circumstances of this case are far from usual."

The judge paused and gave Davina friendly glance.

"It is perfectly plain to anyone who had read this case that you are a relatively guileless young man who has fallen prey to corrupting influences. Firstly, there's your brother. Whereas we may regret his passing, there is little doubt that he was persistently leading you astray. From what I have been led to believe, one could almost say he was manipulating you to his will."

At the mention of his brother Churcher's knuckles went white as he gripped the rail. The prison officers behind him, aware of his potential to explode into violence, tensed themselves ready to restrain him.

"Then we have the Hoskins family," the judge was still speaking. "Suzanne Hoskins may not have deserved to die, certainly not the way she did, but she could hardly be called an innocent victim. Together with your brother, this woman subjected you, over a prolonged period, to certain unnatural practices simply to satisfy their lustful urges. To put it bluntly, she was a leech who had made her living exploiting other people's perversions, and your brother had become her disciple.

"Now we come to her husband, Steven Hoskins. I am mindful of the fact that he has chosen to remain hidden in the

Republic of Ireland rather than attend this court. He has therefore failed to take the opportunity to refute your contention that it was he, and not you or your brother, who struck Mrs Hoskins, causing her death. So, in the absence of evidence to the contrary, I am obliged to accept your version of events.

"I think it is to your great credit, and an indication of the wisdom of your counsel," another smile to Davina, "that you have elected to plead guilty to this charge. I, therefore, sentence you to three years imprisonment, which, according to my calculations, should see you released in just over a year from today.

"I wish you well, Mr Churcher, and on your release, I trust you will enjoy an honest and industrious life and remain a good son to your mother. Take him down."

"I don't know about you, but I need a drink." Johnson had seen the deflated look on his young colleague's face. "I came in the car today, and I've a spare civvy jacket in the boot that I can lend you. We'll just have a quick one then you can get back to Rosemary."

Don left his police van in the car park, and the two men travelled the few hundred yards from the court to The Jolly Brewers in Johnson's car. The lunchtime rush was just finishing, so they had no problem locating a free table in the corner of the lounge bar. Through force of habit, they each sat with their back to the wall, thus giving them a clear view of customers entering and leaving.

No good policeman ever sat with his back to a crowded room.

Don decided to play safe and asked Johnson to get him a lager shandy as the latter stood up to go to the bar. Johnson got himself a pint of Directors Bitter, and they saluted one another before taking a deep swallow of their drinks.

"I needed that," said Don. "My nerves are still shot from yesterday. That woman gave me a right grilling."

"Talk of the Devil, here she is now," said Johnson.

Don looked up from his beer and nearly fell from his chair with surprise. Sure enough, Davina Cooper was strolling into the bar – and with her, chatting away like an old friend, was the prosecution brief, Leslie Smith. The couple spotted the two policemen in the corner and walked over to them.

"May we join you?" enquired Smith.

Don indicated the spare seats at the table and Davina sat down whilst Smith went to the bar to get Davina and him a drink.

"Just a Saint Clements for me," Davina called over to him. She wanted to keep a clear head for later, and the mixture of orange juice and bitter lemon was the ideal choice of refreshment.

"Well, Mr Johnson, we didn't get the chance to meet properly at the court. I'm Davina, how do you do."

"Please, call me Dave." The two shook hands.

"And you, Mr Barton, may I call you Don; I believe congratulations are in order?"

Don looked perplexed. "I don't know what you mean," he said.

"I'm told this was your first homicide case. A successful result like today can only be good for your career, don't you agree, Dave?"

"I'll drink to that," said Johnson with a smile as he lifted his glass.

"A success all round, I'd say," said Smith returning with the drinks. "Churcher would have been looking at a much stiffer sentence if it weren't for you, Davina."

"To be honest, I was all for carrying on and going for not guilty – especially after Mr Steptoe's evidence," said Davina.

"And mine," said Don morosely.

"Nonsense," said Davina. "You did very well, didn't he, Leslie?"

"I think so," said Smith. "You came across as an honest and impartial witness. As an officer of the court, you are not supposed to take sides. Your evidence was perfectly sound."

Don was uncomfortable. "Should we be talking like this?" he asked.

Davina laughed. "I don't see why not," she said. "The case is over, and there are no appeals pending. We are back to being a group of professional colleagues enjoying a quiet drink together. Nothing wrong with that is there!"

"So, Davina, why *did* Churcher change his mind and cop a plea?" asked Johnson.

"We got word that the judge was thinking of a light sentence and the little sod didn't want to take a chance on losing the case. I mean, he probably knew he was guilty, and three years was like being let off as far as he was concerned."

"Well, sorry to spoil the party, but we're just off," said Johnson, finishing his drink and indicating Don to do the same. "We'll leave you two legal eagles to chat."

They all stood up, and Davina shook hands with Don. "Must you dash off? Oh well, perhaps next time we'll be on the same side," she said. "I do quite a lot of prosecution work these days."

Anne Wilson's written testimony had been accepted by the defence, so she'd had no need to be present at the trial. However, Don had promised to drop in on her on his way home to give her the result.

He'd chatted with her a few times since that first time he'd gone to her house, and the two of them had formed something of a friendship. Anne was a very private person, but she knew a lot about the local area – and its people. This made her an ideal, but discreet, source of knowledge and information.

Don was relieved and disappointed in equal measure that Anne had never showed any inclination to take their relationship any further. The fact of the matter was that she came from a different class and lived in a different world to him. It was a world he could never hope to belong in.

For his part, he knew that if he was caught "over the side" again so soon after the last episode, it would almost certainly cost him his job not to mention breaking Rosemary's heart.

No, he decided, this relationship was best kept on a platonic level.

But that didn't stop him thinking about her.

As he pulled through the gate, he was surprised to see a bright red E-Type Jaguar parked on the gravel outside the front door. Don could see It was the much sought after 4.2-litre convertible, and from the number plate he could tell that the car was ten years old. However, the car had been highly polished, and the vehicle gleamed like new.

Don was still admiring the car when the doorbell was answered by a tall, red-haired man wearing a rugby shirt. The man was about Don's age, broad-shouldered and, in addition to the shirt, was dressed in ice blue jeans and brown suede Hush Puppy shoes.

Don disliked him instantly.

The man looked at Don and lifted his head back as if he were shying away. He stood squarely in the doorway in a gesture of blocking any entrance.

"Yes?" he said somewhat defensively, Don thought.

"Er, is Miss Wilson at home?" Don said.

The man turned his head and shouted back over his shoulder. "Anne, darling, there's a policeman here to see you."

"I'll be right there," Anne called from somewhere inside the house. "It'll be about that wretched trial."

There was an awkward silence as the two men waited by the door. Finally, Anne, elegantly dressed in a white silk blouse and a pair of figure-hugging jeans, hurried from within to join them. Don saw that she was also wearing black, expensive-looking, high-heeled shoes.

"Be an angel, Raymond," she said to the man. "The dogs will have to be fed before we go out. I've prepared their food in the kitchen. You couldn't just pop it out to them for me, could you?"

"Well…" Raymond didn't look too impressed.

"Oh, and you'll have to stay and supervise," Anne continued as though she hadn't noticed his discomfort. "Satan will scoff the lot if you don't watch him."

Raymond looked none too happy but, nevertheless, turned and walked back into the house.

Anne watched him go and, when she was sure he was out of earshot, looked at Don and smiled.

"Raymond, I presume?" said Don with a glance into the house.

Anne gave him a wry smile and looked into the distance over his shoulder.

"He turned up yesterday," she said. She looked back at Don. "He says he wants to try again, have another go at it. He says he's been out of the country and didn't know Daddy had gone."

"Do you believe him?"

She looked at her feet. "I'm not sure," she said, "but his family and mine have known each other since forever, so I can't just kick him into touch without giving it a shot."

Don refrained from mentioning that if the families had been that close, it was unlikely Raymond hadn't heard about Daddy's death.

Instead, he said, "Right, well I guess that's the end of our coffee evenings."

"Yes, I suppose it is." Anne looked wistful. "Maybe that's

just as well, though, Don." She briefly touched his hand with hers. "I think you know what I mean."

Don knew exactly what she meant. Part of him wished he didn't.

With a conscious effort, Anne brightened up. "Right, I'll walk you to your van, and you can tell me all about the trial," she said. "I hope they flogged him before they hanged him!"

"It's a good thing they didn't," Don laughed. "That little sod would probably have enjoyed it!"

CHAPTER TWENTY-FOUR
BROMPTON POLICE OFFICE - SIX MONTHS
LATER

For the fourth time in ten minutes, Don checked through the pile of paperwork that had been sent out to him that morning. He even took a forlorn second look into the large plastic dispatch bag in which it had all arrived. However, that elusive form PER 38, the notification of transfer, was nowhere to be found. Don was starting to get desperate

Thanks in no small part to a statement submitted by Dave Johnson, Don's Criminal Injuries Compensation Board (CICB) claim had been approved a couple of months previously. The generous pay-out, together with the savings he and Rosemary had put aside, meant they now had enough money to put down a minimum deposit on a house of their own. However, whilst he remained stationed at Brompton, there was no possibility of this dream becoming a reality.

Don had also recently made friends with a local estate agent who, as well as having a number of affordable homes on his books, assured Don that he could obtain him a mortgage. However, although it was currently a buyers' market, and a lot of nice three-bed properties were still on sale at below fifteen thousand pounds, everyone knew another bout of house-price inflation could kick in at any time.

"This recession isn't going to last forever, Don," his friend had told him. "You'll need to get on that property ladder before prices get jacked up again. Believe me, mate, big rises are just around the corner."

In fairness, Don's divisional commander had been sympathetic to the young officer's request for a move into Newbury – but he had told Don that the young officer needed to be patient.

"You and your missus are perfectly safe while Alan Churcher's locked away," the chief superintendent had told him. "He's not exactly a big-time villain with hitmen all over the place."

"I know that, sir," Don had replied, "but you can understand my position – and why my wife is so concerned, what with being left alone out there as much as she is."

"Look, Don, we'll do our best to get you moved out of the village before that little shit's back on the streets, but I'm making no promises. I don't want you to worry, but every officer in the force wants to buy his own house these days – and we're struggling to keep the rural beats manned, so it won't be easy."

It would be easy enough to move me if I was in the shit and getting kicked off the section for doing something wrong, Don thought to himself, but he wisely refrained from saying so.

Now, back in his office, Don's mind was brought back to the present by a series of sharp raps on his front door. Putting the paperwork to one side, he got up to see who his visitor might be.

He instantly recognised the two women waiting on his doorstep.

"Good morning, Constable Barton," said Emily Pritchard, flourishing the walking stick she'd used to knock on the door.

"Mrs Churcher and I would like a word with you, if it's convenient."

"Yes, of course, come in." Don ushered the two women into his office and arranged the furniture so that they could sit facing him across his desk.

Mrs Churcher, a short, painfully thin woman in her mid-sixties, seemed ill-at-ease. She was wearing an old-fashioned headscarf and an ancient woollen overcoat. Her eyes kept darting around in a manner that reminded Don of a small, frightened bird; and she was nervously clutching an old brown leather school satchel that was covered in grime of some sort.

"So, how can I help you ladies?"

As self-confident as always, Emily appointed herself spokesperson for the small deputation. "Mrs Churcher and I have been friends for a number of years, since we worked together at the school."

"That's right," said the other woman in a voice as small and thin as the rest of her. "Mrs Pritchard was very good to me whenever the boys were naughty."

Don wondered briefly if Mrs Churcher realised how much Emily had enjoyed watching the boys get caned by the headmaster – but he decided not to mention it.

"Well, Mrs Churcher has a message for you," said Emily.

"Yes," the little woman said, "Alan wants you to know he didn't mean it. He's very sorry."

"Didn't mean what, Mrs Churcher?" said Don, perplexed.

"You know, that day at court when he said he'd burn your house down. He was just upset. He's a good boy really; he'd never do a thing like that. So, he hopes you won't hold it against him."

Don was beginning to see some light in the darkness.

"I take it the probation service have been talking to him about early release – on parole that is?"

"Yes, he may only have to do another few months – as long as he's not a threat, that is."

Don knew that, when it came to prisoner release, the Parole Board would make up their own minds without reference to anyone, including him. However, he decided to keep that knowledge to himself for the moment.

"I can assure you, Mrs Churcher, that I harbour no ill feelings towards Alan. But why did he chose you to deliver his apology? There are a number of other means he could have used without bothering you like this."

Mrs Churcher looked vacantly around her, as though searching for an answer.

"Well, Alan didn't exactly send her, "said Emily Pritchard. "My friend here called on me this morning, seeking advice, and I suggested we come and see you."

"He's all I've got left," said Mrs Churcher. "I need him home, and I don't want him getting into any more trouble. That's why I brought this."

She placed the satchel she had been carrying onto the desk in front of her.

"She found it hidden in the barn where the two young men had hidden the stolen Jaguar motor car," explained Emily. "I told her she had to hand it in to you."

"Tell me Alan won't be in any more trouble," said Mrs Churcher, plaintively.

Don opened the flap of the satchel and poured the contents out onto the desktop.

The haul consisted of a number of clear plastic bags. Some contained small blocks of a dark, tarry substance that Don recognised as cannabis resin, others held a white powder that he assumed to be cocaine. There was also an old cutthroat razor, a tiny set of scales and a bag with some little weights. There was also a wad of cash – a couple of thousand pounds at least.

Classic implements as used by drug dealers the world over. Don whistled softly through his teeth.

The satchel was equipped with two small pockets at the front. Don unbuckled the pockets and checked for contents.

The left pocket was empty, but Don found a neatly folded piece of paper tucked into the right-hand side. The paper looked as though it had been torn from a school exercise book and contained writing.

Don examined the paper and went silent.

"So, you did exist after all," he said more to himself than anyone.

"Right, ladies, I have to make some phone calls. But, before that, I need a brief statement from you, Mrs Churcher, explaining exactly how you found this. Don't worry, you won't be getting Alan into trouble. It could be quite the opposite, in fact."

CHAPTER TWENTY-FIVE
WINCHESTER PRISON

The interview room in the prison presented a sparse and functional appearance. The walls had been painted and repainted many times over the years, and the bricks now shone with a stark, pale gloss that harshly reflected the light from the green metallic lamps that hung suspended from the high ceiling.

There was a large oblong table bolted to the brown vinyl floor that dominated the centre of the room, and similarly secured wooden benches were positioned either side of it. Two metal ashtrays had been screwed to each end of the table.

The prison officer who escorted Johnson to the room was an affable man of middle years. He opened the door with a large key from a ring attached to his uniform by a chain and motioned with his hand for the detective to enter.

"I'll go and fetch Churcher for you," he said. "Would you like a cup of tea?"

"That would be great, thanks," Johnson replied. He sat on one of the benches. He looked over at the door that the officer had left ajar and wondered briefly what it would be like to be incarcerated here. He dismissed the thought from his mind and concentrated instead on the job in hand.

Faint sounds could be heard in the distance, but otherwise, the room was deathly quiet. After a few minutes, Johnson could hear footsteps approaching along the corridor. The door swung open, and the prison officer entered followed by Alan Churcher, who was carrying two steaming enamel mugs.

"I forgot to ask if you took sugar," the P O said. "So we just put one in. Is that okay?"

"Great, thank you," said Johnson.

"Sit yourself down, Churcher," the officer ordered, and once the young man had complied, he turned to Johnson. "I'll be outside if you need me. The bell's by the door."

Once they were alone, Johnson took a packet of Embassy cigarettes from his pocket and offered one to the prisoner. Churcher's eyes lit up, he took the cigarette, and the detective lit it for him. Johnson then left the packet open on the table facing Churcher.

"Help yourself when you want another one," he said.

"I will, Mr Johnson, ta. They said you wanted to see me, but they didn't say what it was about."

"I've got some news for you." Johnson went on to explain about the finding of the receipt, together with the other items that Alan's mother had handed in.

Churcher looked crestfallen. "So, that's where he hid it all – Frank, I mean. What will happen to the money?"

"That's not for me to say, but the important thing is this receipt. It puts Steven Hoskins right back in the frame for the killing of his wife."

"So, you believe me now, do you? About what happened?"

"I always did believe you, Alan. I knew you wouldn't lie to me right on top of the death of your brother. You were too upset to make up stories."

"Yeah, but you still nicked me for murder though."

"That wasn't my decision, and anyway, that lovely barrister of yours got the right result, in the end, didn't she?"

Churcher opened his arms expansively and said, "Yeah, a right result. Look around you, I'm as happy as a pig in shit, me."

"So, why did you cop a plea?"

"It was her idea. She said I'd only do a year if I admitted manslaughter. She said I would get a load more if I continued to plead not guilty, and if it all went against me."

"To be honest, she was probably right. But now's your chance to get Hoskins back over here and into the dock."

"What do you mean?"

"If you give me a statement, and support a case against him, I stand a good chance of getting him extradited from Ireland."

"But I already gave you a statement."

"That was a statement under caution. We call it a VS, or voluntary statement. It can only be used against the person that made it. I need a different kind of statement, a witness statement, if I'm to go after Hoskins."

"So, what's in it for me?" Churcher helped himself to another cigarette. He lit it from the stub of the one he was holding.

"I can't promise anything, but I'll make sure the authorities know you're helping us when your case comes up for review for early release."

"What are the chances?"

"Like I say, I can't make any promises, but I'd say they were pretty good given the circumstances."

"Right, I'll do it. It's not as though I owe that bastard anything, is it?"

"Good lad, but before we start there's one thing I'd like you to clear up for me, off the record like."

"What's that then?"

"That dancing in the woods that Danny told us about. What was all that?"

Churcher burst out laughing.

"That's all about bullshit, Mr Johnson, pure bullshit. When we was boys, our dad used to get me and Frank to help him pick things up at the farm. Bits of bone, feathers, smooth pebbles, sometimes herbs. Mum used to sew them into little cloth pouches, and Dad sold them to people who came to the house at night wanting charms and things."

"So, your dad was into all that?"

"He told them he was – but he told us it was a load of nonsense and that they was gullible fools. It paid for his beer and baccy though."

"So, what about the dancing?"

"Well, after dad died, me and Frank found this old suitcase at the house. There were all these robes and masks and stuff, and there was two little notebooks. They were really old with leather covers and had all sorts of funny writing and drawings inside."

"Did you understand any of it?"

"No, our dad never taught us anything like that, but Frank showed one of the books to the mistress, er, I mean Mrs Hoskins, one time and she got all excited. Frank let on he'd been trained and knew all about the rituals and that."

"But he didn't."

Churcher laughed again. "No, but he told her he did. So, after that, whenever there was a full moon and 'the headmaster,' that's what we called her husband, was away we'd all go off to the woods and get her naked and have sex with her."

"So, Danny was telling us the truth then? He just got the day wrong."

"Yeah, it was the week before she died. Frank knew someone was watching us then he caught Danny hiding in the bushes."

"That's what he told us."

"I bet he didn't tell you he was having a wank though."

It was Johnson's turn to laugh. "No, he didn't tell us that – but he did say Frank got a bit rough with him."

"Yeah, he threatened to tell Danny's sister. That scared the boy more than anything. Frank wouldn't have done it though, he only said it to frighten him."

"What about the night Mrs Hoskins was killed, was that one of these rituals?"

"No, that was completely different. The mistress liked playing other games as well. She was wicked with that cane of hers."

He lit another cigarette.

"So, it was one of those games, the same as you told me in your first statement?"

"Well, yeah, but it was less of a game and more a real punishment. She was really angry that we'd taken the boys to see her husband. She said we could all land in prison if we got caught. So, she really laid into us. But then she got really excited doing it, and we all had sex anyway. Then the headmaster turned up."

"Right, well, I'd better get some of this down on paper before our time is up and they kick me out. Help yourself to another fag and put a couple in your pocket for later."

"Thanks, Mr Johnson, what do you want me to say then?"

CHAPTER TWENTY-SIX
THE BLACK NORTH

S teven Hoskins paid off the cab and walked into Conleys Bar. The tiny public house was situated in a quiet, run-down area on the outskirts of the city, and it was exactly the type of place that his handlers had, over the years, repeatedly told Hoskins to avoid.

"Lily-white, Steve, that's what you are. No police record, no connections to the cause, you stay quiet and wait to be activated. You're a respectable Englishman, you stay away from sympathisers, and you watch everything you say. Nobody but chosen members of the army council themselves even know you exist. We'll call you when we need you."

Now, as the barman slowly poured out his pint of Guinness, Steve found himself looking across the bar at framed photos of the Republican heroes of the past. The pub reeked of conspiracy, and there were no prizes for guessing who was to be the beneficiary of the huge collection bottle that stood proudly on the bar – boasting no small quantity of five, ten, and even twenty-pound notes.

Acutely conscious of his middle English accent, Steve said as little as he could as he paid for his drink. He decided to sit at a secluded table, with a view through a window to the street outside.

It was just before noon, and the pub was as quiet as one would expect for an early Tuesday lunchtime. The only other customers were a small group of elderly men huddled together at the bar, each wearing an ancient blue serge suit – the ubiquitous uniform of the respectable working man of days now past.

Steve picked up his glass, took a sip, then wiped the white, creamy foam from his upper lip. He stared out of the window at the row of mean single-storey terraced houses opposite him. A builder's van pulled up across the road, and two beefy workers emerged from the rear. They each took a shovel out of the vehicle which they then proceeded to lean on before engaging in a conversation that involved much pointing up and down the road.

"I wouldn't drink too much of that if I were you, the boys won't be happy if they have to keep pulling over to let you out for a pee."

Startled, Steve looked around to find one of the men from the bar standing behind him. The old codger must have moved as stealthily as a cat to creep up on him the way he did. Steve opened his mouth to speak, but the man held up a warning hand to stop him.

"Listen, I'm just a feckin messenger boy. I don't want to hear one feckin word from you. I'm just to ask if you're the man from the crossroad and, if you are, to tell you to go out there and pick up your transport."

"Crossroad" was Steve's correct activation code, the word used by the anonymous telephone caller the night before when he was ordered to this meeting. He got to his feet and began making his way to the door.

"Don't worry about your Guinness, I'll see it doesn't go to waste."

Steve's frown deepened as he walked out through the door and across the street.

The two workmen replaced their shovels in the back of the van then stood by the open rear door to wait for their passenger. Steve got the message and silently climbed into the vehicle. The Transit van had been designed for utility rather than comfort, and the wooded slatted seats that ran down either side were hard and unyielding.

As Steve sat down, he saw that there was a third man in the driver's seat. This chap seemed a bit more sociable. He turned in his seat and smiled back at Steve, revealing a neat row of large white teeth.

"Are you all right back there, Mr Hoskins?"

Steve nearly jumped out of his skin. He made to get up, but the two men with him made it clear that leaving wasn't an option.

"Am I under arrest, Sergeant Rogan?" Steve said as he slowly regained his composure. "I didn't think I was wanted for anything in the Republic."

"No, no, no, stop worrying. There's nobody on duty here. We're just taking you to meet some people. Just for a bit of a chat, nothing to fret over."

"I'd be happier if I knew where I was going," Steve replied.

"Ah, you'll know that soon enough – but I warn you it's a bit of a stretch, and we'll be using some roads you never knew existed."

Steve felt a moment of panic.

"You do know that I can't go to the north, don't you? The British police are still after me – or is that what this is all about? You kidnap me and take me to your colleagues north of the border?"

"All in good time, Steven, all in good time. Now just you relax and enjoy the ride. It's a grand day for a trip to the country."

The conversation was over. Rogan turned back to the wheel, started the engine, and pulled out into the empty road.

There were no seat belts, and Steve soon found himself bouncing painfully when the van picked up speed as it made its way out of the city. In contrast, his companions on the other seat, and either side of him, sat motionless as though glued to their seats.

The journey seemed to last forever. True to his word, Rogan drove along country lanes, some of which were little more than cart tracks. Endlessly winding into the featureless countryside, these byways had existed for generations, and very few maps revealed their existence.

After a couple of hours, Rogan stopped at a field entrance and let his passengers out to take a brief comfort break. The four men took turns relieving themselves in the bushes, with Steve under constant surveillance.

Rogan produced a pack of Sweet Afton cigarettes which he handed round. Steve felt inordinately grateful to be included in Rogan's generosity, and he relaxed even more when one of the other men offered him a light. Rogan was as garrulous as always and chatted away about such items as the weather, the price of beef – anything but the purpose of their journey.

It was another hour and a half before they reached their destination. Steve, like all professional photographers, was aware of the position of the sun in the sky at any time of the day and this told him he had travelled north and west since leaving Dublin, but exactly whereabout he was, he had no idea. All he knew for certain was that he was deep into the countryside.

The van eventually pulled off the road at the site of an isolated group of buildings that were nestled into the side of a grassy hill. The complex was obviously used for the storage and maintenance of agricultural vehicles, several of which were standing abandoned and partially dismantled, in an area set aside for scrap.

Rogan drove in through a metal gate and came to a halt on a hard standing of concrete outside a wooden building the size of a small aircraft hangar.

"Right, lads, this is it. It's as far as we go," said Rogan.

He went to the rear of the van, opened the door, and motioned for Steve to get out. The other two men made no effort to move.

"What? You're leaving me here?" said Steve. "How do I get back?"

For once, Rogan had nothing to say. He waited for Steve to alight then silently closed the door behind him. He then climbed back into the driver's seat and, without any further ado, drove out of the gate and disappeared down the road.

None of the three men in the vehicle could bring themselves to look at Steve as they left him standing, forlorn and abandoned, watching them drive off.

After a few seconds, Steve heard the creaking sound of a door opening behind him and he turned around to see two men coming out of an access door that was set into one of the two large sliding doors at the front of the large barn. The men were identically dressed in army-style green fatigues and black boots.

Each of them wore a full-face balaclava helmet with separate holes for the mouth and eyes.

One of the men had an automatic pistol in his hand; his companion was carrying an Armalite rifle that he now pointed in Steve's general direction. The first man looked all around the yard then, seemingly satisfied that no-one was around, he started to go back through the door from which he had just emerged. He indicated with the pistol for Steve to follow. Steve did as he was instructed and the man with the rifle followed them both into the barn.

Just inside, and to the left of the main door, was a separate room the size of a large shed. It was apparently used by workers to store their personal equipment, overalls, etc. A coarse wooden trestle table ran the length of the room, and wellington boots were neatly lined up along one wall. The three men went into this room, and the man with the pistol turned and faced Steve.

"Right, Mr Hoskins, take all your clothes off please and put them on the table." He spoke in a matter-of-fact way in a distinctive Belfast accent, like a doctor about to perform a routine examination.

"Don't be bloody ridiculous!" Steve blustered. "I'll do no such thing. In fact, I'll do nothing at all until somebody tells me what this is all about."

The sound of the shot was deafening in the small room and, although the bullet was aimed at the floor in front of him, Steve immediately went into shock. The breath went out of his body, his heart began to race, and he began to shake uncontrollably.

"I'll not tell you again, Mr Hoskins. The next one will be through your kneecap. Now get them fucking clothes off!"

Still polite, but this time the voice was loaded with menace. With trembling hands, Steve began to unbutton his shirt.

Once he was completely naked, Steve felt more vulnerable and wretched than he had ever done in his life. It became even worse when he was told to hold his hands out in front of him, depriving him the illusion of protection that cupping his hands over his genitals had allowed him.

The man put his pistol on the table and retrieved a set of handcuffs from a rear pocket.

Steve looked at the pistol and weighed up his chances of making a grab for it and getting away from these two men. Within the space of a heartbeat any chance of success, however slender, was taken from him.

"Don't even fucking think about it," came a gruff voice

from behind, and Steve felt the muzzle of the Armalite jabbed in to the small of his back.

The handcuffs felt cool on his wrists. They were an obsolete version with an old-fashioned screw-in locking mechanism. Unlike their more modern counterparts, they were fairly slack on his wrists, but still effective. Once his hands had been securely cuffed, Steve was told to face the door.

Suddenly, and without warning, a black bag was pulled over his head from behind, and he was plunged into darkness. The bag smelt of old oil and had presumably been used to hold tools. The effect was claustrophobic, and Steve felt panic rising within him.

One of the men took hold of the handcuffs and, with the rifle still being prodded into his back, Steve was roughly pulled out of the room and into the barn beyond.

The concrete floor beneath his bare feet was cold and gritty, and he felt a definite drop in temperature as he walked twenty paces or so before being told to stop. The man in front kept hold of the handcuffs, but the rifle was taken from the small of Steve's back and he heard the gunman walking away from him. He then heard chains rattling and the unmistakable sound of a hoist and pulley being operated. The noise of the hoist travelled across the room then stopped immediately above him.

There was a click followed by the soft whir of an electric motor as the hoist was lowered. The noise stopped, and Steve's hands were lifted so that the small chain between each of the handcuffs could be attached to a hook. The motor whirred again, and his hands were raised higher and higher until he felt himself being lifted off the floor. Capable hands fastened a belt around his ankles and used it to pull them painfully together – putting Steve in fear of losing his balance.

The weight of his body pulling on his wrists was already starting to become unbearable, so it gave some relief when the hoist was finally lowered sufficiently to allow the balls of Steve's feet to reach the floor and take some of the strain.

Hanging naked and exposed, Steve then heard the sound of other people entering the room. This was followed by the sound of chairs being scraped along the floor as they were moved into place somewhere close in front of him.

The hood was roughly jerked from his head. The fresh air he sucked into his lungs felt wonderful, but the sudden harsh white light that emanated from the overhead lamps was blinding.

"Hello, Steven."

He couldn't make out the speaker's face to begin with, but the voice was unmistakable. A voice he had fervently hoped he would never hear again. The cold fear he was already feeling now became abject terror as he realised that he was at the mercy of a psychopath. A genuine sadist, a woman highly skilled in the art of causing pain.

"Irene," he said despairingly. "Oh God, of all people. It had to be you..."

As well as Irene, there were now four men in the room, including the two who had stripped and bound him. The newcomers were also sporting balaclava masks and were sitting behind a trestle table either side of the red-haired Irene who was wearing a sober-looking grey trouser suit.

"Ah, Irene," said the woman, smiling. "I've not heard that name in a while. I left Irene Silver back in London years ago."

"So, who are you now?"

"Oh, you can still call me Irene, Steven. For old time's sake, I mean."

"Well, for old time's sake, can you please tell me what I'm doing here – and why can't I keep my trousers on?"

"Tell me, Steven, did you really kill Suzanne? To be honest, I didn't think you had the balls for it."

"I didn't mean to kill her. I lost my temper and hit her a bit harder than I intended. You of all people know how she could wind people up. Anyway, I thought you hated her?"

Irene laughed. "That old witch? I hope she burns in Hell! I'd have done it myself, given half a chance."

Steve was confused. "So, why am I here?" he asked her.

Irene spoke calmly and quietly. "Steven, cast your mind back a few hours to that pub where you were picked up. Did you notice the big bottle on the bar?"

"Yes, a collection for the cause."

"Yes, exactly. And the cause could not survive a single day without those contributions. The contributions of decent working people. Some of them often put their entire week's wage into that bottle. To them we are heroes, freedom fighters, patriots. They genuinely believe that God is on our side."

"Yes, Irene, yes, and they're right. You, I mean, we *are* heroes. We have a just cause."

Irene carried on as though Steve hadn't spoken. "So, how motivated do you think would these folks be on their way home from Mass if they associated us with stuff like this?"

She stood up and took a large brown envelope from the handbag beside her. One by one she removed photographs from the envelope. She placed them face up on the table in front of her, where Steve could clearly see them.

"Irene, I can explain. It's not what it appears. There were these two perverts who used to supply drugs in our village. I didn't know it, but they were having an affair with Suzanne. They told me they could get me models; I didn't know they were children. Honest to God, I didn't. They told me they were jockeys and just looked young. I'm not a kiddy-fiddler, honest I'm not. I never have been. Oh God, please, please don't hurt me. I'm innocent, I swear I am."

The woman known to Steven Hoskins as Irene stood up and slowly walked around the table. She went over to her helpless captive, looked him in the eye, and smiled.

Steve frantically looked around the room for support, desperately seeking some glimmer of human compassion from the people in the room. Finding none, he began to writhe and twist in a vain effort to break free.

"D'you know, Steven, I almost believe you. But I'll know the whole truth soon enough, don't you worry."

"You don't need to do this, Irene." He started crying. "I'll tell you anything you want."

Irene just stood there, apparently amused. Still smiling, she clicked her fingers behind her and one of the henchmen walked over to a corner. He returned with a large wooden toolbox that he opened on the table in front of him. Inside the box lay a seemingly innocent selection of everyday tools – including drills, pliers, and even a small blowtorch.

Steve stopped crying and his eyes opened wide in terror.

"They were just a couple of young tearaways," he shouted. "Yobbos from London. Nobody cares what happens to them! Surely I'm worth more to you than this? Or is that it? This is a warning, isn't it?" He actually began to feel hopeful. "Well, you've made your point. Message received and understood. Now let me down so we can get on with the serious work we both believe in."

"But do we, Steven? Do we really both believe in it? I know I do – but how can I be sure about you?"

"You know me, Irene. You can trust me. I swear to God you can!"

Irene became aware of the sound of shuffling feet behind her. Her companions were becoming impatient.

"Well, Steven, I've enjoyed our little chat – but I really must get on."

She took a large pair of pincers from the toolbox, then took a long hard look at her captive. Her eyes roved up and down his body, like a butcher sizing up a side of beef.

"Now, where should I start?" she mused.

Steven Hoskins began screaming.

EPILOGUE
THAMES VALLEY POLICE HQ

I t was nearly four o'clock, and Headquarters canteen was quiet following the afternoon rush. The staff, mostly middle-aged ladies wearing white coats, were busily cleaning the tables, and one or two small groups of people were standing around, huddled together and engrossed in hushed conversations.

Don picked up a cup of coffee at the counter and walked over to join DS Johnson, who was sitting alone at a corner table.

"Hi, Don," said Johnson. "Grab a pew. Thanks for coming, I know it's a pain, but I'm so busy at the moment I just couldn't get the time to drive down your end to see you."

"No problem, Dave, it's not much more than a half-hour drive, and I don't often get to see the Taj Mahal these days," Don replied, employing one of the many nicknames enjoyed by the HQ building complex.

"So, how's it been going, anything interesting happening down your way?" Johnson asked him.

"Well, they're keeping me busy – but it's mostly crap."

"It's a bloody waste keeping you there, I could do with

you up here working with me. I thought you and I made a good team last time."

"Mr Merryweather didn't think so, as I recall. I doubt he'll ever forgive me for the cock-ups I made."

"Nonsense! Once he realised you weren't actually shagging half the females in the county, he decided he quite liked you. The governor's a bloody shrewd bloke you know – and a brilliant detective. He knows a good copper when he sees one. There'll be CID boards coming up soon. If you're interested, I'd be happy to put a word in."

"Thanks, Dave, I really appreciate that, but Rosemary would go ballistic if I applied for a job with you blokes. She's decided she likes having me home once in a while – especially now."

"Does that mean what I think it means?" said Johnson with a grin.

Don smiled and nodded. "About four months gone, we reckon."

"That's bloody marvellous, congratulations! I'm really pleased for both of you."

"Rosemary says I'm to ask if you'd like an invite to the christening when the day comes. A bit soon to ask, I know. But …"

"Don, I'd be honoured. Thank Rosemary very much for me."

"Oh, it gets worse. If it's a boy, she wants to call him David."

"I don't know what to say, I've come over all emotional, not like me at all."

"Well, if it weren't for you…"

"You'd have sorted it all out yourself," Johnson finished for him. "So, how's the application for a transfer coming along?"

"It's going nowhere at the moment I'm afraid, and neither am I. The powers that be reckon I'm in no danger now that

Churcher has withdrawn his threats. And he's started coming up trumps with his info on the drug gangs. In fact, it's him they're more worried about than me now. I could see him being whisked off to a secret hideaway before long."

"So, the bottom line is you're staying in Brompton? What about your CICB claim, did that ever get settled?"

"Yeah, I actually got a good pay-out. Enough for a small deposit on a house – Rosemary and I would like to get on the housing ladder – if we weren't stuck in the tied police house."

"Would you stay in the area?"

"Yes, it's a great place for kids, and I've made a contact with a local estate agent. Actually, he's the same one that's dealing with the sale of the Hoskins house. Not easy, he reckons, given the story."

"I bet! Anyway, that's what I wanted to see you about. You must be wondering what's been happening since you sent me all the gubbings that Mrs Churcher gave you?"

"Well, now Churcher's out of prison, I did rather suspect his cell would be occupied by Steven Hoskins by now. Did we ever apply for extradition, or was it all swept under the carpet?"

Johnson was miffed. "There was never any danger of that, Don. We're not that cynical, you know."

"Sorry, mate, I know I say stupid things sometimes, no offence."

"No problem. Anyway, it turns out things were a bit more complicated than we realised."

"Really? How come?"

"Do you remember Partridge, the Special Branch bloke?"

"Yeah, of course I do."

"Well, gave me some of it the day we flew over to Ireland, but I've got the full story now."

"And?"

Johnson grinned. "You know what I'm going to say next, don't you?"

"Yeah, yeah, keep your gob shut, Don, all highly confidential."

Johnson laughed. "You learn fast, are you sure you don't fancy giving those boards a try?"

"Quite sure, thank you. I'm chasing promotion these days. I'm really getting on with studying for that sergeants exam."

"I wish you luck, but listen, it turns out Hoskins was a bit of a hero according to SB."

"Hoskins? A hero? You're having me on!"

"Responsible for saving loads of lives it seems. A sort of double agent inside the IRA. That's what we'd call him, but PIRA would probably call him a traitor and an informant."

"What did he do?"

"He got recruited a few years back when the troubles were just kicking off. His job was to recce and photograph suitable sites for planting bombs in London."

"Bloody Hell!"

"Well, he completely bottled it and turned himself in to SB. They turned him and persuaded him to carry on, but report everything back to them."

"Christ! He had to have some balls to do that!"

"Well, he hasn't got them now. Take a look at these."

Johnson handed Don a packet of photographs, but then put his hand over it. "Be careful, Don, we don't want to give the canteen ladies bad dreams."

As surreptitiously as possible, Don looked through the pictures. He went pale as each shot proved to be more graphic than the last.

Finally, in a hoarse voice, he asked, "I take it this is definitely Hoskins? We're completely sure are we? I mean you can't tell from these, can you? It's just a bloody carcass."

"The RUC sent them to us. The body was found by a farmer on a remote hill in the border area, and Hoskins was identified by fingerprints."

"Do they know who did it?"

"If they do, they're not saying. It's been put out as a routine sectarian killing to the media over there, not even worth a mention in the mainland press. We're doing what we can to trace next of kin, etc."

"Isn't that a job for the Met?"

"Hoskins' last known address was on our patch, so we cop for it, for now anyway. It's not your problem though, Don, and I probably shouldn't have filled you in on it."

"So, why did you?"

"Well, besides the fact that I think you deserve to know, I suspected you'd be shaking the tree sooner or later trying to find out what was happening."

"People are going to find out he's dead though. You can't expect that to stay secret."

"No, we won't even try to do that. It's just the gory details you need to stay schtum about – that and the Special Branch connection, of course."

Don felt totally deflated. He hadn't particularly liked Hoskins, but he wouldn't have wished the horrific end the man had come to onto anyone.

"So, that's it then?" he said.

"Afraid so, mate, there's nothing more we can do. Go on back to Rosemary and get on with your life."

"Thanks, Dave, and thank you for trusting me. I may as well clear off then."

The men shook hands, and Don headed back to Brompton.

It took Don forty minutes to get home. He pulled up onto the driveway outside the police office and took his official notebook out from the back pocket of his trousers. Before making up his notes for the day, his mind drifted back over the events of the past few weeks.

Three people were dead, one was in prison and several other people's lives had been forever changed.

But, in the big scheme of things, had Don made a difference?

He wasn't sure.

He decided to call it a day, the pocketbook entry could wait. He picked up the radio handset and depressed the toggle.

"HT from Foxtrot Golf Five Zero, over." He said into the mouthpiece.

"Go ahead Five Zero." Came the reply.

"Booking Ten, Ten at Brompton police office, over."

"Thank you, Five Zero, and a very good evening to you. HT to stand-by."

THE END - for now ...

Dear reader,

We hope you enjoyed reading *Nine O'Clock Bus to Brompton* Please take a moment to leave a review, even if it's a short one. Your opinion is important to us.

Discover more books by Kevin Fitzpatrick at https://www.nextchapter.pub/authors/kevin-fitzpatrick

Want to know when one of our books is free or discounted? Join the newsletter at http://eepurl.com/bqqB3H

Best regards,

Kevin Fitzpatrick and the Next Chapter Team

ABOUT THE AUTHOR

Kevin retired from the British police force at the turn of the century, having completed over thirty years of service. He is a father and a grandfather and lives with his wife at their home in Berkshire. He enjoys reading, travel, and motorcycling. This is his first novel. Albeit a work of pure fiction, the story was inspired, very loosely, by his early career.

Lightning Source UK Ltd.
Milton Keynes UK
UKHW020633210422
401849UK00009B/432